Evergreen Christmas

More Christmas romance from Janet Dailey

The Sound of Sleighbells

Somebody Like Santa

Santa's Sweetheart

Holding Out for Christmas

It's a Christmas Thing

My Kind of Christmas

Just a Little Christmas

Christmas on my Mind

Long, Tall Christmas

Christmas in Cowboy Country

Merry Christmas, Cowboy

A Cowboy Under My Christmas Tree

Mistletoe and Molly

To Santa with Love

Let's Be Jolly

Maybe This Christmas

Happy Holidays

Scrooge Wore Spurs

Eve's Christmas

Searching for Santa

Santa in Montana

JANET DAILEY

New York Times **Bestselling Author**

KENSINGTON
PUBLISHING CORP.

www.kensingtonbooks.com

KENSINGTON BOOKS are published by

Kensington Publishing Corp.
900 Third Avenue
New York, NY 10022

After the passing of Janet Dailey, the Dailey family worked with a close associate of Janet's to continue her literary legacy, using her notes, ideas and favorite themes to complete her novels and create new ones, inspired by the American men and women she loved to portray.

All Kensington titles, imprints, and distributed lines are available at special quantity discounts for bulk purchases for sales promotion, premiums, fund-raising, educational, or institutional use.

Special book excerpts or customized printings can also be created to fit specific needs. For details, write or phone the office of the Kensington Sales Manager: Kensington Publishing Corp., 900 Third Avenue, New York, NY 10022. Attn. Sales Department. Phone: 1-800-221-2647.

Kensington and the K logo Reg. U.S. Pat. & TM Off.

ISBN: 978-1-4967-4790-7 (ebook)

ISBN: 978-1-4967-4789-1

First Kensington Hardcover Printing: July 2024
First Kensington Trade Paperback Printing: October 2024

10 9 8 7 6 5 4 3 2 1

Printed in the United States of America

Evergreen Christmas

Chapter One

Black Friday in Noel, North Carolina, looked like any other in a small but bustling town: locals milled about Main Street, elbowing their way in and out of crowded stores, snagging the best deals. Couples, bundled up tight against the winter chill, strolled along sidewalks, walking their dogs, holding hands, and smiling. And children of all ages gathered at the front of Teddy's Toy Store, plastering their noses against the cold glass for a better view of the hot new gadgets and gizmos that were arranged into a mesmerizing holiday display.

But four women, well into their seventies, sitting in the center of Noel's town square, had stuck their noses into something quite different.

A stranger, whom the four women had been eagerly awaiting for well over two months, had just driven into the close-knit Appalachian community, parked her big white truck and trailer across the street and hopped out, smiling as though she owned every inch of America's Christmas Tree Capital.

"I don't like her." Carol Belle Bennett, self-appointed leader of Noel's Nanas (a title townsfolk had bestowed upon the four female friends), eased back in the comfy white rocking chair that sat beneath a green banner emblazoned with the words SIGN UP HERE FOR NOEL'S ANNUAL CHRISTMAS COMPETITION. She crossed her arms over her ample bosom and huffed. "She smiles too much."

The three women seated in rocking chairs to Carol Belle's right remained silent.

Carol Belle scowled. "I said, I don't like her."

"We heard you the first time." Kandy Lyons, who still mourned the grave misfortune of arriving late, which meant sitting in the chair next to Carol Belle, tucked a short curl behind her ear and smiled. "But there's nothing wrong with smiling, Carol Belle. I do it quite often. It's good for the soul, you know? Makes your body and mind feel good. As a matter of fact, I was looking in a magazine the other day while I was getting my hair colored at Patty's salon and there was this whole article about things you can do to make yourself feel better physically. A doctor wrote it. One from way up north—you know, like in Michigan or something? Anyway, he had lots of letters listed behind his name. I have a habit of that, you know? Paying attention to people's names. Like . . . a name can tell you so much about a person. His name was Dr. Kirk Belvedere." She sighed wistfully. "Belvedere. Isn't that a fabulous name? It's the perfect name for a doctor, in my opinion. Strong, rich, sophistica—"

"Oh, please do hush up, Kandy!" Carol Belle narrowed her eyes at the other woman, and the wounded look on Kandy's face made her think better of her harsh response. But then the mere sight of Kandy's new hairdo made her temper flare again.

Why on earth a respectable seventy-three-year-old woman would feel the need to dye her hair hot pink, Carol Belle would never understand. Patty Dalton should've had the good sense to tell Kandy *no* and refuse to color her beautiful silver locks that garish shade. It looked absolutely ridiculous—especially at Christmastime!—and Kandy should've known better than to go and do such a thing right before their big sign-up day. For goodness' sake, they had a reputation to uphold and a task of utmost holiday importance to undertake!

Carol Belle frowned. She should let loose and give Kandy an angry earful but she'd always had a soft spot for Kandy. The woman had kept her tender heart and generous—though somewhat naïve—disposition since childhood which, in a cynical world, Carol Belle knew was a difficult and rare feat.

Kandy had remained a close friend to Carol Belle since they were five years old. Kandy had been widowed in her thirties and she'd stood by Carol Belle through the loss of Carol Belle's husband eleven years ago. That kind of treasured relationship was one a person shouldn't take for granted.

"Please excuse me," Carol Belle said, patting Kandy's knee. "I didn't mean to be harsh. I just want to be certain she's suitable. It'd be disastrous if we made a misstep. What I meant is that the woman smiles very easily for a stranger who just stepped foot in a new town with unfamiliar people. It disconcerts me, is all."

Eve Knight, seated on the other side of Kandy, scooted to the front of her chair, propped her elbows on her knees and tossed in her somber two cents . . . as usual. "There's nothing wrong with smiling when you enter a new town. I'd worry more if she didn't smile."

Holly Wyld, who'd deliberately chosen the seat farthest from Carol Belle, grinned. "I agree with Eve and Kandy." She shrugged. "A smile puts others at ease *and* does a body good. Just look at her." She waved a slender arm in the direction of the stranger who still stood beside her white truck, surveying her surroundings. "She appears young, healthy, and energetic. And she's moving to a new town, getting a new home at Christmas. She has every right to smile."

"And she has a trailer." Kandy perked up at the sound of hooves clanging on metal. "That sounds like a horse, stomping around in there. Do you think she brought a horse with her?"

"More than likely." Carol Belle narrowed her eyes, taking a better look at the tall, slender stranger. "She bought that vacant farm, Chestnut Ridge, with the intention of breeding horses. Least that's what Hal Sutton told me two months ago when he sold her the place. Did you know she bought that land from him over the internet? Paid for it in full without ever even stepping a toe in Noel? Hal said she wanted to snatch it up before anyone else had a chance to buy it but that she didn't have the time to drive up here. She's a barrel racer and has been—what do you call it?" Her brow furrowed. "Touring the circuit?"

Eve nodded.

"Well, supposedly she was too busy competing to make the drive and look the place over, which was a mistake, if you ask me." Carol Belle's frown deepened. "Hal said they completed the whole real estate transaction via phone, email, and . . . Doom." She waved a hand in the air. "Or whatever you call that virtual thing people do from home nowadays."

"Nothing wrong with that." Holly fingered the soft tassels on her cashmere scarf as she eyed the stranger, an excited expression crossing her pretty face. "People buy all kinds of things online nowadays—groceries, furniture, cars, naughty negligees."

Eve gasped. "Holly, please! A little decorum."

Carol Belle clucked her tongue. Holly was in no way demure, and her mere presence always seemed to get under Eve's skin. Eve had always been modest—even as a teen—

and Holly's brazen disposition shocked her on most occasions.

A transplant from Florida, Holly had moved to Noel twelve years ago, struck up a friendship with Kandy and joined the trio of lifelong friends two years after that. Holly came from old money, had decided in her twenties to never marry but enjoyed dating more than anyone Carol Belle had ever met.

Last year, Carol Belle, Kandy, and Eve had made a bet that Holly's latest love interest, Don Jacobs, would manage to steal her heart and get a ring on her finger. After all, the handsome horse trainer had lasted months longer than any other man Holly had taken an interest in, but the moment Don had tried to persuade Holly into making a commitment, Holly had dropped him like a hot coal.

And Carol Belle had lost fifty bucks. She huffed. The memory still stung.

"A person can barely make it in today's world without the internet," Holly continued happily. "Or a cell phone, or Jackpot Millionaire." She smiled wider. "Mm-mm, I do love the Jackpot Millionaire app! I played this morning on my tablet and won sixty-five dollars." She waggled her fingers, her elegant French manicure impeccable. "That's enough to change my nails if I take a notion. What do y'all think of Ruby Red? I think that shade would be perfect for the Christmas season."

Carol Belle frowned as the stranger across the street walked to the trailer and reached between the slats to pet the horse inside. "She has red hair."

Eve, surveying the stranger too, raised one eyebrow. "So?"

"Red hair means she probably has a temper," Kandy piped in, smiling as she twirled one of her hot-pink curls around her finger. "Just like a name, hair can tell you a lot about a person, you know?"

Carol Belle glanced at Kandy's pink locks and shuddered. "Kandy has a point. That gal has a ton o' red hair, almost to her waist, I'd say. If she has a temper to match, she may be mighty hard to win over, and we just have to win her over. Otherwise, Nate Reed'll get the drop on everyone for the tenth year in a row—a whole decade of domination!"

"It's all in the approach," Holly said. "You know what they say—you catch a lot more flies with honey . . ."

Eve exchanged a knowing look with Holly, then lifted her chin at Carol Belle. "And Santa don't like ugly, Carol Belle."

Carol Belle scowled. "Why y'all telling me that?"

Kandy, bless her, reached out and squeezed Carol Belle's hand gently, soothing her stung pride just a bit. "They're just saying that if we're going to pull this off, we need to be on our best and most welcoming behavior, no matter what. That notion applies to all four of us."

Eve nudged her glasses higher on the bridge of her nose. "Exactly."

"No offense," Holly said.

Carol Belle huffed but remained silent.

After a moment, the four took up rocking again, their chairs swaying forward then back in perfect rhythm as they watched the stranger with red hair enter Kringle's Café—a small coffee shop across the street—then emerge five minutes later with a bright red cup in one hand and a shiny silver bag in the other.

Kandy's stomach rumbled. "Oh, I'm so hungry! What do you think she got?" She licked her lips, rubbing her hands across her belly. "Kringle's Café has the best hot chocolate and their red velvet cupcakes are just to die for!"

Carol Belle narrowed her eyes. The wistful look in Kandy's expression as she stared at the café seemed too intense for dessert. Carol Belle suspected Kandy's eagerness to visit Kringle's Café had more to do with the handsome owner rather than with a cup of hot cocoa, and any move on Kandy's part to pursue Max Reynolds would no doubt set Noel ablaze with gossip. And even worse . . . just might break Kandy's tender heart.

"Don't matter what she got in that café." Carol Belle leaned to her left to see past the couple who had walked into the center of the town square, obscuring her view. "What matters is what she's got at Chestnut Ridge."

The other three women nodded then leaned to the left, too, to get a better look at the stranger.

As though sensing she was being watched, the red-headed stranger looked across the street and glanced at each of the four women, meeting their eagle-eyed scrutiny head-on, holding each of their gazes in succession. Then she smiled, tossed her long red waves over one shoulder and . . . winked!

"Did you see that?" Carol Belle pressed her hand against her chest, where her heart thumped wildly. "She winked at us! And it was a sarcastic wink at that." She smiled full blast, her worries melting away like a mini marshmallow tossed into a blazing bonfire. "Boy, she's a feisty one! Exactly what we need. She'll give Nate Reed a run for his money, for sure. Ain't no way Nate'll win the Christmas Crown again this year!"

"Good! Now that we know for sure she's what we're looking for, how about we take our lunch break a little early? Maybe visit Kringle's Café for a spell?" Kandy asked. "We've already had a ton of people sign up for the Christmas competition and we could just leave the sign-up rosters out for them. They'd know what to do. Then after we eat, we can stop by Chestnut Ridge and introduce ourselves to her."

"No! No time for a lunch break." Carol Belle stood. "Let's go, ladies." She hustled toward a nearby parking lot and motioned for the other women to join her as the

stranger climbed into her truck and cranked the engine.
"Come on! We need to follow her. Scope her out a bit
more, then make our first move."

Kandy blinked furiously, her long, false lashes fluttering
against her overly blushed cheeks. "But . . . shouldn't we
give her some space? Let her settle into her new home before we pounce on her?"

Carol Belle stopped in her tracks. "Absolutely not! That
woman right there"—she stabbed her finger at the truck
and trailer as they rolled past, gaining speed and disappearing out of view around the curvy mountain road—"is
Fabio Fraser's new owner. And if she owns Fabio, we need
to own her."

Eve and Holly frowned, protesting in unison, "But,
Carol Belle!"

Ignoring them, she spun on her heel and stalked toward
a cherry-red Cadillac. "Get a move on, ladies. We got to
sweet talk that newcomer into a Christmas war."

Jordyn Banks knew she was being followed, but at the
moment, the four elderly women stalking her in a red
Cadillac hardly registered as the overwhelming majesty of
her new home dazzled her senses.

"Merry Christmas to you, too, Noel, North Carolina!"
Jordyn, squirming in her seat with excitement, laughed as
she eased her large truck and trailer around a sharp curve
in the winding mountain road.

The small town of Noel, sitting at an elevation well over
three thousand feet, completely surrounded by mountains,
was far more impressive in person than in the profession-
ally shot photographs she'd pored over for months. Driving through the center of town had been like cruising
through a snow globe Christmas dream full of quaint shops,
smiling faces and nostalgic decorations. Jordyn couldn't

possibly be more pleased with her decision to move to the charming Appalachian town.

Over the past two years, she'd scoured the internet on her laptop, hoping to find a stretch of land that was not only affordable but that would also offer a potential place to call home. The forty acres of land for sale in Noel listed on Hal Sutton's real estate website could easily support several paddocks, stables, and an arena, and came equipped with an aged—but ridiculously charming!—log cabin, which consisted of one bedroom, one bathroom, and a small front porch suitable for admiring the mountains that sprawled in every direction.

Chestnut Ridge (as the stretch of land was named) was, in fact, the perfect setup for building her new horse-breeding business and luckily, the price had recently been marked down to below market-value, which suited Jordyn just fine. Having tucked away pennies here and there from rodeo wins over the past seven years, she placed high priority on getting the biggest bang for her buck, but the absolute deal clincher for her had been the beautiful town of Noel and its renowned Christmas splendor.

"Christmas," she whispered.

What a marvelous thought! To think . . . *she*—after seven long years of nomadic life on the road—would actually have a home of her very own in a close-knit community full of Christmas nostalgia and hopefully (*oh, hopefully!*) good neighbors who'd adopt her as one of their own.

Smiling, she dug one hand into a shiny silver bag that rested in the passenger seat, pinched off a chunk of red velvet cupcake and popped it into her mouth. The sugary delight melted on her tongue, making her shiver again with excitement as she drove, craning her neck for a better view of the mountain peaks dusted with the barest hint of snow.

Oh, she hadn't had an honest to goodness *real* Christmas in . . . well, ever!

Having been removed by children's services from neglectful parents at the age of four, she'd spent her entire life in foster care, aged out at eighteen and hit the road to tour the rodeo circuit. Her childhood Christmases had usually consisted of simple cafeteria-style meals at youth centers or awkward gatherings in houses with new family who served as makeshift parents for a while, sharing space with their biological children with whom she rarely had anything in common. The foster parents she'd had over the years had done their best to make her feel at home— and she'd had many due to her stubborn behavior—but she'd never felt like more than a number . . . or really loved in any way. Even in her last foster home, where she'd lived for five years, she had still felt like an outsider up to the moment when she left, hopping into her newly purchased used truck, cranking the engine and driving away for a future she hoped would be more welcoming.

Twenty-five years old now, she'd traveled the road, touring the rodeo circuit, for seven years, her only family being Star, an eleven-year-old white mare she'd saved from a fed-up owner seven years ago. A hot, high-powered quarter horse, Star had had the potential to be a champion in the arena, but she was pushy, temperamental, aggressive and—according to those who'd ridden her—had no manners. That alone had been enough to entice Jordyn into taking on the challenge of training the stubborn mare, but the vulnerability she'd noticed in Star's eyes—a wary, wounded look Jordyn recognized immediately—had sealed the deal. And Star must've sensed a kindred spirit in Jordyn as she'd grudgingly allowed Jordyn to lead her through months of training sessions to prepare for their first barrel race.

In the end, Star had a huge motor, was the best at her

job and formed a strong bond with Jordyn, becoming a sweet companion who kept Jordyn's spirits and hopes high during their long journeys on the road. Star had become more than just a horse; Star was her best friend, sister, and only family in the world. And now, for the first time in years, both of them would truly have a home of their own.

Jordyn glanced in the rearview mirror at the trailer she hauled. Star would be ready to stretch her legs by now, and she couldn't wait to get the mare onto the firm ground of their new land.

"Your destination is fifteen feet ahead on the right."

Jordyn slowed the truck at the direction of the voice emitted from the navigation system on her dashboard. "We're almost home, Star."

And just then, the winding mountain road dipped and leveled out, revealing the rolling foothills of the Appalachian Mountains, a dirt road leading to the right and a small log house just visible from the road. Jordyn recognized it instantly.

"That's it!" Jordyn palmed the steering wheel and turned onto the dirt drive. "We're here, Star. We're finally here!"

She drove slowly along the dirt road and placed a palm on the top of the red coffee cup in the cupholder, keeping it steady and avoiding potholes. When she reached the log house, she cut the engine, opened her door and hopped out, inhaling deeply and holding the clean cold mountain air in her lungs.

It was a beautiful sight! Sprawling acres of dormant grass, a small but perfectly adorable log home, and impressive mountains in the distance. She couldn't quite believe she was really here. And though financially broke after the purchase, she had high hopes that Noel and Chestnut Ridge held good things for both her and Star. All she needed to do was build a strong foundation for her new horse-breeding business, find her place among the close-knit locals and hope her presence would be accepted—no . . . welcomed!

That was what she hoped for most of all. To be welcomed into the beautiful town of Noel, to make new friends whom she hoped would one day feel like family. That possibility made the financial gamble worthwhile.

Jordyn clapped her hands and squealed, then jogged to the back of the trailer and opened it, leading Star out of the trailer.

"Ready to check out our new home, beautiful?" Jordyn stroked Star's neck and smiled as the mare shook her head, her long white mane rippling over her broad neck. "I know," she soothed. "You've been cramped up in that trailer for way too long. How 'bout we take a walk around our new property so you can stretch your legs?"

The low rumble of a car drew close and Jordyn glanced over her shoulder, noting the red Cadillac that had been following her from Noel's town square. She could just make out the outline of four bouffant hairdos she recalled spotting in Noel's town square just minutes earlier. For some reason, the four older women sitting in white rocking chairs had taken a keen interest in her the moment she'd arrived. She'd felt their eyes when she'd gotten out of her truck to stretch her legs, and they'd continued to scrutinize her as she entered and exited a local coffee shop for coffee and cupcakes.

It was understandable the women would be curious about her, but she'd hoped to have more time to prepare before meeting the locals. It was imperative she make a good first impression. She needed to do everything possible to blend into the small community and build a successful business if she wanted Chestnut Ridge to become her permanent home.

And she wanted that. Oh, how she wanted to be a part of charming Noel!

Jordyn stroked Star's nose gently as the Cadillac pulled to a stop several feet away. The doors opened and four women exited the vehicle, clutching their scarves, hats, and coats snugly against their chins as they approached.

One of the women, thin with shockingly pink curls, whispered to the silver-haired lady next to her, "She's much taller up close. So much taller than I expected."

"Carol Belle was right," the lady wearing glasses said. "She sure has a ton of red hair."

"It's gorgeous." A third lady, wearing a cashmere scarf and sporting an immaculate French manicure, smiled brightly at Jordyn. "*She's* gorgeous. And have you ever seen eyes that shade of emerald before? They're absolutely stunning!"

"Don't matter if she's pretty or not." The fourth woman, a short, stout lady with sharp hazel eyes, moved quickly to the front of the pack and propped her hands on her hips. "What matters is how tough she is." She stood in front of Jordyn and leaned closer, eyeing her from head to toe along with the three other women. "So, how 'bout it? You tough?"

It was hard to guess exactly what their intentions were and even harder for Jordyn to admit she couldn't figure them out. During her years of touring the circuit, she'd spent more than her fair share of time in rowdy, smoke-filled bars packed with cowboys oozing ulterior motives, and she could spot trouble a mile away. But the four older women standing in front of her were a complete enigma. One she didn't particularly want to deal with at the moment.

But . . . these four women were part of Noel—an important part, if their prominent presence in the town square this morning was anything to go by—and it was imperative she make a good first impression.

Jordyn rocked back on her heels and smiled. "I suppose one could say I'm tough."

The stout woman in front of her, seemingly the leader of the group, nodded slowly. "You do rodeos, right?"

Jordyn's smile widened. "Yes. I compete as a barrel racer."

"You're a barrel racer?" Pink Curls piped up. "Is that your horse?"

The stout woman grunted. "O' course that's her horse, Kandy. Who else's would it be?"

The one wearing glasses nudged her metal frames further up the bridge of her nose. "I'll remind you, Carol Belle, that Santa don't like ugly."

The stout woman, Carol Belle, rolled her eyes. "Go ahead, Kandy. Ask your questions."

The woman named Kandy elbowed her way in front of Carol Belle, wound a pink curl around her finger and beamed at Jordyn. "What are the rodeos like? You ever get hurt on that horse? How many contests have you won?"

"Forget the contest wins." The lady wearing the cashmere scarf stepped closer, held out her French-manicured hand and winked. "I'm much more interested in how many cowboys you've won over. I'm Holly Wyld, by the way."

Jordyn shook her hand. "Nice to meet you Ms. Wyl—"

"Holly, please. We don't stand on ceremony." She shrugged. "Except for the Christmas Crowning, that is."

"The Christmas Crowning?" Jordyn tilted her head and smiled. "That sounds intriguing. I'm Jordyn B—"

"Jordyn Banks," Carol Belle stated matter-of-factly. "Twenty-five-year-old barrel racer. Bought Chestnut Ridge from Hal Sutton over Boom and you'll be cohabiting with Fabio Fraser."

Jordyn frowned. "You know quite a lot about me. Although . . . I'm not sure what Boom is or who Fabio Fr—?"

"She means Zoom." The lady with the glasses stepped forward and held out her hand as well. "I'm Eve Knight. It's a pleasure to meet you."

Jordyn shook her hand, too. "Same here. And may I ask who Fabio Fraser is?"

"Oh, darling." Holly stroked her cashmere scarf and smiled dreamily. "Fabio's magnificent. He's twenty-two-years-old, towers over you, smells divine, and were we to climb him, he's so strong, he could easily accommodate all five of us women without even a quiver."

Jordyn blinked, stepped back then frowned. "Are . . . we talking about a man here? Because I bought this place outright and Hal didn't mention anything about me sharing with a tenant."

"The detestable *man*," Carol Belle said through gritted teeth, "is your new neighbor, Nate Reed." She pointed to the left, toward ornate white fencing visible in the distance. "He owns Frosted Firs Ranch next door and has monopolized our Christmas Crown for nine years in a row now. We refuse to give him the tenth! Fabio is our best shot at success." She ran a hand over her gray hair and inhaled. "Now, as Eve has graciously reminded me, Santa don't like ugly. So we won't impose on you any longer. We'll get out of your hair to let you settle in. We just wanted to introduce ourselves and let you know that we'll stop by tomorrow with a welcome basket and a proposition of utmost importance."

Jordyn studied each of the women. They stared back at her, their expressions an odd mixture of curiosity, excitement and anxiety. It was the strangest thing, being scrutinized in the town square, followed to her property and swarmed by four women before she could even set foot inside her new home. But a good first impression was essential, and Jordyn knew from experience that good manners were critical for success in a small town. If she wanted to be embraced by the heart of Noel's community, she'd do well to get into these women's good graces.

"Well . . ." She shrugged and smiled. "Thank you, I guess?"

"You're welcome." Carol Belle spun on her heel and motioned for the other women to follow her. "Come on, ladies. We need to get back to the sign-up booth. And Jordyn? You might want to go ahead and get acquainted with Fabio, seeing as you've got to partner with him on an important mission." She pointed toward the back of the log cabin. "He's inches from the property line and Nate Reed is probably slinking around him again already. Guard Fabio with your very life."

Eve, Kandy, and Holly looked at Jordyn, nodded in unison, then smiled, waved, and followed Carol Belle back to the Cadillac. Moments later, the engine rumbled and Carol Belle turned the car around and peeled out, the four women dashing off as quickly as they'd arrived.

Jordyn glanced at Star, who raised her broad nose, closed her eyes, and savored the chilly breeze sweeping over the foothills. "Well, that was an interesting welcome. Whatcha say, girl? You wanna go to the back of the lot and check out this Fabio thing?"

Star bobbed her head as though in agreement and Jordyn smiled, then led the way around the log house to the back field. The acres behind the house were even more impressive than the front yard. The wide field offered an unobstructed view of the impressive mountain range. But toward the left corner of the lot, a solitary tree—a Fraser fir, if Jordyn guessed correctly—stood well over eighteen feet, its full, healthy branches the richest shade of forest green she'd ever seen.

"Wow," she whispered, leading Star across the field toward the lone tree. "You must be Fabio Fraser."

A rich aromatic mix of pine and fresh mountain air drifted over her as she drew closer to the edge of the property line. She tipped her head back, taking in every inch of the beautiful fir—a living embodiment of the Christmas tree of her dreams. And it grew right here in the back lot of her brand-new home.

"Can you believe this is ours, Star?" Brisk mountain wind brought goose bumps to Jordyn's skin, but her heart blazed warmer than ever as she admired the sight before her and smiled. "Our first, true Christmas tree."

Chapter Two

"Incoming! The Cheek Pinchers are here!"

Nate Reed, owner of Frosted Firs Ranch, shut the cash register drawer, handed change to the customer in front of him, then frowned as his younger brother sprinted across the gift shop, nearly crashing into the young woman who stood on the other side of the checkout counter.

"Sorry about that." Nate grabbed the customer's elbow, steadying her as she swayed in Tucker's wake. "Tucker is . . ." He smiled ruefully. "Well, you know Tucker."

The young woman standing in front of him—Sandy Simmons, if he recalled correctly—blushed then giggled. "Oh, yeah. I know Tucker." She smoothed her long blond hair behind her ears and grinned. "Everyone in Noel knows Tucker. He gets around more than any one man should in his life. You, on the other hand"—she winked— "are quite the mystery."

Nate smiled politely but nudged the ornament—an ornate reindeer figurine he'd just gift wrapped for her—closer to her hands, hoping she'd get the hint and go on her way. "There's no mystery to me," he said. "I run this place, take care of my daughter, and stay out of trouble."

Her smile fell into a pretty pout. "No drama, excitement, or romance for you then?"

Still holding his polite smile firmly in place, Nate shook his head. "I like things peaceful and predictable. Thank you for visiting Frosted Firs Ranch, Sandy. We appreciate your business and hope you visit us again soon."

Sandy's smile, which had briefly dimmed, brightened at his last comment. "Oh, I will." She gathered up the bag in her arms and eyed him from head to toe, grinning wider. "I definitely will."

Nate stifled a groan as she left, then rubbed his forehead. After nine years, he should've gotten the hang of letting women down gently and discouraging their interest in him. But no matter how many times he declined dates, a new woman would show up, poking around his ranch in an effort to catch his attention or entice his interest.

That was Tucker's fault though. His younger brother made an art form out of catching a woman's eye, and while Nate disliked being the center of attention, Tucker reveled in it, delighting daily in the flirtatious advances of women and enjoying each opportunity to use his charisma and charm. Tucker's behavior was an irritation Nate could do without, but considering that his twenty-five-year-old brother had abandoned his bull riding career and left the rodeo circuit to return to Noel and partner with Nate to run Frosted Firs Ranch, he couldn't complain too much.

Tucker had been a lifesaver in more ways than one. He'd picked up the slack at the ranch when Nate had lost his wife, Macy, six years ago due to childbirth complications.

Nate's polite smile vanished as quickly as he'd summoned it. A heavy weight of grief settled in his gut like a stone. As a thirty-year-old widower and single father who ran a thriving ranch that boarded horses and doubled as a Christmas tree farm, Nate had little time and no interest in pursuing a romantic relationship with any woman.

Macy and his six-year-old daughter, Roxanna, occupied all of his thoughts and every bit of his heart.

"Nate!" Tucker, hiding behind two women who were shopping in the snow globe aisle, slung one brawny arm over each of their shoulders and peeked between their giggling faces at him. "Did you hear what I said? They're here!"

Nate frowned. "Who's here?"

"The Cheek Pinchers!" He pointed frantically at the wall of windows that lined the front of the gift shop. "They're out there right now, looking for us."

Nate jerked his head to the right, scanning the parking lot through the wall of glass panes, his gaze homing in on four elderly women exiting a red Cadillac. "And you left Roxie out there to fend for herself?" A smile, a sincere one this time, tugged at his lips. "How could you? What kind of uncle are you anyway?"

Tucker shook his head, the look of abject horror on his face almost comical. "I don't care what kind of uncle that makes me. The kid's gonna have to fight 'em off herself. Ain't no way I'm getting pinched by them women again."

Nate rolled his eyes, then rapped his knuckles on the checkout counter. "Then take over the register and help the customers while I go see what they want."

"Now that I can handle." Clearly relieved to be well away from the Cheek Pinchers, Tucker straightened his muscular physique, slipped between the two young women he'd hidden behind, then swept his arm toward the snow globe aisle. "You ladies find what you're looking for? Because I'd be more than happy to check y'all out." He winked.

Groaning, Nate dragged his hand over his face as the young women giggled.

It was a blessing Tucker had the good looks to go with his oozing charm, and that his charismatic presence had increased foot traffic exponentially over the past six years, otherwise Nate would've cut him loose from the business long ago. But as things stood, he couldn't imagine running Frosted Firs Ranch without his brother. Not only had Tucker's presence eased the workload, but he also made the day more enjoyable . . . if, at times, in a somewhat aggravating way.

Nate left the checkout counter, grabbed his jacket from his office, and shrugged it on as he exited the gift shop, then strode across the gravel parking lot to where his six-year-old daughter, Roxanna—or Roxie, as they'd nicknamed her—stood helpless in the grip of the Cheek Pinchers.

"Oh, my gracious, how you've grown!" Holly Wyld, decked out in a warm cashmere scarf and dressy pantsuit, squeezed one of Roxie's cheeks gently while Kandy Lyons tugged at the other. "You are absolutely precious."

"I do believe she's grown at least three inches since we last saw her," Kandy said. She smiled down at Roxie, who seemed enraptured by Kandy's pink curls. "Do you like my hair, sweet girl? I had it done special just yesterday."

Roxie tilted her head back for a better look at Kandy's pink hair and the two women's hands moved with her, maintaining their gentle pinch on her cheeks. "Yes, ma'am. I like pink."

Nate smiled. Roxie had been born with a sweet, gentle disposition and never wanted to disappoint anyone. Her manners had always been impeccable without much prompting from him. Which, if Nate were being honest, was a godsend, because he had no idea how he and Tucker would've instilled such ladylike qualities in Roxie. Goodness knows, they'd unintentionally brought out the tomboy in her already.

"Oh, let go of the girl and let us have a look." Carol Belle Bennett shoved Kandy and Holly aside, lowered to her haunches with a grunt and opened her arms. "Merry Christmas, Roxie, darling. The season is finally here, you know?"

Roxie smiled, and when Holly and Kandy released her cheeks, she moved into Carol Belle's arms and hugged the older woman.

"Aw, you're just as sweet as sugar, aren't you?" Carol Belle's tone was surprisingly tender given the backbone of steel Nate knew she possessed. "How did you get so sweet despite those two brutes who look after you?"

Eve Knight squatted down beside Carol Belle, adjusted her glasses and grinned. "Why, she was born that way. Weren't you, doll baby? You take after your mother—just as kind and gorgeous as our Macy was." She tugged at Carol Belle's arms. "Now let her go, Carol Belle, so I can get my turn."

Roxie smiled wider, hugged Eve, then stepped back as the two women continued to smile down at her.

Nate grinned. Eve was the most reserved woman in the group, but her exuberant greetings and joyful expressions around Roxie over the years had made it clear that she held his daughter in high regard. From what he'd heard, Eve had never been married or had children of her own but loved doting on the children living in Noel. During his interactions with Eve over the years, Nate had noticed a quiet grief hanging on the older woman, and the shadows in her eyes had spoken of a secret sorrow she carried.

"She's just an angel," Eve said softly. "Don't you think she's an angel?"

Carol Belle nodded, love glowing brightly in her eyes. "Yes. A perfect angel."

Then, as usual, both women's hands found their way to Roxie's cheeks, pinching again gently as they crooned down at her. Roxie's polite smile morphed into a wince.

"All right, ladies," Nate said, smiling as he strode over. "Let's not cut off my daughter's circulation."

Carol Belle frowned but she and Eve released Roxie's cheeks, put their hands on the ground and tried to shove themselves back to a standing position. Grunts and moans escaped their pink, wrinkled lips but neither of them made any progress toward standing.

Nate bent and reached for their elbows. "Please, allow m—"

"No, siree! You keep those grubby Christmas Crown paws to yourself." Carol Belle motioned toward the women behind her. "Holly, Kandy. Help us up, would you?"

They did, and soon all four women were lined up in a neat, confrontational row, all four pairs of eyes fixed firmly on Nate.

He shifted from one boot to the other, then hugged Roxie against his leg, hoping the four women wouldn't notice his discomfort. During his childhood, the three women, affectionately known as Noel's Nanas, had doted on him. Every time he'd crossed their paths, they had patted his shoulders, kissed his forehead, and pinched his cheeks much as they—and Holly, who'd joined the group of women later—had Roxie's. The women were fun, spunky, and energetic. For as long as he'd known them, he'd enjoyed being around them as much as they had enjoyed being around him.

When he'd turned twenty-one, they'd attended his

birthday party and later, his wedding to Macy, showering them both with gifts and attention. And six years ago, they'd even come to the hospital the night Roxie had been born and consoled Nate during his darkest days of grief, cradling Roxie in their arms as though she were their very own granddaughter.

But their outpouring of love and support for him had changed over recent years when his winning streak in Noel's Christmas competition had continued without fail. Apparently, he had—as Carol Belle had so bluntly put it—a monopoly on winning the Christmas Crown, and she believed it was time he gave it up. She'd even gone so far as to insist he drop out of Noel's Christmas competition altogether.

Nate admired Carol Belle and wanted to please her—he truly did!—but bowing out of Noel's Christmas competition was out of the question. He and Macy had begun participating in it ten years ago, shortly after they'd married, and had continued up until her death. Macy had loved every aspect of the twelve Christmas competitions sponsored by the town, but her favorite had been the tree contest. She and Nate had built Frosted Firs Ranch together and lovingly tended to the Christmas trees they'd grown, picking out the best one each year and entering it into the Christmas tree contest. One October, the year before Macy died, one of their eighteen-foot Fraser firs had even been chosen as the White House Christmas tree, beating out other trees from all over the US. Macy had been so proud of their success.

Each Christmas season was an opportunity to celebrate Macy's memory and help Roxie get to know the mother she'd never met by sharing Christmas memories he'd cherished with Macy and creating new ones that he hoped Roxie would carry with her into adulthood.

No. Bowing out of Noel's Christmas competition—no matter how much Noel's Nanas wanted him to—was completely out of the question.

As though reading his thoughts, Carol Belle narrowed her gaze on his face. "You haven't changed your mind about sitting out the Christmas competition this year, have you?"

Nate sighed. "No, ma'am."

Carol Belle looked down at Roxie and smiled. "Dear, would you be so good as to go inside and ask your uncle Tucker to bring out a load of firewood for us?" She reached into her pocket, pulled out a set of folded bills and handed them to Roxie. "That should cover the cost of one trunk-load and provide a nice tidy tip for your uncle and you. There's a sweetie."

"Yes, ma'am." Roxie took the money, spun on her heel and skipped toward the gift shop, her long blond ponytail swishing across her back.

"Now that we're alone," Carol Belle said, leaning close to Nate, "I feel it's only fair that I warn you."

Nate frowned. "Warn me about what?"

Carol Belle smiled, a hint of devilry gleaming in her eyes. "That you have some competition this year."

"Fierce competition," Eve said, crossing her arms over her chest.

"And she has red hair and a white horse," Kandy whispered, grinning.

"And they're both gorgeous," Holly said, spreading her manicured hands. "Stunning, actually."

Nate made a face. "Look, I know what you're saying makes sense to y'all, but I'm not quite followi—"

"Chestnut Ridge has been sold," Carol Belle said. "And Fabio Fraser has a new owner. One that we're going to sweet-talk"—she glanced at her wristwatch—"in precisely twelve hours, into entering Noel's Christmas competition and kicking your burly butt."

Nate chuckled. "Now, Miss Carol Belle, I know you think I'm hogging the Christmas Crown, but I honestly don't mean any harm. I'm simply doing what any good citizen of Noel would do by participating in the annual Christmas celebration that the four of you created. Roxie loves it, Tucker likes it, and I enjoy it on most occasions, so I don't really see the problem."

"The problem," Carol Belle said, poking her finger in his chest, "is that you've won the Christmas Crown and the Christmas Tree competition every year for the past nine years. Participation in our annual competition has decreased five percent every year since you started winning. Since you manage a Christmas tree business, everyone knows you'll have the best tree and that they'll be no match for you, so some of them give up before they even start. They'd rather not enter than lose for another year in a row." She huffed. "We cannot grow participation in this competition if the same person wins the Christmas Crown every single year."

Nate rubbed the back of his neck. "I understand that, Ms. Carol Belle. But I take pride in my work and participating in this competition is important to me and my family. I can't help it if we just happen to win every y—"

"Well, we're going to help you out with a loss this year," Carol Belle stated matter-of-factly. "We're bringing new blood into the mix—strong, feisty blood—and she has Fabio. You know as well as I do that it'll be tough to find a tree that's more perfect than Fabio."

Yep. Nate nodded. He was well aware of that... though he still cringed every time he heard the ridiculous name Noel's Nanas had bestowed upon the tree. Still, that hadn't stopped him from taking an interest in the evergreen.

As a matter fact, he'd eyed the impressive tree bordering his property for years, never ceasing to be impressed by its growth and stature. The tree had grown wild into a perfectly trimmed shape all its own, as though God had fashioned it for himself as his very own Christmas tree. Nate had offered to buy it from the former owner of Chestnut Ridge several times over the years, but the owner had always refused, and Nate knew exactly why. Noel's Nanas had paid his neighbor a tidy sum every year to preserve the tree and allow it to continue to grow until it reached a suitable height for entry into Noel's Christmas tree contest.

It was a stroke of brilliance for Noel's Nanas to lay claim to that tree, but it seemed their scheme might not pan out. Chestnut Ridge had been sold and there was a good chance the new owner with red hair and a white horse might be willing to hand the tree over to him if he played his hand right.

The corner of Nate's mouth lifted. "Seeing as how I have a new neighbor, I ought to stop by for a neighborly visit."

The four women scowled.

"You watch that, Nate Reed," Carol Belle said.

He laughed. "Watch what?"

"That cunning mischief-making of yours!" Carol Belle propped her hands on her hips. "We're stopping by Chestnut Ridge first thing tomorrow morning, givin' that gal a rundown on the competition and talking her into competing. She'll know better than to let you bribe that tree out from under her."

The hint of uncertainty in Carol Belle's voice made Nate smile wider.

"Oh, my," Holly whispered to the other women. "You see that passionate fire in his eyes?"

Kandy beamed. "I sure do. It's been ages since he's had that spark in his eyes. It sure is nice to see our Nate finally excited over something again."

Eve nodded, smiling. "I agree."

"Well, he better watch it," Carol Belle said, thumping his chest. "Don't even try pulling a fast one, Nate. We've got our eyes on you. And don't even think about going over there and bribing that woman with your big bucks, gift shop coupons, or free firewood!" She glared at the other women. "And don't go soft on me now, ladies—too much is at stake this year. Nate's not our innocent little boy anymore. He's a wily thirty-year-old man bent on stealing our Christmas Crown!"

The bell over the gift shop door jangled and Tucker emerged, carrying a bundle of wood in each muscular arm. He strode across the gravel parking lot, carefully averting his gaze as he passed the four women, then headed toward the trunk of their red convertible. "Afternoon, ladies."

The frowns on each of the four women's faces disappeared, bright smiles replaced them, and a collective giggle emerged. The four women huddled around Tucker as he opened their trunk and began loading the firewood into the Cadillac.

"We so appreciate your help, Tucker," Kandy crooned.

"It's so cold at night now," Eve said. "It's nice to have extra firewood on hand to keep our toes warm. We're quite delicate, you know."

Carol Belle nodded. "At our age, it's important we stay warm."

"I'll say." Holly leaned on the car's bumper and ran one manicured finger over Tucker's biceps, which strained the long-sleeved flannel shirt he wore. "But I can think of a lot of other ways to stay warm besides lighting firewood."

Tucker tossed the last log into the trunk, shut it, then backed away slowly. "Glad I could help, ladies." He gestured over his shoulder. "But Nate's available, too, you know? He can load firewood in your trunk anytime just as well as I can."

"Yes, but we enjoy talking to you," Holly said as Tucker turned and started walking away. "And seeing you, too."

Her gaze was fixed on his rear as he made a hasty retreat.

Nate choked back a laugh as Tucker made sure to position his backside in the opposite direction from the women.

"You're all loaded up and ready to go." Tucker's face flushed as he added under his breath, "Thank God."

The women smiled and waved, blew kisses at Roxie, then climbed back into their Cadillac, cranked the engine and drove away.

Tucker groaned. "Man, you gotta watch out for those four."

Nate chuckled. "The last time I turned down a date, wasn't it you that told me attention from a woman was a blessing from God that I shouldn't decline?"

Tucker snorted. "That's different." He jerked his thumb toward the road. "Those four are trouble."

Nate nodded as he watched the cherry-red Cadillac ascend a mountain curve. "Yep. They're definitely up to something."

The four women were probably sitting in those leather seats, plotting against him right now, discussing ways to convince the new owner of Chestnut Ridge to give them that perfect tree so they could steal a win right out from under him, ending a nine-years-long tradition that had been dear to Macy and was now just as precious to Roxie.

As distasteful as it might be to play dirty, he'd have to find a way to beat them at their own game.

"What are the Nanas up to, Daddy?"

Nate looked down and smiled. Roxie had joined them and stared up at him, her blue eyes innocent, her expression worry-free . . . as he believed every child's should be. "The Nanas are determined to keep us from winning the Christmas Crown this year." He bent, scooped her up in his arms and kissed her warm cheek. "But we're not giving it up without a fight, are we, darling? We're gonna win that crown again this year and put it in the display case beside all the others, for your mama."

Roxie beamed. "Yes, sir. No one can beat us at the Christmas competition. You, me, and Uncle Tucker are the best team on earth and we're gonna keep the"—her brow furrowed—"ta-dish-un going!"

Laughing, Tucker nodded. "That's right, baby girl. Keep that same fire in your belly when you're building your gingerbread house for the competition."

Roxie high-fived him. "I will, Uncle Tucker!"

Nate lowered Roxie to the ground and rubbed his chin as she skipped back into the gift shop. "We might have to play a little dirty this year. The Nanas claim they're going to recruit our new neighbor at Chestnut Ridge to compete against us in this year's tree competition."

"Oh, yeah?" Tucker asked. "Who bought the place?"

"A feisty redhead with a white horse, apparently."

Tucker's eyes sparkled with male interest. "Oh? Want me to check her out for you?"

Nate grinned. "Nah. I know exactly what kind of checking out you'd do. Besides, I need to handle this one myself. I don't want to drag you into my feud with the Nanas. I'll pay our new neighbor a visit right now and ask her to sell us the tree. I doubt she'll give me a hard time considering she just moved here and probably has no use for it. In any event, she couldn't possibly give us more trouble than the Nanas."

"You got that right. The Cheek Pinchers are the worst."

The small log cabin Jordyn had purchased showed signs of age and neglect, but had a vaulted ceiling fit for a choir of angels.

Lying on her back, sprawled across the hardwood floor of the living room, she stretched her arms and legs in opposite directions, arched her back and gazed up at the dark hardwood planks that comprised the high ceiling. Two thick wooden beams supported the ceiling and spanned its length, and a stone fireplace was centered on the wall beside the front door. The two windows on either side of the stone fireplace were small, but large enough to let in a pool of sunlight that added warmth to the cold hardwood floor beneath her.

Sighing, she closed her eyes, swung her arms and legs out in wide arcs as though creating a snow angel, then opened her eyes and smiled brightly at the impressive ceiling above her. "I don't know exactly how you feel about me," she said, "but I sure like the looks of you. I got a feeling you and I are gonna get along just fine."

The vaulted ceiling remained silent.

Jordyn smiled wider. "I know you probably think it's strange having some stranger lie on the floor and talk to you like this, but the thing is, you're all I got aside from Star and a dream. But I've been pretty successful making my dreams come true. I wanted to compete in barrel racing, so I taught myself how to do that, saved my money to pay for proper training, and won several championships on the circuit." She rose to her elbows, craned her neck, and glanced around the small log cabin. "If I can do all that, I know I can make this place into a real home."

But where to start?

She had bare floors, bare walls, and a beautiful vaulted ceiling. That was it. She had no furniture, no dishes or silverware, no bed, no cute homey trinkets, and no food. She'd had no need of any of those things during her years traveling the circuit. She'd spent her nights in motels—and occasionally her truck—never entertained anyone and lived off food from restaurant buffets and grab-and-go items from convenience stores.

It was vital that she make a good first impression as a hostess tomorrow when the four women who'd bombarded her earlier returned with their welcome basket and a proposition of *utmost importance*, as they'd termed it . . . whatever that would be. If she didn't pull something together today, the four women would have nowhere to sit, nothing to admire, and nothing to eat.

Well, she did have one bit of food.

She rolled her head to the side and glanced at the silver bag that lay open on the hardwood floor beside her, revealing a lone red velvet cupcake with thick cream cheese icing.

Her stomach rumbled. She'd already consumed two of the three mouthwatering delicacies she'd purchased earlier. A jumbo cupcake by anyone's standards, the remaining one could easily serve three to four people if it were divided equally. She should stick the last one in the refrigerator, pull it out in the morning, slice it up and offer each woman a taste when they came for their visit. Surely that would go over well—at least better than offering them nothing—and score her at least one point as a good hostess.

Jordyn frowned. "Forget that!"

Her hand shot out, withdrew the last cupcake and

brought it to her mouth. She chomped off almost half in one bite. Its sweetness burst against her tongue, and a shiver of excited pleasure stole through her whole body at the realization that she was finally sitting in her own home.

"No way am I saving this for someone else," she mumbled around a mouthful. "This is a time for celebration." She swallowed, licked her lips, then took another bite of the cupcake. "Matter of fact, when I finish this one, I'm probably gonna go back to town and get myself some more."

What was to stop her? She'd stayed fit and healthy for years while she toured the circuit, forgoing greasy food and sweets in favor of more healthy options that would fuel her performance in the arena. But now she was a homeowner, an entrepreneur. A young single woman living in a Christmas town known for its holiday cheer and spectacular mountain views. She had a charming log cabin all her own where she could roll around on the floor anytime she felt like it, basking in the celebratory glow of a fresh start and new life!

Something moved in front of one of the windows, blocking the sunlight. A knock on the glass pane jerked her upright into a seated position, her gaze shooting toward the source.

A man—tall, blond, and muscular—cupped his big hands around his face and peered through the window, his rich blue eyes finding hers.

She stopped chewing. *Holy holly!*

"Sorry to disturb you," the man called out, the deep tone of his voice muted as he waved one hand. "I knocked but I guess you didn't hear me. I'm your neighbor. Saw your truck outside and thought I'd pay you a visit."

Jordyn stared. A Christmas town full of holiday cheer, a charming log cabin, spectacular mountain views, *and* a hot man? What sweet Christmas dream had she been lucky enough to fall into?

The man rapped his knuckles gently against the glass pane again. His brow furrowed as he peered through the window. "Are you okay in there? Do you need some help?"

Jordyn shook her head, mumbling around the chunk of red velvet cupcake in her mouth, "I'm fine." *He* was fine! The finest of male specimens she'd ever laid eyes on. Chewing furiously, she scrambled to her feet and smoothed her hand over her long, tangled hair. "Hold on." She chewed twice then added, "I'll let you i—"

Oh! Oh no! Red velvet cupcake! Choking, she doubled over and coughed, struggling to clear the crumbs from her windpipe.

"You okay?"

At the sound of the man's voice, she nodded and waved furiously for him to come to the front door.

Oh, Lord, Jordyn prayed, her throat burning, *please don't let me go like this. Not now. And not by cupcake. I promise I won't ever be selfish with baked goods again!*

One heavy cough later, the obstruction cleared and she drew in a deep, ragged breath, glancing up at the vaulted ceiling where she almost expected a choir of merciful angels to appear. "Oh, hallelujah! Thank you, thank you, thank you."

She smoothed her hands over her long-sleeved shirt and jeans, inhaled deeply, then opened the front door.

The man was even more impressive up close, with chiseled features and a sensual mouth. It was as though he'd been plucked from her romantic dreams—a strong, handsome prince sent to sweep her up and carry her away.

He grinned. "Hi."

She blinked, her body swaying toward him. Did he feel that electric sizzle between them, too?

"Hi," she breathed.

His grin widened. "You, uh, have a bit of . . ." He lifted his hand and tapped his lower lip with one blunt fingertip.

Jordyn licked her lips, the sweet taste of cream cheese frosting hitting her tongue. Face flaming, she spun away, dragged the back of her hand over her mouth, wiped it clean on her jeans then pushed her hair away from her face and lifted her chin, doing her best to summon a bit of dignity.

"Thank you," she said, her voice slightly hoarse as she faced him again. "I was, um, strangled by a cupcake."

His eyes narrowed and one blond brow rose, amusement appearing on his face. "Strangled by a cupcake?"

"Yep." She forced a strained laugh. "First time I've had one of Noel's famous red velvet cupcakes. I gotta say, those things are dangerous."

One corner of his mouth lifted in a boyish grin. "I have to agree with you on that. I have a hard time turning 'em down, too." He held out his hand. "I'm Nate Reed, owner of Frosted Firs Ranch next door."

She shook his hand, the feel of his warm palm against hers sending a fresh surge of female appreciation through her. "I'm Jordyn Banks. New owner of Chestnut Ridge," she stated proudly.

He nodded, his gaze lowering to her mouth again. "I didn't mean to barge in on you, but I wanted to welcome you to town. And I . . ." His lean cheeks darkened slightly as he gestured toward her chin. "You . . . you've still got a bit of frosting there."

"Oh!" She scrubbed her fingers over her chin. "Sorry. I usually have better manners! I promise." She looked down

at her fingers, which were coated with icing, briefly considered wiping them on her jeans again but, seeking a po-
liter option, stuck them in her mouth instead, quickly
licking the icing from her fingertips.

He looked away, averting his eyes.

"Sorry," she blurted. "That was rude of me. Just don't
want to waste that money I spent on the cupcakes, you
know?"

He rubbed the back of his neck and issued a half-
hearted laugh.

Great. Fantastic first impression! Wallowing on the
floor, choking on a cupcake, then disgracing herself with
bad manners . . . The poor man probably thought she was
a fruitcake.

"Look, I'd love to invite you in but as you can see"—
she gestured behind her—"I don't have any furniture yet."

He held up his hands. "No worries. I didn't mean to in-
trude. I'm sure you'd rather settle in before having company. You just arrived today, I take it?"

"Yeah." She gestured toward the stable to the left of the
log cabin. "Me and Star, that is."

His brows rose.

"My quarter horse." She smiled widely. "Star's been my
partner for years."

"Ah." He nodded. "You barrel race, right?"

"I see word travels fast around here."

He tapped his lips. "From your mouth to all of Noel's
residents' ears . . ."

"Indeed."

They both laughed, then fell silent.

"Well, as I mentioned," Jordyn said, "I'd like to invite you in but I don't even have a chair to offer anyone a
seat yet."

She laughed self-consciously, eager, at this point, to retreat in embarrassment and try to impress him another day when she had time to make herself presenta—

"Hey, wait!" She snapped her fingers. "You said you're my neighbor. Nate, right?"

Smiling, he nodded.

"Neighbor Nate Reed," she repeated slowly. "Owner of Frosted Firs Ranch and that long, white fence bordering my property?"

"Yep."

She grinned. "The one who lurks around my fabulous fir tree from time to time?"

He chuckled. "I see Noel's Nanas have already warned you about me."

"Noel's Nanas?" She tapped her chin. "Has a nice ring to it. I suppose those were the four women who followed me from the town square this morning and told me to guard Fabio Fraser with my life?"

He groaned and dragged a broad hand over his face. "I hate that name."

"Not your first choice, huh?"

"No. It's demeaning. First of all, I don't name trees—each species has already been named—but if I did, I would've chosen something much more dignified."

She tilted her head, trying to focus on his eyes rather than his mouth. "Like what?"

He shrugged. "I don't know. Frederick? Bill? Carlton Brandon Holmes the third, maybe?"

She laughed. "All suitable choices, but a bit stuffy, if you ask me. Fabio Fraser has a much more mischievous—and fun—ring to it. I take it Fabio's the reason you're here?"

He winced. "Not that I'm trying to take advantage of anyone, but—"

"But you'd like to get an up-close look at him, huh? Get your Christmas fix?"

He held her gaze, his mouth twitching. "I suppose that's what I'm after."

"Then how 'bout we take a stroll out back and admire him?" Jordyn grabbed her jacket from the floor, shrugged it on and slipped past him outside, pausing on the front porch. "While we're out there, would you mind showing me the property line between my place and yours? I was thinking of putting up some fencing for an additional paddock and I don't want to encroach on your property."

"I'd be happy to."

He ambled down the steps, joining her, then strode across the property, his long legs matching her pace. The wind had grown blustery, pushing against them as they walked, ruffling their hair. By the time they'd walked across the back lot, Nate's blond hair had been tousled across his forehead and ears.

"The white fencing to your left marks my property line, and"—he pointed to the right—"the Fraser fir marks the back edge of your property bordering mine." His steps slowed as they reached the tree in question and he dragged a hand across the back of his neck, adding sheepishly, "Have to admit, this one caught my eye a long time ago. It has a natural shape I haven't been able to replicate in my own trees." He lifted his hand, his long fingers gently cradling the needles of a low branch.

She drew to a stop, too, standing behind Nate, doing her best to keep her eyes above his waist. Good grief, the man was built! And after an inconspicuous glance at his left hand, she noticed he wasn't wearing a wedding ring. Something about his reserved, quiet, gentlemanlike approach pleased her unexpectedly.

Most of the men she'd met when traveling the rodeo circuit were decent guys, but they tended to be a bit rowdy, overly assertive and usually only interested in one thing: a good time with no strings and no commitment. They all sought a casual relationship. The exact opposite of the type of romantic relationship she'd always dreamed of having.

But judging by first impressions, this man—Nate Reed— seemed to have put down roots in this beautiful town and might be inclined to embrace commitment rather than run from it. In any event, he was a man she definitely wouldn't mind getting to know a little better.

"... willing to part with it?"

Jordyn blinked. Nate faced her now, his gaze, expectant, focused intently on hers. "I'm sorry, what did you say?"

"I was wondering if you'd be willing to part with it?" He reached out and touched one of the tree's branches again. "I'll pay top dollar for it."

She shook her head in confusion. "You want to buy Fabio Fraser?"

He nodded.

"You want to cut it down?"

Smiling, he nodded again.

"But . . ." Frowning, she shoved her hands in her jacket pockets, pulling her coat tighter around her chest. "I kinda like it in the ground, you know? Healthy and alive? Able to be admired year-round? It's a rather perfect tree, I think."

"That it is."

"You know . . . the Nanas mentioned they were coming back to visit me tomorrow with a welcome basket and a proposition of utmost importance." She raised one eyebrow. "Got any idea what they want to propose? Anything to do with this tree?"

Nate chuckled. "Chances are, they're going to come by

to talk you into competing against me in Noel's annual Christmas competition."

"Christmas competition?" Her frown vanished and she smiled, her stomach fluttering. "That would be fun. I've never stayed put anywhere long enough to participate in a community event. Sounds like a blast!"

He shrugged. "It is. But it's also pretty cutthroat." He leaned closer and lowered his voice, his mouth twitching. "The Nanas are in charge of the competition and they take the whole thing very seriously."

"And that's why you're both interested in this tree?"

"I'd like to buy it and enter it into Noel's Christmas tree contest," he said. "It's the culminating contest of the Christmas competition. And the Nanas probably want to buy it, give it to one of my competitors to make sure I lose the Christmas tree contest along with all the other contests in Noel's Christmas competition this year."

"Oh yeah?" She stifled a giggle. "And what did you do to deserve such poor treatment?"

He laughed. "Nothing, I assure you. I board horses and grow Christmas trees next door on my ranch and generally keep to myself. Producing spectacular Christmas trees is my specialty and it's more than a full-time job. But I guess I won the tree contest in the Christmas competition too many years in a row and the Nanas think it's time someone else gets a shot."

"And you don't want to give up the title?"

"Not a chance."

Jordyn crossed her arms over her chest and smirked. "I get it. I'm pretty competitive myself."

"That's what they're counting on." He rocked back on his heels and glanced up at the tree. "They're planning on talking you into competing against me and using this tree to clinch the win." He spread his hands. "But considering you just moved in, I imagine you'll have a lot to do to get settled and probably won't have time to participate in the Christmas contests. By the way, if you need a hand getting moved in and settled, I'd be happy to help you out. I know a few folks who'd be willing to give you discounts on—"

"Are you trying to bribe me?" She lifted her chin and held his gaze, the hint of mischief in his eyes making her smile wider. "You are, aren't you, Neighbor Nate? You're just trying to get to my tree before they do."

Holding her gaze, he grinned. "You think?"

"I know." She leaned in, too, bringing her nose inches from his, then whispered, "And I'm gonna tell you right now, Nate Reed—neighbor and not—if I were to enter this competition, I'd wipe the floor with you."

He laughed softly, his warm breath brushing her chilled cheek. Oh, he smelled delicious. His muscular physique, tender voice and sensual mouth were enough to melt any woman into a puddle at his feet—even in the midst of a winter chill.

"What if I sweeten the deal?" he whispered. His gaze lowered to her mouth, a subtle flare of heat in his eyes. After a moment, he stepped back, straightened to his full height, and withdrew a business card and pen from his jacket pocket. He flipped the business card over and scrawled something on the back, then handed it to her. "If you go to town to pick up some things—furniture, linen, household supplies, whatever—show this to the owners of the stores you go to and they'll give you my business discount. You can even flash it at Kringle's Café for a hefty markdown on those red velvet cupcakes."

She flipped the card over and read his note on the back: *Please extend my discount to Jordan Banks upon purchase.* His signature was beneath the note.

She glanced up at him and grinned. "I spell my first name with a y."

"Oh." He dipped his head in apology, then plucked the

card from her hand, corrected it, and returned it to her. "There. Good to go now."

"You think this will do it, huh?" She tapped the business card with her fingernail. "You think offering me a discount on some furniture and jumbo cupcakes is going to persuade me to sell you this tree?"

Biting his lip, he squinted up at the Fraser fir. "Well . . . I'm hoping it'll at least be a jumping-off point for negotiation." He met her gaze again and smiled. "And if you're into decorating for Christmas, I sell every decoration imaginable in the gift shop next door. Swing by when you have the time and I'll make the deal even sweeter."

He spun around on the heels of his worn boots and left, striding across the dormant grass, but paused several feet away and glanced at her over his shoulder. "I mean it. Stop by Frosted Firs Ranch anytime you like. We'd be happy to welcome you to Noel properly."

We?

Jordyn watched him amble away, then looked up at Fabio Fraser and smiled. "You're in rather high demand, dude. Though I'm not sure who's more handsome—you, or our neighbor."

At the sound of an engine, she glanced at the driveway, watching as Nate's big red truck moved slowly along the driveway and returned to the main road.

Looked like Noel had even more to offer than she'd thought. Though she was eager to get to know Neighbor Nate better, make a good impression on Noel's Nanas and possibly participate in Noel's annual Christmas competition, she was rather fond of her new Christmas tree and had no desire to give it up to anyone. And most especially, she didn't want to cut it down. How could anyone hack down a perfect, living embodiment of Christmas?

But she did want to make a good impression on Noel's

Nanas, become a part of the close-knit community and create a home here. There was no better way to get a jump on that than to participate in the annual Christmas traditions.

Problem was, whom could she afford to disappoint the least? Neighbor Nate, Noel's Nanas . . . or herself?

Chapter Three

Nate had discovered years ago that chopping firewood was an excellent distraction. Swinging an ax through the air was an antidote to every unwelcome emotion in the human body: anger, grief, regret, frustration—you name it! And it certainly would've relieved the unexpected—and unwelcome—desire that lingered within him long after he'd left Chestnut Ridge . . . had his younger brother and daughter not joined him the moment he'd returned to Frosted Firs Ranch an hour ago and picked up his ax.

"So, she had red hair like the Nanas said?" Tucker, hands on his hips and an eager gleam in his eye, stood several feet away and stared at Nate intently. "Was it long or short? Straight, wavy? Or was she wearing a hat?" He grinned. "You know, those barrel racers, they love them some hats. Wear 'em well, too."

Nate hefted his ax in the air and swung, splitting a log on the low stump in front of him. "It was long. Kinda wavy."

But it wasn't totally red. Up close, Jordyn's hair had a hint of gold in it. Or maybe that was just the way the sunlight had highlighted the long strands. Either way, his fingers had itched to trail through the soft waves. The rays of sunlight cutting through the cold mountain air had cast a golden glow at her back. That's what had made those long locks of hers attract his attention. He'd never seen a shade of red quite like it before.

"What about her eyes?" Roxie, standing near Tucker, walked across the pile of logs as though each piece of wood were a balance beam, hopping from one log to another each time she reached its end. "What color eyes did she have?"

Nate placed another log on the stump, swung his ax and split it. "Green. They were green."

A mesmerizing, deep shade of emerald with more tiny flecks of gold. They'd darkened ever so slightly when she'd looked at him, and every time those long thick eyelashes of hers had blinked slowly, it was as though they were casting a sweet, dreamy spell over him. It'd been hard to look away and even harder to walk away from his alluring new neighbor. He didn't know what he'd expected when he'd arrived at Chestnut Ridge, certainly not the gut punch of desire he'd experienced when she'd opened the door.

No. He hadn't felt an attraction that intense in a long time. Not since his teenage years when he'd first begun dating and discovered what attraction was all about.

"Her name's Jordyn, right?" The spark of male interest in Tucker's eyes was unmistakable.

Nate rolled his shoulders, trying to dispel the tension that knotted between his shoulder blades and burned clear through to his chest at the thought of Tucker taking a shine to their new neighbor. "Yes. Jordyn. Spelled with a *y*—not an *a*."

Roxie smiled. "Oh, that's neat. I like that."

Grinning, Tucker rubbed his chin thoughtfully. "How old is she?"

"Didn't ask." But considering the youthful spark he'd

admired in her playful gaze . . . "If I had to guess, I'd say she's probably around your age."

"Twenty-five," Roxie supplied. "That's how old you are, right, Uncle Tucker?"

Tucker grinned. "Yep, sweet pea. And your dad here is an old man who just turned the ripe old age of—"

"Watch it." Nate bit back a smile. "I might be five years older than you but I can still pin you down."

"How tall is she, Daddy?" The wind ruffled Roxie's bangs across her eyes and she pushed them back with one gloved hand. "Is she a whole lot taller than me?"

Nate smiled. "Yeah. She's almost my height, save for an inch or two."

Tucker whistled low. "Leggy, then?"

Grunting, Nate chopped another log. "You've got a one-track mind, Tucker. You ever think of moving intelligent conversation to the top of your priority list for a woman and putting appearance at the bottom?"

"What's a pri-or-ty list, Daddy?"

Nate stilled, the wide-eyed, innocent look in Roxie's eyes making his cheeks burn. "It's a . . . well, a priority just means something that's important. That's all." He cut his eyes at Tucker and cleared his throat. "Aren't you getting cold out here, sweetheart? You could take Tucker up on his offer of some hot chocolate and go warm up inside the gift shop with him."

And maybe then, he could finish the task at hand without being interrogated by Tucker.

"Nope. I ain't cold." She hopped onto another log and grinned. "And I want to hear more about the new lady next door."

Tucker wiggled his eyebrows. "Me, too, brother. You said she asked about the property line 'cuz she's planning on adding a paddock?"

Nate sighed. "Yeah."

"And she's got a white quarter over there?"

Nate positioned a new log on the stump and swung again. "Yeah."

"White?" Roxie stopped walking along her log, hopped off, then propped her hands on her hips as she looked up at Tucker. "But quarters are silver, Uncle Tucker. All coins are except for pennies."

Nate chuckled. "He's talking about a horse, sweetheart. Not a coin."

"Oh." Roxie smiled. "You mean like the one you put in our stable last week?"

Nate nodded. "Just like it. But this one was white as a pearl. I caught a glimpse of her in the stable at Chestnut Ridge as I was leaving."

Tucker squatted on his haunches beside Roxie and gently tugged her blond ponytail. "Those quarters are magicians when it comes to circling barrels. You know the ones I showed you on the video the other day? The ones that compete in the same arena where I used to ride bulls?"

Roxie grinned, her eyes lighting up with excitement. "Yep. I remember. You said you'd take me to see them run one day."

"Well, we won't have to go too far for that now, will we? We've got a real-life barrel racer living next door." Tucker, brow furrowing, held up one finger and looked at Nate. "Say, what's the horse's name? I'll look 'em both up. If they're any good at competing, there'll be some highlight videos on them somewhere."

Nate swung his ax again, splitting another piece of firewood, then stuck the blade of the ax into the stump. "It's a white mare named Star."

And how he wished he'd had the opportunity to mull over all of this information in silence.

On the short drive home from Jordyn's place, he'd been looking forward to some solitude in the brisk, winter wind, swinging his ax, relishing the sharp split of oak and dispelling each of the bothersome—but intriguing—thoughts of his new neighbor that buzzed in his mind. Jordyn Banks and the effect her presence had on him had been nothing short of a shock.

When he'd knocked on the front door of her log cabin, he'd planned to greet her politely, welcome her to town and feel absolutely nothing—the same reaction he'd experienced with every woman he'd encountered since losing Macy. But from the moment he'd caught a glimpse of Jordyn through her cabin window, her pretty features and pink, kissable lips had snagged his attention. And when she'd opened the door and stood in front of him, he couldn't help but notice she had a fantastic figure—soft but strong—and as he discovered later, a sassy attitude to boot.

But it was her fun, flirtatious demeanor that really made him relax in her presence. The open, casual way she'd greeted him as though they were already familiar acquaintances or perhaps even old friends had made him feel an almost instant connection with her. And the teasing tone in her voice and admiring glances she'd sneaked at him when she thought he wasn't looking had filled him with pleasure. Her easygoing disposition and bubbly welcome were an intoxicating combination. A reaction quite different from the calm, tender emotions he'd felt for Macy.

That realization had sobered him up and dispelled the giddy attraction he'd felt for Jordyn as he'd driven home from Chestnut Ridge over an hour ago. The thought of admiring another woman who was so different from Macy had instantly reminded him of how rare the loving bond he'd had with Macy was.

At first glance, Jordyn Banks was nothing like Macy and therefore, logically, she should not have appealed to him.

But there was something about her. Something about the sweet tone of her voice, the gentle look in her eyes and the way she'd fallen so easily in step with him as they'd walked beside each other across the back lot of her property. Her charisma had made being in her company easy. So much easier than the time he spent with women he'd known all his life, whose advances he'd ended up politely rejecting.

Jordyn Banks was a stranger. It should be easy to get her out of his mind. The emotion she'd stirred inside him had been desire, plain and simple. Nothing more. He just needed to shrug off the attraction he had for her and get down to the business of negotiating a fair price for that magnificent Fraser fir.

"We've got a real shot at persuading her to sell us that tree." Nate dragged the back of his forearm over his sweaty forehead and sighed with satisfaction at the sight of the tall stack of seasoned firewood he'd chopped. "To get off on the right foot, I extended my business discount to her so she can buy furniture and supplies at a good price in town, and"—he gestured toward the stack of firewood—"once I drop this off on her front porch with a neighborly note, she'll be so pleased with our welcome that she'll be happy to sit down and negotiate."

Roxie skipped over and hugged his leg. "She's gonna give us the perfect tree?"

Throat tightening, Nate looked down and smoothed his hand over her soft hair. "I hope so, sweetheart. Your mom loved watching that tree grow. She used to say God grew it special just for the Noel's tree competition."

"And if we have it," Roxie said, "we'll win the Christmas Crown again, won't we?"

Nate nodded. "That's what I'm counting on. Ten wins in a row. That way, the Reed family tradition of winning will still be going strong and we'll have a new Christmas Crown for your Mom's Christmas case."

"Shouldn't be too difficult to pull off." Tucker spun on his heel and started walking away.

"Hey," Nate called out. "Where you going?"

Tucker stopped and looked back. "I'm gonna bring my truck around, load up the firewood and take it over to her." He grinned. "Introduce myself to her properly and turn on the charm. We'll have that tree within the hour."

"Oh, no." Nate waved a hand in the air. "No way. Right now, it's best that we back off and give her some time to settle in. And since she has an empty house, with the Nanas expected to drop by tomorrow, I'm thinking a gift of firewood to make her cabin cozy would be welcome. I'm gonna bribe her a little bit—like the Nanas suggested." He took off his gloves and glanced at the sky, noting the sun had dipped behind the mountain range in the distance. "I'll take care of loading this up in my truck after supper, then I'll drive over after dark and leave it on her front porch." He could feel Tucker's suspicious gaze on him, and his skin prickled under his brother's scrutiny. "I'm gonna wrap a bow around it and leave a card, you know?" He strove for a blank expression, then looked Tucker in the eyes. "Do it up real nice as a neighborly Christmas gesture."

"A neighborly Christmas gesture?" Tucker cocked one eyebrow, searched Nate's expression, then burst out laughing. "Oh, man. You want to have a real conversation now? Maybe actually tell me what's going on here?"

The knowing look in Tucker's gaze made Nate's cheeks burn.

Frowning, Roxie glanced up at Nate. "What's he mean, Daddy?"

Nate cleared his throat and dragged his hand across the back of his neck. "Nothing, sweetheart. Your uncle Tucker's just babbling nonsense like he usually does. Now, did you bring the Christmas card out with you like I asked?"

"I sure did, Daddy." Roxie stuck her hand in her jacket pocket and pulled out a small Christmas card with a festively trimmed Christmas tree drawn on the front. "I picked the prettiest one from the gift shop," she said, smiling broadly. "Scott helped me."

"That was nice of him," Nate said.

And even nicer that he and Tucker had been able to afford to hire Scott, a local senior in high school, as well as two other teenagers to run the gift shop at Frosted Firs and sell Christmas trees during the late afternoon and evening hours this Christmas season. That way, he and Tucker had more time to devote to enjoying the holidays with Roxie while she was on vacation from school.

"Thank you for helping me, sweetheart." Nate took the Christmas card from her, pulled a pen from his jacket pocket and sat down on the stump. He placed the pen to the card then paused, hesitating.

Tucker guffawed. "What you gonna say, Casanova?"

Roxie's brows rose. "What's a cass-a-rova, Daddy?"

"Nothing," Nate said softly, shooting a stern look at Tucker. "I'm just going to write a nice, neighborly Christmas message."

And he tried. He really tried.

Sitting there in the back lot of Frosted Firs Ranch, he stared down at the blank side of the Christmas card on his thigh and tried several times to write something festive and catchy. This was harder than he thought. What did a man say to the new, attractive woman next door that couldn't be construed as an invitation for something more than just "being a good neighbor"? 'Cuz Lord knew, as a happy single man who preferred to remain so, he didn't need to send any mixed signals.

But he did need to make his message kind so that, hopefully, his welcome gift would make a good impression on her and convince her to consider his offer for the tree.

Tucker, who'd been staring a hole through Nate's head for the past five minutes, seemed to read his thoughts. "How about you just write, *Give us your tree, woman?*"

Nate rolled his eyes.

"Or"—Tucker spread his hands—"here's some free firewood in exchange for giving me a leg up in the Christmas Tree Competition."

Nate rubbed his aching forehead. "No. I said all I needed to say regarding that when I went over there earlier. This just needs to be a simple welcome. It can even be just one word. Just something short and pleasant, you know?"

"One word?" Roxie asked, bouncing with excitement by his side.

Nate nodded. "Sure."

"You're giving her firewood." Roxie smiled, approval in her eyes as she glanced at the large stack of split logs. "That's so she'll be warm and cheery at Christmas, right? That's what you say to me every time you make a fire in the fireplace—that you're keeping me warm and cheery."

Nate reached out and nudged her chin affectionately with one knuckle. "That's right, sweetie."

"Then how about you write *joy?*" she asked. "Because I always feel joy when you make a fire to keep me warm."

Nate kissed her forehead. "That's perfect! Kind and to the point."

He pressed the pen to the card, amended Roxie's word slightly, and wrote, *Enjoy!*

Roxie peered over his shoulder. "But make it happy, Daddy. Put a smiley face."

Nate grinned. "You got it."

He drew a smiley face underneath the word, *Enjoy!*

"Happier, Daddy. Give it a Santa wink, okay?"

"Sure thing." He added a wink to the smiley face which, judging by the proud expression on Roxie's face, met with her approval.

"Perfect!" Roxie giggled.

"Nothing like a useful gift and benevolent message to inspire goodwill in a neighbor at Christmas," Nate said. "Hopefully, she'll be so grateful, we'll have a decent shot at getting that tree."

And with a little luck, his gentlemanly gesture would help Jordyn, and maybe even the Nanas, see the good in him.

"Of all the . . . !"

The next afternoon, Jordyn, coughing and sputtering, ran over to one of the living room windows in her log cabin, jerked it open, stuck her head outside and heaved in a lungful of ice-cold winter air.

"Oh, for goodness' sake!" she gasped. There went her plan for extending a warm welcome to her guests!

"Jordyn?"

There they were—Noel's Nanas. Arriving for their afternoon visit just in time to witness her predicament. All four of the women, dressed in elegant holiday-themed sweaters paired with either a skirt or dress pants, hustled across the front yard and up the front steps of the log cabin as fast as their shiny high heels would allow. Kandy, straggling behind, carried an oversized white basket decorated with a shiny red bow.

"What in heaven's name is going on?" Carol Belle asked.

Leading the pack, she halted in her tracks at the front door, her mouth hanging open as a thick cloud of black smoke rolled out of the window, engulfing Jordyn's face and prompting a new round of hacking coughs.

"Oh, my Lord!" Kandy squeaked, clutching the basket to her chest. "She used the fireplace! I told you we should've—"

"That's quite enough, Kandy," Carol Belle said hastily. "Are you okay, Jordyn?"

"I'm"—*cough*—"okay." Jordyn coughed again, peering through the fine particles of black soot.

The front door banged open, several sets of high heels clacked across the hardwood floor in the living room and a second window whooshed open. A chorus of dismayed murmurs peppered the air as the four women waved their arms, dispelling as much of the black smoke as possible.

"What in the world?" Carol Belle's gentle but firm hands hooked around Jordyn's waist, tugging her away from the window and back across the living room to a small pocket of clean air near the kitchen. "Did Hal Sutton not tell you the fireplace is a dud?"

Jordyn cupped her hands over her mouth and released a horribly croupy cough. "He told me the place needed some repairs and that the chimney needed to be inspected but I bought the place as-is and I decided to give the fireplace a try anyway." Finally able to drag in some much-needed oxygen, she lowered her hands, lifted her face and inhaled. "It's not Hal's fault. I was in such a hurry to buy this place and settle in, I didn't ask or worry about any problems the place had and I declined to have the home inspected to close the deal sooner. I should've had the chimney inspected before I tried using it like Hal suggested."

Her cheeks heated as all four pairs of eyes leveled on her with a hint of disbelieving judgment. Oh, how could she have been so impulsive and irresponsible!

"But, well . . ." Jordyn added sheepishly, "I've never had a home before—let alone one with a fireplace—so I don't know all the ins and outs of owning a house and I was so excited to have my own home and my own fireplace—especially at Christmas!" She looked down, her cheeks heating. "I just opened the flue, threw the wood in and lit it."

The Nanas were silent for so long, she couldn't help but lift her head and glance at them. Instead of the criticizing looks she expected, their eyes had warmed with a mixture of surprise and a hint of sadness.

"You've never had a home before?" Holly fiddled with the tassels on her cashmere scarf and bit her lip. "A home . . . or a house?"

Jordyn shrugged. "Neither, really."

"But what about when you were a child?"

"I grew up in foster homes," Jordyn said, waving away the women's concerned glances. "It wasn't bad, you know? I met some really great people, lived in a lot of different places . . ." She forced a smile. "I guess that's why I enjoyed traveling the circuit so much. Bouncing around felt more familiar to me than staying in one place."

A soft sound of dismay escaped Eve's lips as she surveyed Jordyn with a wounded expression.

Kandy stepped over the big basket she'd placed on the living room floor and hurried over, taking Jordyn's hands in hers. "And you chose Noel as your safe landing?" She kissed Jordyn's cheek, her pink hair tickling Jordyn's skin briefly before she stepped back and smiled. "We're so glad you decided to join us—especially during Christmas!"

"Yes, indeed!" Eve clacked across the hardwood floor on her high heels and hugged Jordyn. "You came at the perfect time!"

"Absolutely perfect," Holly chimed in, hugging Jordyn, too.

"Quite right," Carol Belle said, nodding. "Noel is gorgeous all year round, but at Christmas, it really shines."

Jordyn smiled. Kandy's gentle kiss still lingered on her cheek and warmed her heart. She looked at each of the Nanas, her chest filling with a pleasant tenderness at the thought of potentially having four caring women in her life. How wonderful it would be to have friends to visit and laugh with during Christmas, and maybe even learn from and lean on from time to time throughout the rest of the year.

"That's kind of why I caused such a scene," she said. "I was given a huge stack of firewood last night and I knew y'all were coming this afternoon to visit with your proposition, so I thought I'd try to make a cozy seating area for us and well . . ." She glanced around at the five lawn chairs she'd arranged into a circle in the middle of the living room, the cheap red fabric covering them barely visible amid the dark cloud of smoke. "Well, I was . . ." Her shoulders sagged. "I was trying to make a good impression."

But she'd failed miserably.

Carol Belle exchanged an odd glance with the other Nanas, a hint of accomplishment in her eyes. "You say you were given firewood? As in for free?"

"Yeah." Jordyn licked her lips as she drew in another lungful of clean air. "I went to town yesterday evening to get some lawn chairs and a few supplies, and when I came back, Nate Reed was driving off in his truck. He left a stack of firewood with a big, red bow on it and a Christmas card."

"You . . . you say Nate brought the firewood over himself?" Holly asked, her expression brightening with pleased surprise.

Jordyn nodded. "It was so nice of him—it's a shame we didn't have a chance to enjoy the firewood."

"Mm-hm." What sounded like a low growl escaped Carol Belle's lips. "May I see the card in question?"

Jordyn waved away an errant puff of smoke that drifted toward her nose. "O-of course. It's in the kitchen." She walked into the kitchen, waving away more smoke as she went, grabbed the small card off the counter, then returned to the living room and handed it to Carol Belle. "It's a beautiful Christmas card, and he wrote a nice message."

She hid her grin. Nate's gift had been unexpected, as had the cute smiley face he'd drawn on the back of the card. Perhaps her hunky new neighbor had a flirtatious—and possibly sensitive—streak after all. Had he felt the same electric chemistry between them that had taken hold of her yesterday?

Carol Belle studied the colorful Christmas tree on the front of the card, then flipped it over. For a moment, Jordyn could've sworn Carol Belle's mouth twitched with humor, but the amused look vanished in a flash and Carol Belle's eyes grew round and angry.

"This wasn't a considerate gift and Christmas card, Jordyn," Carol Belle said. "This was a warning!" Her hand shot out, jerking the small card toward the three women who stood nearby waving their arms to dispel the last vestiges of smoke. "Have a look, ladies, and tell me what you think."

Eve plucked the card from Carol Belle's hand and peered at it through her glasses.

"Notice what's on the front?" Carol Belle prompted.

"What's on it?" Kandy asked, hurrying over to Eve's side, the bells on a silver bracelet she wore jangling.

"A Christmas tree," Eve said softly as she exchanged a knowing look with Carol Belle.

"A Fraser fir just like our Fabio," Carol Belle grumbled.

"And on the back?" Holly asked as she pressed close to the other women for a look. She still waved a hand in front of her perfectly made-up face, warding away the tendrils of smoke lingering in the living room.

Eve flipped the card over. "He wrote one word. *Enjoy.*" Her brows rose. "And he drew a smiley face." She looked up, her surprised gaze roving over each of the women standing around her. "A smiley face that's winking."

The Nanas exchanged meaningful glances; then, moments later, Kandy gasped, Holly tutted her tongue, and Carol Belle stomped one high-heeled foot.

"That mean-spirited, nasty, grinch of a man!" Carol Belle huffed. "I knew he meant it when he said he wasn't going to bow out of the Christmas competition, but I never dreamed he'd try to sabotage an innocent woman he didn't even know just to get his hands on a tree!"

"Sabotage?" Jordyn frowned, bewildered by the overly righteous indignation in Carol Belle's voice and mixed signals coming from all of the Nanas. "Wait . . . what exactly is it you think he did?"

Carol Belle scowled. "He tried to smoke you out to send a message." She stabbed her hand at the still smoking fireplace. "That right there's a warning!"

Jordyn laughed. "You think Nate did this on purpose? You think he knew my chimney was damaged and gave me firewood so I'd burn it and smoke up my cabin?" A low laugh escaped her lips. "Please forgive me, but I think that's a bit of a stretch—"

"Really?" Carol Belle scowled. "He lived next to Beau Manning, the former owner of this place, for almost a decade. Beau was a frugal man and would use up every last bit of good in something before he replaced it. I, myself, know Beau had to call the fire department twice before he moved out because of the cracks in that chimney. And if I knew about it, I bet Nate did, seeing as how he lives right next door." She shook her head. "I wouldn't put a thing past Nate when it comes to the Christmas competition. And by the way . . ." She leaned closer to Jordyn and tilted her head. "Did he happen to approach you about Fabio yesterday?"

Jordyn hesitated. "Well, yes, but—"

"See!" Carol Belle stomped her foot again. "He wanted to buy the tree, didn't he?"

"Yes, b—"

"But nothing!" Carol Belle said. "You can't let him get away with this or he'll stomp all over you during the competition. You need to go over there and give him a piece of your mind!"

Oh, boy. What was she getting herself into here?

"Let's slow down a bit, please?" Jordyn gestured for the Christmas card and when Eve handed it to her, she turned it over, studying the cheery Christmas tree illustration. "I really think this was just a kind, neighborly act that backfired. And I do want to participate in Noel's Christmas competition, but I did just move in. I have to agree with Nate that I'll be spending a lot of time sprucing this place up and may not have time to fully partici—"

"He said that?" Eve peered at her over the rim of her glasses. "Nate said you'd be too busy to participate in our Christmas competition?"

Jordyn nodded slowly.

"Oh, my." Holly clamped a hand to her chest.

"Let's not be hasty." Kandy clapped her hands together and smiled. "Nate didn't mean anything by it. He was probably just making conversation and watching out for his new neighbor. After all . . ." She glanced around at the lawn chairs in the living room. "Jordyn *will* need some time to settle in." She smiled brightly at Jordyn. "I'd be happy to help you decorate. There's a wreath at Nate's gift shop that would be just perfect for—"

"Excellent point, Kandy." Carol Belle crossed her arms over her chest. "Jordyn does have a lot to do and she'll need a helping hand to guide her through the Christmas contests." She pursed her lips. "The rules allow for a mentor for newcomers, and I think any situation involving Nate necessitates one. There are twelve contests and you'll need someone to guide you through the rules of each—especially the Christmas tree contest."

Jordyn grinned. "Rules, a mentor, and twelve contests? This Christmas competition must be a big deal for Noel, huh?"

"The absolute biggest, my dear," Carol Belle said. "We've been managing the contest for ten years now. Ever since . . ." Kandy glanced at Carol Belle, her tone softening. "Well, ever since Carol Belle lost George."

Jordyn hesitated then asked, "I don't mean to pry but . . . who was George?"

"My late husband." Carole Belle's voice trembled. She looked away and cleared her throat. "George and I grew up together. Right next door, actually. Both of us were headstrong and we fought like cats and dogs when we were kids, but when we got older, that animosity turned to something sweeter." She smiled. "We married young. Had a lot of good years together. But I lost him to cancer eleven years ago."

Jordyn winced. "I'm so sorry."

Carol Belle sniffed and waved away her concern. "Not your fault. Everyone loses someone at some point in life, but I lost George on Christmas Eve, so that made the pain a whole lot worse." Her chin trembled. "He loved Christmas. Every year, he spent days decorating our lawn and house—inside and out. He always used to say Noel needed a formal Christmas tradition of some kind other than the lighting of the town tree. He said he thought a contest of some sort would lift everyone's spirits, boost community relations and maybe even bring some of our loved ones home." She cleared her throat. "Our daughter left home years ago after she and I had a falling out, and she hasn't returned to Noel since. I've never met my grandchild, and now George never will. He loved her so much and used to hope Christmas might one day be the catalyst for her return."

Kandy reached out and squeezed Carol Belle's hand. "I lost my husband, too. I was only thirty-three when Carl died of a heart attack and it was quite a shock, so I knew how difficult things would be for Carol Belle for a while after losing George. So one day, Carol Belle and I sat down with Eve and Holly and discussed how we could best honor our late husbands and make Christmas joyful for Carol Belle again." She met Carol Belle's eyes and smiled. "The Christmas competition was a hit and grows bigger every year with us Nanas at the helm. When the four of us work together, there's nothing we can't accomplish."

"If it hadn't been for Kandy, Eve, and Holly," Carol Belle said, "I don't know how I would've overcome my grief. Organizing the Christmas competition kept me busy and optimistic, and it's become a well-loved tradition in Noel." Carol Belle smiled wider as she patted Jordyn's shoulder. "And you're going to be our guest of honor this year. Since Kandy is great at motivating others, I'm assigning her as your mentor and will add your name to the sign-up list. Opening day is tomorrow at dusk in the town square."

Kandy squealed and did a little dance, her pink curls bouncing over her shoulders. "This is so exciting! I'm going to teach you everything I know about getting a leg up on the competition—especially Nate!"

"Oh, but wait just a sec." Jordyn rubbed her temple, her mind swirling. "I thank you for the support, but twelve contests will take a lot of time and commitment. I wouldn't want to let anyone down by promising to do something that I can't carry through with—especially seeing as how the Christmas competition is so special to all four of you. I wouldn't want to do anything to jeopardize its success. And I still have a ton to do around here. I mean, I don't even have a bed yet. I'm still using my sleeping bag on the floor."

"We'll take care of that right now." Kandy looped her arm around Jordyn's and tugged her toward the door. "We pounce on any excuse to shop, and holiday sales just kicked off in Noel. We can shop while your cabin airs out."

"Do you prefer a storage, adjustable or simple bed frame?" Eve asked, clicking along on her heels behind them.

"Metal or wood?" Carol Belle asked, joining them.

"And what about bedding?" Holly smiled and looped her arm around Jordyn's free one as they tugged her outside. "Do you like comforters or quilts? Cotton, flannel, or silk sheets? And what type of pattern? Solid, floral or . . ."

Jordyn, her mind swirling, threw caution to the wind, allowed the women to lead her along the driveway, bundle her up in their red Cadillac and start the drive to downtown Noel. It was a welcome new joy to be swept up among the women as though she were one of them, and chances were, if she agreed to sign up for Noel's Christmas competition, she might even win over more residents of the town.

But winning the Christmas competition for Noel's Nanas would mean Nate's tenth Christmas Crown win—and Fabio would have to be sacrificed. And Neighbor Nate would—according to the Nanas—have to become Christmas enemy number one!

Chapter Four

When competing on the circuit, Jordyn always played things straight. She prepared, followed the rules and wished her competitors well. So the day after the Nanas' visit, a Sunday afternoon and the day of Noel's Christmas kickoff, she drove over to Frosted Firs Ranch, determined to do just that.

A low whistle escaped her as she reached the end of the long, paved driveway and parked her truck.

White fencing wrapped with deep green garlands, red and gold bows, and white lights stretched as far as the eye could see, encompassing the expansive grounds of the ranch, then disappeared out of view as it bordered the narrow road that ran alongside acres upon acres of lush evergreens growing in perfectly aligned rows below the high peaks of the mountains and the wide, blue sky. A beautiful farmhouse-style building stood proudly at the front of the property and served as a gift shop with an antique red sign etched with the message: DASH INTO A FROSTED FIRS CHRISTMAS FOR ALL YOUR HOLIDAY DECORATIONS AND GIFTS!

Beyond the gift shop stood several white stables with steeples, two large barns with decorative cupolas, and a breathtaking three-story Victorian farmhouse with a wrap-around porch and black metal roof. Every structure on the ranch had been lovingly decorated with evergreen garlands, wreaths, and potted trees and all of it had been trimmed with bright red holly berries, pine cones, and solid and patterned bows in red, gold, white, and silver.

"Talk about a Christmas dream . . ."

Jordyn hopped out of her truck and walked slowly into the gift shop, taking her time to savor the view outside as she went, glancing around at the rural mountain splendor like a child in a toy store. A bell jangled over the door as she entered and a soothing atmosphere of cozy warmth, soft holiday music, and at least fifteen thousand square feet of Christmas decorations, handcrafted toys, and the decadent aroma of rich hot chocolate enveloped her.

"Well, hello."

Jordyn glanced to her left. A a tall blond man with a come-hither smile stood beside an ornate metal log rack stacked with dozens of bundles of seasoned firewood tied with red bows.

"I've seen one of those somewhere before." Grinning, Jordyn removed the sunglasses she'd donned during her drive over, slipped them in the pocket of her jean jacket and smiled. "You work here?"

The man grinned wide. "Yep. I'm one of the owners of Frosted Firs Ranch." He sauntered over to her, his swagger surprisingly reminiscent of the cowboys she'd encountered on the rodeo circuit, and held out his big hand. "Tucker Reed."

"Jordyn Banks." She shook his hand, the flirtatious gleam in his eyes making her smile. This guy was definitely a heartbreaker—she could spot one a mile away—but the boyish charm in his expression was just endearing enough that she suspected a woman who had the misfortune of falling for him might be inclined to forgive his roguish tendencies. "Any chance you dropped off a bundle of that firewood by my place yesterday?"

"Depends on which place is your place." He cocked his head to the side and tapped his chin, his mannerism somehow familiar as he surveyed her. "Wavy red hair and deep green eyes." He raised one blond brow. "I'm guessing you're our new neighbor at Chestnut Ridge."

She laughed. "You'd be guessing right."

"Then, yeah. A bundle of firewood was dropped off at your place yesterday. But it wasn't me that left it and it wasn't one of these bundles right here," he said, patting a log.

"It was Nate, right?"

"Yep. You received a freshly chopped stack of our finest—and perfectly seasoned—oak from my brother, the primary owner of this ranch." His gaze veered over her shoulder and his blue eyes narrowed on something in the distance, his mouth twitching. "From what he told me, he dropped it off like Santa Claus. Just tossed it on your porch and left like some common big-gut, holiday-gift-giver from the North Pole." Grinning, he refocused on her face and winked. "Did you get his note? The one with the little smiley face that—"

"Please excuse my brother," a deep, familiar voice drawled at Jordyn's back. "I have my doubts that he ever matured beyond twelve years old."

Jordyn spun around to find Nate and a little girl, a cute blonde with Nate's crystal blue eyes and warm smile, standing behind her. Judging by her appearance, the child was unmistakably related to the two brothers, and by the way the girl held Nate's hand and leaned affectionately against his leg, she couldn't help but wonder . . .

"We." Her voice faltered with surprise at the word escaping her lips.

Nate frowned in confusion. "I'm sorry?"

Clearing her throat, she carefully maintained a neutral expression and polite smile as she continued. "You said 'We'd be happy to welcome you' yesterday when you asked me to stop by your gift shop. I guess this is what you meant." She gestured toward the little girl, then Tucker. "You have a brother and a niece?"

"Daughter," Nate said.

Oh, heavens! The little girl was his daughter. He *was* married. And she'd admired and flirted with him like a lovestruck fool yesterday.

How humiliating!

She smiled wider, despite the scorching heat in her cheeks. "How wonderful."

Smiling back, Nate smoothed his hand over the young girl's ponytail and gently squeezed her shoulder. "Roxie, would you like to introduce yourself to our new neighbor?"

Nate's daughter released her father's hand and stepped forward, extending her hand to Jordyn. "Merry Christmas! My name is Roxanna Dawn Reed but I like Roxie best. It's nice to meet you."

Jordyn's polite smile warmed with tenderness as she shook the little girl's hand. "The pleasure is mine," she said, crouching down in front of her. "You have a beautiful name, and I love the nickname, Roxie, too. Did your dad give it to you?"

Roxie glanced up at Nate, beaming with pride. "Yes, ma'am. He and my Uncle Tucker did."

"They have good taste."

Roxie's tangled ponytail and a small smudge of dirt on her rosy cheek stirred a wave of nostalgia in Jordyn. She remembered being Roxie's age, running wild outside, playing until her breath left her lungs, trying to hold on to every drop of daylight. And in a place as beautiful as

Frosted Firs Ranch, nestled in the beautiful Christmas wonderland of Noel, she imagined—and hoped—that Roxie took advantage of the perfect outdoor playground.

"What've you been up to today?" Jordyn asked. "Enjoying the fresh mountain air?"

"Yes, ma'am. We got out of school last week for Christmas break." Roxie scratched her neck where a piece of hay clung to her skin. "I helped my dad in the stables and met the new quarter horse we're boarding." Her expression brightened, her blue eyes roving over Jordyn's face and hair. "You have a quarter horse, too, don't you?"

"I do."

"And you race him?"

Jordyn smiled. "Her. We used to barrel race together, but I'm taking a break to settle here in Noel. But when my Star was in the arena, she could beat any horse, any day, any time."

"Even the boy horses?"

"Especially them!" Jordyn laughed.

"Ms. Jordyn's a fierce competitor. She enjoys wiping the floor with the other riders." Nate grinned when Jordyn looked up and met his eyes. "Least, that's what I've been told."

Despite her awkward embarrassment, Jordyn couldn't help but laugh. "I do like healthy competition, so long as everyone plays by the rules." She smiled at Roxie then stood, glancing around at the dozen or so customers traversing the aisles of Christmas decorations. "Which, I have to admit, is one of the reasons I stopped by today. I wanted to talk to you about the tree."

"The perfect one by our fence?" Roxie asked, bouncing in place with excitement. "Dad and Uncle Tucker said we'll win the Christmas Crown again for Mama with that tree. It'll be our tenth year in a row of trad-dish-pun!"

Mama. Jordyn winced. Oh, boy.

"Tradition," Nate corrected. "Roxie, would you mind giving Ms. Jordyn and me a chance to talk?"

"Yes, sir." Roxie waved at Jordyn. "Bye, Ms. Jordyn. It was nice to meet you."

"Same here," Jordyn said.

After Roxie skipped off to the toy section of the store, Nate looked at her with a pleased expression. "You're ready to negotiate a price?"

"Um, well . . ." Jordyn shrugged. "That's not exactly what I wanted to discuss, though the tree does have something to do with it."

Tucker, who still stood by the firewood rack with a rapt expression, burst out laughing. "I know that tone." He dragged his finger across his neck. "No deal, man. Your negotiation's dead. She ain't selling you that tree."

"Tucker." Nate frowned at his brother. "Would you mind giving us some privacy? Help Scott ring up the customers or go set up a new display or something."

Tucker made a face but complied, saying over his shoulder as he ambled away, "I don't do displays. I'll help the hands round up the horses and get 'em settled for the night."

Nate sighed. "You got one of those?"

"One of what?" Jordyn asked.

"A younger sibling who aggravates you no end?"

Jordyn shook her head. "Nope. It's just me and Star." She glanced around the store again and dragged her trembling hands over her jeans. "Since, according to Roxie, this tree competition seems to be a tradition for your family, would you like to ask Roxie's mom—er, your wife—to join our conversation?"

Nate's expression changed instantly. The relaxed warmth

in his eyes faded and sad shadows took its place as he said softly, "I lost my wife, Macy, six years ago."

"Oh." Jordyn's chest tightened. "I'm so sorry. I—"

"You didn't know."

"No," she whispered. "When I met Roxie, I just assumed . . ." Her face heated. "M-may I ask how old Roxie is?"

His mouth flattened into a thin line. "Six."

Oh. *Oh, no.* Jordyn looked down at the toes of her worn boots, a lump forming in her throat as she compared the numbers. Six years ago, he'd lost his wife and Roxie had lost a mother before ever having the chance to meet her.

Jordyn's own pain at losing her mother, though dulled by time, was still present and would probably never completely dissipate. "I . . . um, lost my mother when I was young, too. I hate that Roxie is having to go through that kind of grief."

"She passed away?" Nate asked.

"Uh, no." Jordyn looked down at the toe of her boots again. "She wasn't really skilled at being a good mom and my dad was angry at the fact that I was around to begin with. That combination didn't make for a good upbringing." She glanced up, avoiding the intensity of his gaze. "I grew up in foster care, then hit the rodeo circuit when I aged out. Being here"—she pointed at the mountain ranges in the distance, visible through the large windows lining the front of the store—"is like having a home for the first time. I have my own house, my own property and, hopefully, will be able to build a new business soon."

He was quiet for a moment, then asked, "What kind of business are you looking to build?"

"I'm going to breed horses and offer training for young,

upcoming barrel racers." She smiled. "When I was first starting out, a retired barrel racer and horseman helped me learn the sport and clinch my first win. I've never forgotten how good that felt—to have someone supporting me and cheering me on. I want to pay that forward to other riders."

Nate smiled. "That's admirable. And you won't be at a loss for customers here. You picked a prime location. We board horses at the ranch, and due to the scenic view, open space, and rural location, we've rarely had trouble finding owners eager to entrust us with their horses' care. A few words to the right owners and it'd be easy for you to drum up some clientele. I'd be happy to help you out on that front when the times comes."

Jordyn's eyes met his, a rush of excitement flooding her veins. "Would you? Oh, that'd be fantastic! I could really use—" Her throat closed. She dodged his gaze again and swallowed hard. "Well . . . that would be nice but I'm not sure you'll be as interested in helping me out once I say what I came to tell you."

The smile on Nate's face faded. "And what's that?"

Better to get it over with fast. Like ripping off a Band-Aid.

"I've decided to participate in Noel's Christmas competition," she stated firmly. "And unfortunately for you, that means I need to hang on to my tree."

The disappointment on his face was obvious. "I see."

She wrung her hands together. "And there's something else."

He held her gaze, trepidation in his eyes.

"The Nanas came by my place yesterday like they promised they would, and they just happened to stumble upon a misfortune of mine." She searched his eyes. "I tried out the firewood you left on my porch—thank you for that, by the way—but after I lit it, I discovered pretty quickly that my chimney has some major issues that the previous owner, Hal, warned me about."

Concern flickered through his expression. "What happened? Was the flue not working? Did your cabin suffer any damage?"

"The flue was fine and there was little damage aside from a few hours of smoke. And the whole embarrassing incident is entirely my fault for not being a more savvy home owner but from what the Nanas said, they knew the chimney had caused trouble for Hal in the past . . . and they thought you were aware of the problem as well." She glanced at him beneath her lashes, looking for any potential of guilt. "They tried to convince me that the Christmas card you sent me was a warning of some kind and that you might've been hoping to cause deliberate damage to my cabin with your gift of firewood in hopes of getting my tree."

He scoffed, disbelief in his eyes. "That's the most ridiculous thing I've ever heard."

The affronted tone of his voice, reflecting a blow to his male pride, coaxed a laugh from her chest but she closed her mouth and held it back. "I thought so, too. But they seemed inclined to believe that you might've been mocking me."

He frowned. "Mocking you?"

"With the smiley face. I think it was the wink that did it."

Nate sighed. "The wink was Roxie's idea—as was the smiley face. I . . . wasn't sure what to write."

Jordyn smiled. "I see." She added gently, "But I think it's only fair that I let you know that the Nanas hold a very big grudge against you for monopolizing their Christmas festivities and they're pretty intent upon using me to give you a run for your money this year."

"No doubt." Some of the irritation left his expression as a slow smile spread across his face. "And you're here to tell me that you're going to wipe the floor with me, right?"

She laughed. "Yep. I play fair, you know? Giving you warning that I'm in it to win it is the right thing to do. The Nanas have assigned Kandy as my mentor, and I've been told I need to attend the official kickoff of the competition tonight in the town square."

"And I should brace myself for your wrath?"

"You bet."

He laughed. "Well, I suppose we'll have to agree to be friendly enemies rather than helpful neighbors until the competition ends."

"For the integrity of the competition, I think that's best." Her attention lingered on his smile, that same rush of attraction streaming through her veins.

Oh, boy. Keeping her distance from a man she was this impressed by was going to be tough.

"Um . . ." She swallowed hard. "Is it okay for friendly enemies to shake on it?"

He held out his hand, the teasing light in his blue eyes making her wish they were on the same team. "I wish you luck, Jordyn—with a *y*—Banks."

"Good." She slid her hand in his and squeezed, the warm press of his skin against hers causing her breath to catch in her throat on her next words. "You're gonna need it."

And maybe this brief touch would help get him out of her system a little bit? Even if it didn't, it'd have to be enough to tide her over until they were free of the competition, because as susceptible as she was to this man's charms, there was no way she could let her guard down around Nate Reed and still win the Christmas Crown.

Three hours later, dusk had settled over the town square of Noel. The setting sun cast a pink-toned glow over Noel's Nanas, who stood on a stage positioned in the center of the town square amid a swelling crowd of Noel's residents. Several vendors had set up in the square, some selling crafts, others Christmas decorations, and a few selling snacks such as popcorn, baked goods, and caramel apples. Hot apple cider and the sweet scent of hot chocolate drifted on the crisp winter air, and children's laughter was all around as little ones chased each other across the dormant grass.

An undercurrent of excitement vibrated in the air. This moment was the big event Noel's residents anticipated all year.

"Oh, opening night always makes my stomach churn!" Kandy, standing on stage beside Carol Belle, rubbed her middle as people continued gathering in the town square.

Carol Belle scoffed. "I don't think it's opening night churning your stomach so much as the amount of hot cocoa you downed at Kringle's Café earlier."

Kandy blushed but her eyes returned to the crowd in the town square and homed in on one face in particular. Max Reynolds, owner of Kringle's Café, six-foot-one and gorgeous, looked up and locked his gaze with hers, the corners of his blue eyes creasing as he smiled up at her. He lifted his hand and waved.

A lock of his salt-and-pepper-hued hair fell over his forehead and her fingertips longed to delve into the thick strands and smooth them back.

"I couldn't help it." Kandy smiled, waving back. "That hot cocoa is addictive."

Carol Belle nudged her. "Kandy. There's a world of difference between you and Max Reynolds."

Kandy's smile dimmed. "I know."

"I know he's taken a shine to you, but he's fifteen years younger than you."

Kandy lowered her hand and looked away, refocusing on the crowd. "I know."

Carol Belle sighed. "Any man would be lucky to have you in his life, Kandy, and I don't mean to offend you or butt into your business, but you know how much female interest there is in Max around here and—"

"I know exactly what people would think," Kandy whispered. "And say. Which is why I keep my distance. The only time I see him is when we go to Kringle's Café, so there's never been—and never will be—anything other than hot cocoa and red velvet cupcakes between us."

Carol Belle sighed. "I don't mean to—"

"It's okay." Kandy looped her arm around Carol Belle's. "I know you're just being a great friend and watching out for me. And I also know how far along I am in life and how much younger Max is." She shrugged. "It's just a nice fantasy. The way he looks at me . . . I've never had a man look at me that way before. Not even Carl noticed me the way Max does. Max thinks I'm interesting and fun." She wound a pink curl around her finger and grinned. "He even complimented my hair."

Carol Belle laughed. "Maybe he deserves more respect than I give him."

"He does." Kandy held her gaze. "He's respectful and kind. In all these years, I've never felt like I was missing anything by not dating or marrying again. I've been fulfilled by Carl's memory and happy with you and the girls. Max is the first man I've been interested in since I lost Carl, and my attraction to him was a complete surprise.

Do you know how great that feels? To admire someone again? To *be* admired again?"

Carol Belle nodded. "I can imagine."

Kandy squeezed Carol Belle's arm. "Anyway. That's all there'll ever be between me and Max Reynolds. Admiration, hot cocoa, and red velvet cupcakes. A nice fantasy of what might've been if circumstances were different. But now, it's time to honor the memory of Carl and George by kicking off this competition." She tipped her chin toward the crowd and grinned. "I see our top two contenders for the Christmas Crown have arrived. And from the looks of things, I think they might be scoping each other out."

Carol Belle followed Kandy's gaze and scanned the crowd, her eyes focusing first on Nate then on Jordyn, who stood on the other side of the town square. "Well, what do you know? I think you might be right . . ."

"It's almost time, Daddy!"

Nate glanced down and smiled at Roxie, who practically vibrated with excitement at the scene unfolding before her in Noel's town square. She'd been anxious for tonight's celebration and had even welcomed his suggestion two hours earlier that they both spruce up a little bit before attending the evening's ceremony. Normally a rough-and-tumble type of girl, Roxie usually chose to wear jeans and a sweater. But tonight, she'd insisted upon wearing her favorite red Christmas cardigan which had little bells sewn into the cuffs, and she'd even insisted that Nate tie a red ribbon around her ponytail.

"Do you think Ms. Jordyn will wear a ribbon in her hair tonight, too, Daddy?" she'd asked, looking up at him with wide eyes as he'd combed her hair.

That had been the first of many questions Roxie had peppered him with as they had prepared for the celebration, climbed into his truck and driven into town.

Roxie, seated in the back seat of the extended cab, had begun asking questions the moment they left the driveway and had continued up until the second Nate parked the truck near the town square. She'd wanted to know exactly how tall Jordyn was, if Jordyn curled her hair or if it was naturally wavy, and where Jordyn had found cowgirl boots with blue stitching like the ones she'd worn at the gift shop. Was Jordyn's quarter horse a pearl white or an ivory white like the one they were currently boarding at Frosted Firs Ranch? How fast did a barrel racing horse run on average and did Nate think Jordyn's horse would be faster? Did Nate think Jordyn would mind if they came by Chestnut Ridge to visit Jordyn and see her horse? And if they did visit Jordyn, did Nate think Jordyn would let her ride Star?

By the tenth question, Tucker, who was seated in the passenger seat during the ride to town, had grinned, shot Nate a sly look and whispered under his breath, "Looks like you're not the only one who's taken a shine to Jordyn."

At the time, Nate had brushed Tucker off and changed the subject, but he had to admit to himself that he had as much trouble getting Jordyn out of his mind as Roxie did.

He hadn't expected Jordyn to ask about his being married, though the question and her interest was understandable considering she'd met Roxie. But he'd been unprepared for the opposing mix of emotions he'd experienced at the relief in her eyes when he told her he wasn't married and that his little family consisted of only him and Roxie.

On the one hand, saying he'd lost Macy out loud had stung as painfully as it always did, but realizing Jordyn's interest in him might be as intense as his interest in her also filled him with a sweet ache of pleasure.

It felt good to be wanted—especially by a woman as intriguing and beautiful as Jordyn. And he couldn't help but wonder, for the first time in years, what it might feel like to date a woman he was truly attracted to again. What would it feel like to spend some part of his day as a single, carefree man rather than a somber businessman and bone-weary single dad? Would he feel that same rush of heady emotion every time he was with Jordyn? Or, after spending some time together, would this pull of attraction he felt for her fade a bit?

Surprisingly, he found himself wishing he could throw caution to the wind and enjoy exploring a romantic relationship with Jordyn while still maintaining the status quo at the ranch.

But as a single father, he couldn't undertake any sort of personal change without considering Roxie's best interests first. Besides, he and Jordyn could only be friendly enemies now that she'd broken the news to him that she planned to enter the Christmas competition and use the Fraser fir in her backyard to secure a win.

And he had to give Jordyn credit. She'd been honest and direct about her intentions when she'd visited him at the gift shop earlier; he admired her determination. It was clear she was a strong competitor.

What was it she'd said?

I've never forgotten how it felt to have someone supporting and cheering me on.

It was a shame they weren't on the same team. He would've enjoyed working with her, supporting and cheering her on . . . or at least he thought he might. But at the same time, the thought of spending Christmas with another woman—even in an innocent fashion—filled him with a sense of betrayal. Christmas had always been the most special time of year for him and Macy.

"Can I, Dad?" Roxie stared up at him expectantly.

"Can you what?" Nate asked, shaking his head slightly to clear his mind of Jordyn.

"Can I go say hi to Miss Jordyn?" Roxie pointed to the left, where Jordyn stood several feet away.

Just as Nate spotted her in the crowd, Jordyn looked over at him, their eyes meeting. She looked different than she had three hours ago. She wore the same boots she'd worn earlier but she'd changed into a darker pair of jeans, a white sweater, and a green scarf that matched her eyes perfectly. The long waves of her hair were loose, spilling around her shoulders, the red hue highlighting the pink blush in her cheeks put there by the wind.

Jordyn smiled at him, and he smiled back, that familiar hum of pleasure zipping through his veins.

"Yeah," Tucker drawled beside him. "Why don't we all go over and say hello?"

The teasing gleam in his eyes made Nate shift uncomfortably from one boot to the other as his smile vanished.

Friendly enemies, he reminded himself. That's what he and Jordyn had agreed to be for the duration of Noel's Christmas competition, and he was going to stick to their agreement. They'd even shaken on it.

"Not a good idea." Nate smiled down at Roxie, wincing as she frowned with disappointment. "I'm sorry, sweetheart, but we're on a different team from Ms. Jordyn right now. And the Nanas have very strict rules when it comes to the Christmas competition."

"Oh, yeah." Tucker rocked back on the heels of his boots and grinned at the Nanas, who were lining up in a neat row on the stage. "No cross-conspiring," he stated in a monotone.

Roxie made a face. "What's cross con—con . . . ?"

"Conspiring," Nate stated slowly. "It means working

together with someone in secret in order to get around the rules in some way."

Roxie's expression turned serious. "It's not good to break the rules is it, Daddy?"

Nate smiled with pride. He had a good and honest daughter and he hoped, despite the increasingly cynical world they lived in, that she'd carry those attributes with her into adulthood. "That's exactly right, sweetheart."

Nate stole one last glance in Jordyn's direction, but the sun had set, the pink glow surrounding them dissolved, and several long sets of Christmas lights, which had been strung on tall poles that surrounded the town square, burst into a warm glow.

Cheers erupted from the crowd that surrounded the stage and a soulful Christmas carol streamed from loud-speakers that were positioned strategically among the crowd. Singing, joyful whoops, and boisterous applause erupted all around the stage as Noel's Nanas, dressed in matching Christmas sweaters and dancing to the music, stepped up to a microphone positioned center stage and smiled.

Carol Belle took to the microphone first. "It's that time of year again, my friends!" She clapped her hands and Noel's residents followed her lead, bursting into applause, the excited energy of the crowd waving through the throng of people. "Tonight is the night we kick off Noel's annual Christmas competition, and this is going to be one of the best years yet! We have strong, returning competitors—and brand-new ones—who are going to make each of the twelve contests more exciting than they've ever been!"

Kandy stepped up to the microphone next. "And on that note, we'd like to welcome our newest resident of Noel and first-time competitor in our annual Christmas competition, Jordyn Banks!"

As Kandy spoke, she lifted her arm and pointed out into the crowd. A spotlight, positioned at the edge of the stage and manned by a teenager, swept chaotically over the mass of people below, then landed on Jordyn.

Caught off guard, Jordyn squinted up into the bright blaze of light and held her hand up in front of her face, smiling and blushing as the crowd applauded, their attention now focused on her.

"Jordyn Banks," Kandy continued, "has moved into Chestnut Ridge and will be joining our competition this year. Let's give her a very happy Noel Christmas welcome, shall we?"

The applause grew louder and a chorus of *welcome* broke out from the crowd. Roxie, still standing in front of Nate, bounced with excitement and waved enthusiastically, shouting welcome along with Nate.

Nate grinned. Oh, man, Jordyn was embarrassed. He could tell from a mile away. But despite her obvious discomfort at being singled out by the Nanas, she looked over and met his eyes again, and the delighted gratitude in her expression as she mouthed the words *thank you* made him smile even wider.

"Now that we've greeted our newest participant," Carol Belle said into the mic, "we need to get down to business." After the cheers died down, she continued speaking. "As you know, we want everyone to have fun and enjoy themselves during these contests, but there must be rules to ensure that the competition is as fair and equitable as we can make it. And those rules must be properly adhered to and enforced every year."

Eve, nodding as she stood beside Carol Belle, leaned in toward the mic. "Rule number one. If you have signed up to participate in the Christmas competition, you may compete individually or in a group of four or less. Once teams—comprised of an individual or a group of individuals—have been established, all participants must remain on their chosen teams for the duration of the competition."

"This rule," Carol Belle interjected, "is meant to promote community and collaboration among our residents."

"There will be twelve Christmas contests," Eve said. "Whoever wins the most contests will win the Christmas Crown at the town square tree-lighting on Christmas Eve. Until that time, scores will be tracked on our Tree Scoreboard and will be updated immediately after the winner of each contest is announced."

The spotlight moved over the crowd until it settled on a tall wooden board, carved into the shape of a large Christmas tree, positioned at the opposite end of the stage.

"Whoever is in the lead," Eve said, "will have their name appear at the top of the tree. Everyone else will be ranked, according to winning points, below, and the number of points each group or individual has earned will be listed beside their name. Transparency has always been and always will be a core principle in our Christmas competition."

"Which brings us to the most important rule of all," Carol Belle said, holding up one finger. "There will be no cross-conspiring in this Christmas competition. It bears repeating that once you have signed up for a team or as an individual competitor, you must operate solely within your team or as an individual. No teams or individual competitors are allowed to cross-conspire, plot, plan, discuss, strategize, or manipulate any aspect of the Christmas contests in order to sway the win or gain an advantage over other competitors. If you are found to be a cross-conspirator, you will be immediately disqualified from the competition and, depending on the circumstances of your violation, may or may not be banned from future Noel community competitions."

The excited cheers of the crowd died down and a hush settled over the town square.

"I mean it," Carol Belle stated firmly.

Holly, standing beside Eve, cleared her throat and made her way to the microphone, edging Carol Belle back a few steps. "Well . . ." She clapped her hands and smiled. "Now that we've gotten the rules out of the way, let's get to the fun stuff!"

The crowd cheered again, and Roxie tugged on Nate's shirtsleeve and grinned up at him, her expression filled with delight.

"Kandy," Holly prompted, sweeping an arm toward the other side of the stage, "please begin the drawing to determine the order of this year's contests."

Kandy, who stood beside an oversized snow globe with folded pieces of paper fluttering around inside like snowflakes, lifted the top off the snow globe, reached in and withdrew one piece of paper. She unfolded it, smiled, then announced, "The first competition will be Snowman Fight at First Snow."

A collective squeal and laughter erupted from the crowd.

Kandy reached back into the snow globe and withdrew another folded piece of paper, then announced, "Our second contest will be Candy Cane Fishing."

The drawing continued, Kandy reaching into the large snow globe and withdrawing folded pieces of paper in succession until she collected twelve. Each contest was announced as it was drawn and Carol Belle announced the final contest lineup once the drawing was completed.

"Here it is in order: Snowman Fight at First Snow, Candy Cane Fishing, Terrible Tinsel Triathlon, Christmas

Cookie Crumble, Sexy Santa's Eggnog Nod—which I'll remind you counts as two contests and is solely for adult participants—Gingerbread Architect, Christmas Karaoke, Christmas Dance Craze, Ugly Sweater Wrapping Pretty, Christmas Light Delight, and Noel's Christmas tree contest."

The four Nanas arranged themselves into a neat line again, looped their arms with one another and shouted out in unison to the cheering crowd, "At first snow, let the Christmas competition commence!"

Chapter Five

Two days later, the first snow of the holiday season fell on Noel. Jordyn stood in the open entrance of Chestnut Ridge's stable, admiring the white landscape and feeling as giddy as a kid as big, fluffy snowflakes fell in a thick blanket around her.

"Wow!" She stuck her hands out, palms cupped, tilted her head back and smiled as she savored the burst of snowy winter wind across her face. "Does it snow like this often?"

Kandy, who stood next to her, shivering, glanced up at the sky with a worried expression. "More than most people would expect. Noel is at the highest elevation east of the Mississippi—even higher than Boone. Heavy and light snowfalls hit us sporadically. One day it can be in the fifties and the next it could be in the low twenties. Snow's a guessing game around here in terms of when it'll hit, but we get at least a few feet several times each year. Some of our best tourist business happens in the ski resorts around us, and the owners rely on snowfalls like this one."

"Well, light or heavy—I love it!" Jordyn stuck out her tongue, catching a snowflake, then grinned. "Most of my foster homes were in the Deep South and we never got anything like this. Most we ever got was a few flurries—

maybe a couple inches at most—one or two days a year and that'd be enough to make everything shut down. But this!" She stuck out her tongue again but it felt slightly frozen, so she pulled it back into her mouth and shivered with cold and excitement. "This is truly magnificent!"

As though in agreement, Star, snug and warm inside her stable, neighed gently. She looked especially beautiful today, draped in a thick, red Christmas blanket, her mane and hide freshly brushed.

Jordyn walked over to her stall, touched her forehead to Star's broad nose and whispered, "I won't be gone too terribly long, my beauty. From what Kandy has told me, the Snowman Fight doesn't last very long, and I'll be home right after to tell you all about it while we watch the snow fall this evening." She stroked Star's neck with a gentle hand, a shiver of delight running through her at the thought of her and Star having their very own land. "I bet you're just as eager as I am to enjoy the view of those glorious mountains covered in snow."

"Jordyn." Kandy, her pink hair dotted with melting snowflakes, beckoned for Jordyn to join her outside the stable. "The contest is set to start at noon and"—she glanced at the festive snowman watch on her wrist—"it's almost that now. We really should get going."

Jordyn kissed Star's forehead and gave her one last pet before joining Kandy. "So, the point of today's contest is to build a great-looking snowman as fast as I can—when time is called, the snowmen will be judged and the winner announced, right?"

Kandy's boots crunched in the snow as they walked across the grounds to Jordyn's truck. "Partially. But there's quite a bit more to it than that."

Jordyn, preoccupied with the snow around her boots, giggled. "Oh, isn't this wonderful? Will it snow like this on Christmas Day? I hope it does. I've never experienced a white Christmas before and with those peaks"—she waved an arm toward the mountain range in the distance—"I can't imagine the view being more spectacular!"

"Well, every year, we have about a sixty percent chance of snow on Christmas Day," Kandy said. "Some of the locals make a habit of betting on it, but I don't partake in that. When I gamble, I lose my money more often than I win, so I've learned not to take the chance."

"Well, I'd be okay with it." Jordyn pulled her keys from her pocket, unlocked her truck, and they both climbed in, settling into the front seats and rubbing their hands together as the engine warmed. "How many people place a bet? Is it a big jackpot?"

Kandy held up her gloved hand, a worried look in her eyes. "Look, we can discuss the snow bet later, but right now, as your mentor, my job is to prepare you for the first contest. If I don't do a good job, Carol Belle is going to have my hide. So could you please focus on what I'm telling you for the time being?"

"Oh, boy. I'm in trouble, aren't I?" Wincing, Jordyn turned up the heat, settled back against her seat and gave Kandy her full attention. "You're absolutely right, Kandy. It's just that I'm so excited to be a part of an actual community Christmas celebration that I can hardly sit still, much less listen to rules. But for you, I'm all ears. And I did do something you asked me to do already to prepare for this contest. I had the best night's sleep in my life last night! And that's thanks to you and the other Nanas. Thank you for helping me pick out the perfect bed frame and mattress for my bedroom."

Kandy smiled and shrugged. "It was nothing. I love to shop anyway."

"It was much more than nothing for me." Jordyn reached out, took Kandy's hands in hers and squeezed gently. "I can't tell you how much I've appreciated your welcome and your help getting settled. I doubt too many people would've gone to as much trouble as you and the other Nanas have to make me feel at home."

Over the past two days, the four women had escorted Jordyn to almost every store in downtown Noel, helping her shop for every little thing she needed to spruce up her new log cabin and feel at home. Kandy had helped her pick out a bed frame and soft mattress while pillows, sheets, and a comforter had been carefully chosen by Holly to suit Jordyn's taste.

Eve, thrifty and practical, had listened carefully to Jordyn's wishes regarding living room furniture and had found a living room set consisting of a sofa, recliner, coffee table, and one end table at a better bargain price than Jordyn could've imagined. She'd measured every piece of furniture carefully, ensuring the entire set fit into the living room of Jordyn's log cabin as though it'd been built into place right along with the rest of the cabin.

Kandy had taken on the task of choosing dishes, silverware, pots, pans, and cups for the kitchen. And Carol Belle had focused her efforts on adding a decorative and inviting touch, by choosing handcrafted rocking chairs for the front porch, garland over the mantel piece, a fresh poinsettia plant on either side of the front porch steps, and strings of white Christmas lights along the banisters. She'd even installed new bulbs in the old-fashioned porch lanterns by the front door, giving the cabin a warm, welcoming glow.

The Nanas had also arranged for Jordyn's chimney to be repaired at a fraction of the cost she would've spent had she done the hiring herself.

All in all, Jordyn had settled into her new home in record time. Last night she'd enjoyed a warm fire (without billowing smoke!) in the living room, rested comfortably on her cushy new sofa, and after relaxing for a bit, had crawled into bed, pulled the soft comforter up to her chin, and slept more soundly than she ever had in her life.

"I mean it," Jordyn said, squeezing Kandy's hand once more. "It's not just the material things y'all helped me pick out. It's your presence. It's so nice to have your help and company. I'd be honored to be able to call all of you my friends."

Kandy beamed. "We feel exactly the same, dear."

"Well, then." Jordyn rubbed her hands together briskly, shifted the truck in gear, and started driving down the road. "The least I can do after everything y'all have done for me is listen closely and abide by the rules of today's contest." Turning onto the main road, she grinned. "Shoot away, Kandy."

During the short drive from Chestnut Ridge to Noel's town square, Kandy gave her a rundown on the ins and outs of the Snowman Fight contest. It was difficult for Jordyn to concentrate, however, as the passing scenery—impressive on any day but mesmerizing on a snow day!—demanded her attention.

"You have twenty minutes to build your snowman, that's all," Kandy said. "But the difficulty level will be at an all-time high for you, since you're doing this on your own. You won't have time to make even a fraction of the ammunition the other teams will have at their disposal."

Jordyn, distracted by the dazzling snowflakes that peppered the windshield, frowned. "Ammunition?"

Kandy nodded. "Snowballs the size of your head, I'm telling you, will be lobbed your way from everyone! Especially the Stones."

"Stones?" Jordyn's mouth gaped open. "They throw rocks during this thing?"

Kandy laughed. "No! I'm talking about the Stone family. They're your biggest competition apart from Nate, and you'll need to be alert at all times around them." Her tone turned serious. "And don't let the Stone children fool you. They might be young, but they show no mercy and they're devilish. Downright devilish!"

Jordyn hid a smile. Boy, Noel's residents sure seemed to take this Christmas competition seriously, but surely it wasn't as aggressive as Kandy suggested. After all, it was a Christmas contest!

"I'll be fine, Kandy." She patted the older woman's knee for good measure as she parked the truck among the other vehicles surrounding the town square. "No need to worry. I can handle myself." She glanced at the energetic scene before them and grinned. "Now, let's get out there and join the party!"

And, she discovered shortly, it was indeed a party.

Dozens of people, gathered in small groups, were positioned throughout the snowy town square, huddling close amid the blustery wind, casting glances all around to check out the competition while rubbing their gloved hands in anticipation. The stage the Nanas had used to kick off the Christmas competition two days ago was still positioned in the center of the town square and Eve, Carol Belle, and Holly stood near the microphone, waiting for all participants to arrive so they could begin the contest. When they noticed her, they waved, their faces lighting up.

Smiling, Jordyn waved back.

"Now, you're sure you are warm enough?" Kandy, who had walked with Jordyn to the edge of the town square, got busy, checking Jordyn's attire. She tugged at Jordyn's gloves, fluffed her scarf higher on her neck, and verified that all of the buttons on her jacket were properly fastened to ward off the cold. "And one more thing," she said, pulling a green, knitted wool hat from her purse. "Keeping the head covered helps keep the body warmer, and we don't want you catching a cold now, do we?"

Feeling treasured, Jordyn closed her eyes and smiled as Kandy gently tugged the hat into place on Jordyn's head, then tucked her long red waves over her shoulders. The older woman's touch was caring and kind, much as Jordyn imagined a mother's hands would be.

"Now, you're all set." Kandy squeezed her shoulders. "Just don't forget that you need to be on your guard against the snowballs just as much as you must focus on building the snowman. Twenty minutes. That's all the time you have to build."

Jordyn hugged her and grinned. "No problem. How hard can it be?"

The expression of consternation on Kandy's face said it all.

"Okay, folks!" Carol Belle's voice echoed with authority across the town square. "It's time to begin. Take your places, please."

Jordyn hugged Kandy and thanked her one more time, then dashed across the town square, glancing around her for an empty spot in the snow to build her snowman. Toward the center of the town square, near the stage, Roxie stood with Nate and Tucker. When the little girl noticed Jordyn, her hand shot up in the air, waving feverishly.

"Ms. Jordyn!" Roxie was waving both hands in the air now, beckoning Jordyn over. "We saved you a spot over here! Come and join us!"

Jordyn hustled over, weaving between the teams as she went, bounding across the freshly fallen snow. When she reached them, she smiled down at Roxie. "Merry Christmas, Roxie! I'm glad to see you here this snowy afternoon."

Roxie, just as cute as ever in her festive Christmas cardigan and knitted wool cap, beamed up at Jordyn. "You've got the same hat as me. 'Cept yours is in a different color."

Jordyn gently tapped the tip of Roxie's nose. "Seems we do. Did you by any chance get yours from one of the Nanas?"

Roxie nodded. "Yes, ma'am. Ms. Kandy gave it to me."

"That's where mine came from as well. You wear yours beautifully. The color red suits you."

Roxie blushed. "I like your green one. It matches your eyes." She looked away briefly, then pointed to an empty area nearby. "We saved you a spot to build your snowman right over there."

Jordyn glanced up, her eyes moving past Roxie and finding Nate's. "We?"

Shrugging, Nate lowered his hands onto Roxie's shoulders and smiled. "Roxie did. She insisted that you would need a little help getting settled for the competition this morning."

Jordyn raised one eyebrow. "So you had no hand in it then?"

"Not a chance." He grinned. "We're friendly enemies now, remember?"

The teasing note in his voice sent a delicious shiver through her. Even now, in a town square full of men, Nate stood out among them. His impressive height, muscular body and charismatic grin enticed her even more than they had upon their first meeting.

The man was positively hypnotic!

"Well," she said softly. "I'm grateful for Roxie's help." She glanced down once more and winked at Roxie. "Thank you very much for thinking of me."

Roxie smiled even wider. "You're welcome."

Tucker, standing next to Nate, pointed to the empty spot Roxie had saved for Jordyn. "You best take up your position or you're liable to fall behind before you even start." He lifted his fists in front of his face. "And keep your dukes up! Competitors are ruthless around here."

Jordyn issued a sly smile and narrowed her eyes. "Oh, I got this."

Moments later, the Nanas began counting down and Jordyn hurried over to the empty space Roxie had reserved for her, ensured her gloves were still tugged snugly over her fingers, and readied herself for the competition.

"When I say go," Carol Belle spoke into the mic, "you may begin building your snowman. The timer will be turned on and you'll have twenty minutes to construct until time is called. Remember that snow is your material for this contest. You may utilize it in any way you wish to aid in building, defending, or preventing the creation of a snowman."

Jordyn hugged her midsection and bounced in place with excitement. Here she was, in a beautiful new town with a beautiful new home and beautiful new friends, competing in her first ever Christmas competition. She couldn't imagine today being any more fun or exciting.

And speed being a factor in who won this contest? Oh, she had this in the bag! Racing to a finish was her specialty.

"In three, two, one," Carol Belle counted off. "Go!"

A flurry of activity broke out across the town square, bodies, warmly bundled, dashing from here to there, arms serving as shovels as they gathered up heaps of snow and gloved hands furiously assembling snowballs and snowmen.

Jordyn joined the fray and dug into the snow at her feet, clearing a spot for the base of her snowman and patting snow together to form the foundation of what she hoped would be the best snowman Noel had ever laid eyes on. She enjoyed the feel of snow in her hands, the satisfactory pat of snow upon snow and the laughter surrounding her as others worked.

She gathered a second armful of snow, patted it down

onto the foundation she'd made, propped her hands on her hips and smiled broadly. Yeah! Things were going nicely. She had this in the ba—

Something rock-solid and cold slammed into the side of her head then crumbled into her right eye. "Ow!"

A black-haired boy around ten years of age faced off with her from several feet away, an evil grin spreading across his face. "She's unprotected, Ma! Get her!"

A stout woman with the same black hair and fierce expression as the boy, picked up a snowball from a large stockpile that lay near the boy's feet, pulled back her arm in tandem with the boy's reloaded hand, and threw it in Jordyn's direction.

Both snowballs slammed smack into Jordyn's middle and she doubled over, clutching her gut and squeezing her eyes shut as a heavy barrage of snowballs continued to pummel her back.

Oh, boy! What in the world had she gotten herself into?

"Man! Jordyn's getting creamed."

Nate patted down a fresh scoop of snow into the second sphere of the snowman he, Roxie, and Tucker had been building, then glanced to his right. Jordyn was on all fours in the snow, cradling her middle with one hand and desperately tossing snow into a pile with the other while trying to avoid an onslaught of snowballs coming at her from every direction.

Though being snowballed was a given during the Snowman Fight contest, the majority of ammunition aimed at Jordyn seemed to be originating from the Stones, who were building their snowman directly opposite Jordyn. The four-member family was feverishly assembling their snowman and taking turns projecting hard snowballs at Jordyn.

Chester Stone was the main culprit. Young, but a veteran of Noel's Snowman Fight, Chester was well-known to be the reigning serial snowball attacker. His younger sister, Angelina, was a close runner-up, however. The little girl, only two years older than Roxie, was a wiry little eight-year-old with good aim and a vicious hunger for domination.

For every snowball Chester threw, Angelina propelled two more in Jordyn's direction. The little rascals aimed for her head, neck, back, and—more recently—her knees, forcing Jordyn into a defensive heap on the ground.

Just then, Chester picked up a particularly dense snowball, hefted it over his shoulder and hammered Jordyn right in the head. She yelped, dropped the snow she'd gathered in her arms and covered her head with both hands.

"That devious little snowball-throwing rascal," Nate grumbled.

Roxie, who was patting down a fresh layer of snow on their snowman, glanced up at Nate in surprise. "Who're you talking about, Daddy?"

Nate grimaced. "No one, sweetheart. That was an awful thing to say about someone and I shouldn't have said it."

"Sometimes calling people names is necessary," Tucker said, bending swiftly to the ground, packing together a snowball and propelling it across the town square at another team. "That Chester Stone has hit Jordyn with more snowballs in the past five minutes than I've thrown during this contest altogether over the past two years. That kid deserves a taste of his own medicine."

With that, Tucker scooped up another hefty handful of snow, packed it into a snowball and hurled it in Chester's direction as the boy bent over for another armful of snow. Tucker's snowball smacked him square in the backside.

Chester, the little devil, rubbed his backside and frowned,

ceasing his attack on Jordyn momentarily to yell at Tucker. "Hey! You can't do that."

Tucker, undeterred, made another snowball and threw it at a team nearby. "I can do whatever I want, kid. There are no holds barred in this competition."

A slight grin spread across Chester's face at the prospect of a new confrontation. He bent over, patted together another snowball and, aiming with precision, hurled it, smacking Roxie on the arm.

"Ouch! That hurt," Roxie said, dropping the snow in her hands and rubbing her arm.

"Hey, kid, you watch that," Nate said, narrowing his eyes at the boy. "Roxie is a builder, not a fighter."

"Ain't no difference between the two during a Snowman Fight," Chester yelled. "Anyone's fair game. Like Tucker said, I can throw my snowballs at whoever I want!"

Drake Stone, Chester's father and big-bellied bartender in downtown Noel, stopped adding snow to the family snowman and took a moment to pat Chester's back instead. "That's right, son. You tell them!" He glared at Nate and Tucker. "You mess with the bull, guys, you get the horns. I put some snow in my boy's hand, and he can take down any man. Can't you, son?"

Chester puffed out his chest. "Sure can, Pop!"

Nate dragged his hand over his face and groaned, the frigid dampness of his glove against his cheek making him shiver slightly. This was all they needed. The Stone family's snowball attack on Jordyn was within the competition's rules, but it was certainly dishonorable—and at the very least, rude—to target her, considering she was participating as a one-woman team. But the last thing Nate wanted was for Roxie to become the Stones' target instead.

"That's some real chivalry you're teaching your son

there, Drake," Nate shouted over the laughter surrounding them. "Can't say I'd be proud if I had a son who relished throwing snowballs at females. It'd do your son good to take on a male for a change this year. Far as I've seen, he only attacks girls and women."

"Stop your whining, Nate!" Drake picked up a snowball in his beefy hand and threw it at Nate, who ducked, the snowball missing his forehead by a mere inch. "You don't want none of this."

Nate glanced down at Roxie, who still rubbed her arm with one hand and struggled to pat down a new layer of snow on their snowman with her injured arm. Then he glanced to his right where Jordyn had risen from her hands and knees to a standing position. She'd managed to form the bottom foundation of her snowman and was feverishly adding her second layer, shooting anxious glances at the Stone family in between motions.

She darted a glance Nate's way and the hopeful gratitude in her eyes as she held his gaze stirred indignant anger within him at the thought of the Stones taking advantage of her vulnerable state.

It was unconscionable, really. Lighthearted contest or not, it had never been in Nate's nature to stand by and leave a woman defenseless to the whims of a stronger attacker.

But stepping in on Jordyn's behalf was against the rules. Cross-conspiring was a huge no-no on the Nanas' list of rules, and one team aiding another—even if the other team was comprised of one vulnerable individual at the mercy of many—would be a breach of honor according to the rules.

The choice was clear. Either he turned his back on Jordyn, refocused his efforts on building his own team's snowman and secured a win, or he would have to act inconspicuously on Jordyn's behalf.

Nate glanced at Tucker, who paused in his efforts to defend their snowman, glanced over his shoulder at Nate and nodded firmly. "Let 'em have it. They deserve it."

"Yeah, Daddy." Roxie, forming the head of their snowman, looked up at him with fierce encouragement in her eyes. "Help Miss Jordyn. Give them some of their own medicine. I won't tell."

Grinning, Nate bent and kissed her cheek. "Good girl. But only this once and only because it's a question of honor."

Roxie nodded solemnly. "Like you said, we're always supposed to help others when they are hurt or in need."

"There are five minutes remaining," Carol Belle announced over the microphone.

The flurry of activity across the town square increased as each team doubled and tripled their efforts. Most of the teams surrounding them had already finished their snowman or were close to finishing. Jordyn was the only participant who had yet to form the second sphere of her creation.

Five minutes wasn't much, but five minutes less of being pummeled by snowballs might give Jordyn a fighting chance in the contest and would be worth the effort.

Ducking behind his team's snowman, Nate gathered a pile of snow at his boots, packed together several snowballs, then leaned around the snowman, waiting for Chester to turn his back and project another snowball at Jordyn.

"Let it loose," Tucker said in a hushed voice over his shoulder.

And Nate did just that.

Still hidden behind the base of their snowman, he threw several snowballs in quick succession, each one aimed for a different member of the Stone family. Three out of four snowballs hit their mark, smacking Chester, Drake, and Chester's mother, Betty Stone, square in the gut. The move was enough to distract the Stones from their attack on Jordyn, prompting them to glance in every direction, looking for the source of their own assailant.

Chester and Drake's eyes narrowed in Nate's direction, but they were unable to pinpoint him as he crouched low in the snow behind his snowman, shielded by Tucker's tall form.

"That you, Nate?" Drake shouted. "I can't see you, but I know what you're up to. Chuck another one of those at me and I'll turn you in to the Nanas for cross-conspiracy. And from what I've heard, they're out for you anyways."

Tell me something I don't know! Chuckling under his breath, Nate remained crouched out of view behind his snowman as his eyes met Jordyn's. She patted a fresh layer of snow onto the midsection of her snowman, and mouthed, *Thank you!*

The grateful admiration in her pretty features sent a wave of warmth through him.

"Four minutes," Carol Belle announced.

Jordyn, a frantic look in her eyes, returned to the task at hand, chucking handfuls of snow on top of her entry and desperately trying to construct a snowman before time ran out.

With the Stone family's attention now focused on Nate, she was able to add a great deal more snow to her haphazard creation, but when time was called, her snowman remained unfinished.

Nate winced. Well, it could barely be called a snowman, considering it was just one sphere topped with un-leveled clumps of snow that failed to form a shape of any kind.

"Step away from your snowmen, please," Carol Belle directed over the speakers. "The judges will be around momentarily to evaluate each team's snowman. In the meantime, the very gracious owners of Kringle Café have provided a warming station on the north end of the town square with free hot chocolate and hot apple cider. Let's give them a hefty thank-you for their donations, shall we?"

Nate clapped along with the rest of the crowd and Roxie bounced in place, shouting, "Hot chocolate! I'm gonna get whipped cream on mine."

"Now, please disperse for the judging and enjoy a warm beverage while you wait," Carol Belle directed the crowd.

Excited voices and holiday music peppered the air as everyone left their snowmen, made their way to the north end of the town square and huddled by the warming flames of small, outdoor firepits while enjoying cups of hot chocolate and apple cider.

"You did an awesome job, sweet girl," Tucker said, crouching beside Roxie and giving her a high five. "Why don't you and I grab us a cup of hot chocolate and bring one back for your dad?"

Roxie smiled, her blue eyes full of joy. "And Ms. Jordyn, too? Can we bring her one?"

"I don't see why not." Tucker looked in Jordyn's direction, lifted his chin and shouted, "Hey, Jordyn! Me and Roxie are grabbing some hot chocolate. You want us to bring you one back?"

Jordyn paused in the act of brushing snow off her jeans and nodded in Tucker's direction. "That'd be great. Thanks!"

Tucker took Roxie by the hand and they left, Roxie skipping beside him as they made their way toward the north end of the town square.

Moments later, Nate felt an elbow gently nudge his arm.

"Thank you," Jordyn whispered near his ear.

Nate stilled, his heart kicking his ribs, then faced her, his breath catching at the pink in her cheeks and tempting lips. Her green eyes, the deepest shade he'd ever seen, sparkled with mischief and merriment. "For what?" he asked.

"For holding off that evil little boy and his family."

Nate strived for an innocent expression. "I don't know what you're talking about."

She grinned, leaning closer. "Oh, you know exactly what I'm talking about. You, my friendly enemy, helped me out in my time of need."

Man, up close, she was even more gorgeous. The teasing lilt of her voice, her admiring expression and the warmth radiating from her body after the bout of exercise tempted him to lean in, lower his head, and brush his cheek against hers. But, somehow, he managed to hold back.

"I did nothing of the sort," he said softly. "Cross-conspiring is against the rules, you know."

"Oh, I know." She grinned, those beautiful emerald eyes of hers roving slowly over his face. "But you did anyway. Even though it might cost you in the long run."

"If you're thinking of turning me in for breaking the rules," he said quietly, "you'll have a hard time. The Nanas require proof before they take action on things like that, and you'll be hard-pressed to show them any concrete evidence."

Lips curving, she eased even closer, her arm brushing his. "I have no interest in turning you in. All I'm interested in is thanking you."

With that, she lifted to her toes, leaned even closer and brushed a kiss across his cheek. Her warm mouth was a soothing balm to his chilled cheek and his eyes slowly closed as he gave in to temptation, leaning into the soft touch of her lips, savoring her touch.

Maybe it was the warmth of her presence, the aromas of sweet chocolate and spicy cider mingling on the air between them or simply the nostalgic joy that remained after a good old-fashioned snowball fight, but whatever it was, he wanted more. He wanted to turn his head, press his mouth to hers and explore the taste and feel of her mouth against his.

But the moment was over.

Jordyn stepped away, her gaze lingering on his mouth briefly before she met his eyes and whispered, "I'm no damsel in distress, Neighbor Nate. But sometimes, it's nice to have a knight like you around."

Chapter Six

Normally, Jordyn didn't handle defeat with a very jovial heart, but coming in last at the Snowman Fight yesterday didn't sting quite the way she'd thought it would.

As a matter of fact, as she sat on the loveseat in her cabin, opposite the Nanas, who sat on the sofa, she had difficulty focusing on what they were saying. As the Nanas spoke, her gaze continued to stray toward the window and the snowy mountain peaks in the distance, her mind and heart drifting back to the day before when she'd touched her mouth to Nate's cheek. His skin, though chilled by the wind, had held an earthy, enticing scent, and she'd had to stop herself from nuzzling her nose against him. As her mouth had brushed his cheek, the warmth emanating from his burly frame had surrounded her, making her long to lean even closer, press her chest against his and slide her arms around his waist.

She'd kissed other men before—and had been kissed properly by other men—but she'd never felt the rush of emotion that had overwhelmed her at the briefest touch of her lips against Nate's cheek. Last night, she'd lain awake in her new bed, mulling it over, replaying the sweet, pleasurable moment in her mind. By dawn, she'd realized that the reason the chaste kiss had held such power was because it involved more than just physical attraction, but also a heady combination of admiration and a sensation of having met a kindred spirit.

From the very moment she'd met Nate, she'd fallen into conversation with him easily. They'd teased, laughed, and conversed with each other with the ease of lifelong friends. Simply being in his presence was familiar to her somehow, prompting her to feel as though she had . . . come home.

She'd never believed in love at first sight and to be truthful, she didn't believe in it now either. But she did believe—especially after their kiss—that there was something special between her and Nate. Some sort of connection that went beyond sheer physical attraction, and she found herself yearning to explore what might lie between them.

"Jordyn, you're not listening to a word we're saying."

The gruff tone in Carol Belle's voice yanked Jordyn's wayward attention back to her. All four Nanas sat opposite her on the sofa on the other side of the coffee table, their eyes focused intently upon her.

"I'm sorry," Jordyn said, rubbing her hands over her jean-clad knees. "I'm listening now. Please continue."

"I said, placing in this afternoon's contest is extremely important," Carol Belle said. "Candy Cane Fishing is not a terribly challenging event, but it does require some finagling and strategy."

"And stretching." Holly held up a finger. "If you don't stretch properly beforehand, you'll injure your neck and you'll be no good to us in the Terrible Tinsel Triathlon tomorrow."

"And that's a very important event," Eve chimed in. "It's a short course but a real test of endurance, and you can't afford not to place in either the Candy Cane Fishing contest or the Terrible Tinsel Triathlon and expect to still have a chance to win the Christmas Crown."

"And judging from Nate's actions yesterday," Kandy said softly, "I think the Stone family will have it out for you from this point forward."

The Nanas fell silent but kept their gazes fixed firmly on Jordyn, a speculative gleam in their eyes.

Jordyn attempted to maintain a blank expression. "I . . . don't know what you're talking about."

Carol Belle grunted. "Oh, you know exactly what we're talking about. What occurred yesterday was cross-conspiring—no doubt about that!"

For a moment, Jordyn panicked, her eyes darting around her living room as she racked her mind for a suitable excuse to combat Carol Belle's accusation. After all, Nate had gone out on a limb to help her in yesterday's Snowman Fight and she had no desire to sabotage him even if it would give her a leg up on winning the Christmas Crown.

Then, it occurred to her that Nate had said Carol Belle always demanded concrete evidence for cross-conspire disqualifications.

"Nate did attack the Stone family with snowballs," Jordyn said slowly. "But everyone was attacking everyone during the event. So, what makes you think he was throwing snowballs at the Stone family on my behalf?"

"Because of who he is." Kandy smiled sweetly. "Nate is one of the few gentlemen left in the world." She sighed wistfully. "Chivalrous, kind, and true. There's no way he would've just stood by and let the Stone family pummel you with snowballs all afternoon."

Holly nodded in agreement, delight in her eyes. "Absolutely. It was very apparent that Nate had his eyes on you for most of the event. And it was rather curious that he didn't begin attacking the Stone family until after they'd hit you several times with snowballs."

"That's a very good point," Eve said. "Not to mention that we heard through the grapevine that—"

"Now, Eve," Kandy said softly. "There's no need to bring that up now."

"There is every need!" Carol Belle scooted to the edge of her seat and propped one elbow on her knee, leveling her gaze on Jordyn. "You kissed Nate Reed yesterday, didn't you?"

Face heating, Jordyn looked down and fidgeted with the hem of her jeans. "I—I might've given him a peck on the cheek."

Carol Belle narrowed her eyes. "Right during the Snowman Fight contest? In the middle of town square? In front of the sweet Lord and everyone?"

Jordyn blinked and shook her head. "That's not entirely accurate." She winced. "I kissed him after the contest ended."

"Moments after," Holly said, grinning.

"It doesn't matter when she kissed him," Eve said. "We all know it was a bad move that doesn't bode well for her."

Jordyn sat up straighter and folded her hands in her lap. "Excuse me, what do you mean it doesn't bode well for me?"

The four Nanas fell silent again. Carol Belle stared at the ceiling, Eve looked at the floor, Holly stared out the window, and Kandy twirled her pink hair around one finger and hummed nervously.

"Come on, now," Jordyn prompted. "You can't say something like that and then not explain."

Carol Belle cleared her throat. "I'm afraid we can't share any more information until after you've practiced at least one round of Candy Cane Fishing."

"But surely, any fallout from my chaste kiss with Nate is more important?" Jordyn shook her head. "You can't expect me to focus on a Christmas contest when I'm concerned about—"

"Why not?" Carol Belle frowned. "You're going to have to deal with distractions during every contest in the Christmas competition, so you might as well start practicing now." She gestured toward a dozen candy canes that she had hooked onto the edge of a glass bowl and set on the table shortly after arriving at Jordyn's cabin. "Now, do your neck stretches and give it a go, please." She lifted her wrist and pressed a button on her watch. "I'll time you."

Stifling a groan, Jordyn complied. Over the next ten minutes, she completed Carol Belle's strict regimen of neck stretches, clenched the end of one candy cane between her teeth and lowered her head to the glass bowl, fishing candy canes from the edge of the glass bowl by hooking them with the candy cane in her mouth. Each time she snagged a new candy cane from the bowl, she jerked her head to the side and flung the candy cane she'd fished out into a pile at the other end of the table.

"Time," Carol Belle called.

Jordyn dropped the candy cane from her teeth, sat up, rubbed the back of her neck and groaned. The dipping and tossing of her head from one direction to the other had taxed her neck and jaw much more than she had expected. "Gracious, that hurt quite a bit more than I thought it would."

Eve raised her eyebrows and nodded abruptly. "See? We told you."

Holly pointed at the pile of candy canes Jordyn had fished from the glass bowl. "Try not to sling those candy canes quite as hard during the contest. Competitors sit close together at the same table and if you toss the candy canes too hard, they're liable to land in someone else's pile and then you'll lose credit. We've caught more than a few participants cheating at Candy Cane Fishing."

Kandy clapped her hands and smiled. "I think she did rather well for her first fishing trip! I think she has a really good shot at placing in this contest."

Jordyn dipped her head in gratitude. "Thank you, Kandy. I appreciate the compliment. And now that I've done as you've asked and practiced, can we get back to my question?"

The Nanas immediately sank back against the soft sofa cushions and avoided her eyes.

Jordyn sighed. "Look, I know this isn't a very pleasant conversation to have because y'all aren't getting along with Nate right now, so I'll come clean with you and admit that I do like him. So far, I think Nate's a great guy. He's been nothing but polite and neighborly to me, and no matter what you might think, he didn't deliberately try to sabotage my chimney. He was just being a good neighbor. So what's the harm in my giving him a little friendly peck on the cheek during a fun Christmas contest?"

The Nanas remained quiet for a moment. Then Carol Belle said, "Well, there's your reputation to think of."

"Yes," Eve said. "Unfortunately, you must consider how kissing Nate during the contest might look to others who don't know you well. You're a newcomer to the competition and, well, kissing a man who happens to be your primary competitor . . . that gets people talking." She grimaced. "They might jump to conclusions."

"Yes," Kandy said. "Noel is a very small community and everyone loves to talk about other people's business." She looked down at her hands, resignation in her tone. "Once word spreads—"

"What are you ladies saying?" Holly asked, an indignant expression on her face. "Are you trying to say that Jordyn should prioritize what other people think above her own thoughts and emotions? She's a grown woman. She's allowed to live her life the way she pleases regardless of what others may think."

Kandy looked up, her gaze meeting Jordyn's. Her expression was thoughtful as she considered Holly's comments.

"No one's disagreeing with the fact that Jordyn should live her life the way she pleases," Carol Belle said. "The kiss potentially compromising Jordyn's victory—should she win the Christmas Crown—is just one concern. The other is more significant."

"Oh, I see." Holly's anger receded a bit, consternation taking its place as she looked at Jordyn. "Unfortunately, Jordyn, I share the second concern."

Jordyn leaned forward, eyeing each of them. "And what is the second reason why I shouldn't have kissed Nate?"

Carol Belle looked at the ceiling again. "Well, how much do you know about him?"

Jordyn shrugged. "I know he owns Frosted Firs Ranch. He's my neighbor. And he has a brother named Tucker and a daughter named Roxie."

Holly smiled gently. "Is that all?"

Jordyn laughed. "Well, I know he's hot, chivalrous, and interesting. And I know that I'd like to get to know him better."

Kandy issued a soft sound of dismay. "That's the problem. He may not be inclined to want to get to know you better."

Jordyn stilled, her hands curling around her knees tightly. "What do you mean?"

"Nate lost his wife six years ago," Eve said gently.

"Yes," Jordyn said. "He told me."

"Did . . ." Holly hesitated, picking at her nails. "Did he tell you anything else about his late wife?"

"Not really," Jordyn said.

"Nate loved Macy very much," Kandy said quietly.

"So much," Holly said, "that he has refused to even consider dating anyone for six years. He's made it very clear to every woman who's approached him that he's not interested in dating or pursuing a romantic relationship."

Jordyn's stomach clenched. "O-other women have asked him out? A lot of them?"

Grimacing, Holly nodded. "More than a few. And they've all received the same answer from what I hear—he's not interested or available."

"He's been very clear about that," Carol Belle confirmed. "And I just don't see him changing his mind. We and Nate may have our differences right now regarding the Christmas competition, but one thing Nate is and has always been, is a fantastic father. He loves that little girl of his so much, he's not willing to take up with another woman who might disappoint either of them in any way."

An ache spread through Jordyn. "But . . . I'm trying not to disappoint anyone. And I certainly wouldn't want to hurt Nate or Roxie."

"No one's saying that," Holly said urgently. She hopped up, sat on the loveseat beside Jordyn, reached out and placed a hand on Jordyn's knee. "All we're saying is that he prefers to be single and focus his energy on Roxie."

"Yes," Eve added. "What we're trying to say is, Nate is not available."

"And all of us—especially me—forgot that for a little while," Carol Belle whispered. Grimacing, she looked down at her hands and wove her fingers tightly together in her lap. "When we heard Chestnut Ridge was getting a new owner, we were excited. For years, we've been subtly trying to persuade Nate to step away from the Christmas competition and focus his energy on rebuilding his own interests."

Jordyn shook her head. "But I thought Nate loved the Christmas competition."

"He does," Carol Belle hastened to explain. "But for all the wrong reasons. You see, for him, the Christmas competition—and the tree contest, especially—has become another way for him to dwell on his loss." She held up her hand. "Not that we want to discourage Nate from remembering Macy, treasuring the time he had with her and sharing those memories with Roxie. The reason we began the Christmas competition in the first place was for Kandy and me to honor our late husbands' memory while moving on with our lives. But instead of celebrating Macy's memory during the Christmas competition and finding new joy, Nate uses the festivities to fuel his grief and remain stagnant. It's just that, well, he's so fixated on the past that he won't embrace any possibility of a new future for himself. Macy loved the Christmas competition and winning the Christmas tree contest and Christmas Crown was her goal every year. Nate even built her a trophy case to store all of the Christmas Crowns she'd won. When she died, Nate took it upon himself to carry on that tradition to the detriment of healing after her loss."

"We've been searching for a way to encourage him to take a break from the Christmas competition and refocus his attention on himself for a change," Holly whispered. "We love Nate and want him to be happy. Misguided intentions or not, we hoped a break from the competition would do him good."

"And when we heard you had bought Chestnut Ridge," Eve said, "we saw an opportunity for a newcomer to use Fabio to kick Nate out of the Christmas tree competition this year."

"But we didn't expect you to be so . . . so . . ." Carol Belle struggled for words, her face flushing.

"So beautiful," Holly said, smiling softly. "And vivacious. And appealing. And it hasn't escaped our notice that Nate has noticed, too. And that you have taken an interest in him."

"And that," Carol Belle stressed, "we didn't count on. Please don't misunderstand us—we were over the moon when we noticed he'd taken an interest in you. We were ready to encourage it even! Maybe do a little matchmaking!"

"But it wasn't until you kissed him that we thought the situation through properly," Eve said. "Nate still hasn't truly let Macy go and, well, we've come to think that he may not ever be ready. And when we saw you kiss him, we guessed you might have already fallen for him a little."

"We may still be getting to know you," Kandy whispered, "but we already care for you—very much! And the last thing we'd ever want is to see your heart get broken, especially right after you moved to town." She reached out and patted Carol Belle's knee. "Looking out for each other's well-being is what we do best as friends."

The two women shared a meaningful look.

"Yes," Carol Belle whispered. "And we're very protective of each other when it comes to romantic entanglements."

Jordyn sank back in her seat, her heart thumping in her chest, and an awkward embarrassment singeing her neck. She hadn't stuck around yesterday after kissing Nate. Rather, she'd walked away, focused only on the pleasurable tingle running through her. She hadn't thought about how Nate might have reacted to her kiss.

Poor man. Had she actually accosted him with an unwanted advance? And in doing so, had she unwittingly given Noel's residents the wrong impression of her? What if Nate really wasn't interested in pursuing a new romantic relationship? What if she had mistaken the chemistry she thought existed between them, and what if he didn't feel the same attraction for her that she did for him?

Heaven help her! She clapped her hands over her face. She'd made an utter fool of herself.

"Oh, Jordyn," Kandy said quickly, leaving the sofa, sitting on the loveseat beside Jordyn and gently tugging Jordyn's hands from her face. "Please don't be embarrassed. You did absolutely nothing wrong. You were just being a kind neighbor and friend."

"And were enjoying a bit of innocent flirting with a man you're interested in," Holly added. "There's absolutely nothing wrong with that."

"Nothing at all," Eve said.

"We're just looking out for you is all," Carol Belle said. "Something we should've done sooner than this by giving you fair warning about endangering your heart."

Jordyn surveyed the Nanas for a moment, the heat in her cheeks receding as she mulled over their words.

What if they were wrong? What if there was a chance, however slight, that Nate actually felt the same attraction and interest for her that she did for him? What if pursuing a potential romantic relationship with her would appeal to Nate enough that he'd take a chance?

She didn't know the answer to any of those questions, but she knew that if she didn't take a chance herself, she'd never know what might have been. And taking a risk had never been something she'd shied away from.

"I just need to ask him," she said quietly.

The Nanas continued staring at her, apprehension in their eyes.

"What do you mean?" Carol Belle asked.

"I mean . . ." Jordyn smiled and glanced at Holly and Kandy who sat beside her, her chest lifting with confidence that she hoped would stay with her throughout the Candy Cane Fishing contest. "I'm going to ask Nate Reed if he's available."

Two hours later, Nate sat at one of many long tables that lined Noel's town square, waiting with several other competitors for the Candy Cane Fishing contest to begin. He warmed up along with the others, stretching his neck and doing his very best to keep his eyes on the wide metal buckets filled with candy canes that sat in the center of the table in front of him, but the temptation to get a glimpse of Jordyn was too strong.

He glanced around the town square again, scanning the small groups of people that milled about, some greeting each other with bright smiles as they arrived, several stopping by vendors who were positioned throughout the town square selling snacks and Christmas decorations, and others eyeing seats at each of the long tables for the best position to participate in Noel's Candy Cane Fishing contest.

Nate, having a favorite strategy of his own, had scoped out the other participants as soon as he'd arrived at the town square, chose a seat beside the least agile and most ungraceful competitors, plopped down in a chair in front of a metal bucket filled with candy canes, and hoped for the best. That was as much as anyone could do to win the Candy Cane Fishing contest. And today, Nate needed to do his very best. Not only was he representing Frosted Firs Ranch but he was also representing Roxie and Tucker.

Sighing, he glanced over at the Tree Scoreboard, which kept a running tally of the Christmas contest wins. The Nanas assigned a certain number of winning points to each contest based on the level of skill and commitment it required. The first place winners of each contest earned either one or two points based on the level of difficulty of the contest and the second and third place winners each earned half a point. At the end of yesterday's Snowman Fight contest, Noel's Christmas competition judges had awarded the Stone family first place, giving the Stones one point and positioning them at the top of the scoreboard. Luckily, Frosted Firs Ranch had been awarded second place, which ranked them directly below the Stones and well above all of the other competitors.

Jordyn, unfortunately, had come in at the bottom of the list, her hastily arranged molehill of snow not even ranking high enough to allow her name to be placed on the scoreboard. But that was no surprise. Due to the Stone family's onslaught of snowballs, she hadn't had a chance to finish her snowman, much less craft an impressive one.

Nate glanced to his left where the Stone family sat further down the table, whispering in hushed tones and strategizing for the contest in which Angelina would represent them. The young girl had already begun casting suspicious glances in Nate's direction.

The bitter expression on eight-year-old Angelina Stone's face was enough to make Nate shudder . . . though he hated to admit that sad fact.

Trying to let bygones be bygones and exhibit good sportsmanship, he lifted his chin and called out to the Stone family, "Good luck today! I wish you well, Angelina."

Noel's Christmas competition had always been a notoriously cutthroat business, but Nate figured there was nothing wrong with being kind and neighborly. And considering he'd stepped in on Jordyn's behalf in the Snowman Fight yesterday, the least he could do was to be neighborly to the Stones today and make it clear he had no personal ax to grind with them during the remainder of the competition.

Angelina, however, was apparently not impressed with his gesture. She narrowed her eyes, balled up one fist, lifted it high into the air and growled, "Eat dirt, Mr. Reed! You're going down!"

Nate's smile froze. The little girl's antagonistic expression struck a chord of fear in even him. She might be small, but she was definitely feisty.

"Don't pay her no attention, Nate," Tucker hollered from the sidelines where he stood with Roxie, both holding jumbo candy apples in their hands. "She's just a little girl." He bit a hunk off his candy apple, chewed, then shouted, "Give as good as you get, man. Give her a taste of her own medicine!"

"Yeah, Daddy," Roxie called out around a juicy bite of apple. "Take her down!"

In unison, Tucker and Roxie nodded, took large bites of their candy apples and scowled in Angelina's direction as they chomped.

Nate closed his eyes and rubbed his forehead. One thing he couldn't deny was that Tucker and Roxie had inherited the Reed family competitive streak. But at least they were honest and fair during competitions. Much like someone else he knew . . .

Nate opened his eyes and his gaze strayed as he began scanning the crowd again. It was ridiculous to be this obsessed with one woman. But for some reason, ever since Jordyn had kissed him yesterday, he couldn't get her out of his mind. Even now, over twenty-four hours later, he could still feel the tender press of her lips against his cheek, her soft breath against his skin and could still recall the sweet scent of her hair.

A pleasurable thrill rippled through him at the memory of her kiss and he couldn't help but imagine—for the millionth time since yesterday—what it might feel like to *really* kiss her. To cover her mouth with his, part her lips and explore her mouth thoroughly.

More than that . . .

What would Jordyn feel like in his arms? If he slid his hands around her slim waist, tugged her close and tucked her head beneath his chin, how would she feel against him? Would she fit perfectly? And would she hold him in return?

Stifling a groan, he squeezed his eyes shut again and rubbed the knot forming at the base of his neck, reminding himself that his focus needed to be on the contest at hand and not on his sexy new neighbor.

"Hello, again."

At the sound of Jordyn's soft voice, he stilled, opened his eyes, and drank in the sight of her as she sat down opposite him at the table.

Jordyn's deep green eyes held his gaze for a moment; then she smiled. "How are you today?"

Clearing his throat, he casually propped his elbows on the table and adopted a relaxed tone. "Good."

"Did you sleep well last night?" she asked softly, wiggling her eyebrows.

His cheeks burned. "Yes. W-why wouldn't I?"

She shrugged. "I just thought that with all that snowball throwing, your arm might've gotten sore. You were quite the defender of my honor, you know."

His shoulders relaxed and a deep chuckle rumbled up from his chest. "I'm not quite old enough yet to get sore after a short snowball fight, even though I may have a few years on you."

She tilted her head. "And how old are you exactly, if you don't mind me asking?"

"Thirty. You?"

"Twenty-five." She grinned. "So, you got five years on me."

"Good to know." He imitated a serious expression. "I'll take it easy on you today, kiddo."

"Maybe I don't want you to go easy on me." Leaning forward, she slid her hands across the table and rested them, palms flat on the table, on either side of his elbows. "Maybe I want you to give me a run for my money. What would you say to that?"

Something had shifted in her tone. Instead of the light, teasing note, a dangerous hint of challenge had entered her voice, as though she wanted something from him. Something he might not be able to give.

"I'm not sure what you mean," he said cautiously.

She leaned even closer, her face mere inches from his, then glanced around, noticing the interested looks of others who sat near them. "Hey." She crooked her finger in a come-hither gesture and when he leaned closer, whispered in his ear, "What if I wanted you to compete with me in this competition to the best of your ability?"

"I'd say, I'd be happy to do that," he whispered back, struggling to focus on forming a complete sentence rather than the soft waves of her hair that tickled his cheek. "I do, after all, want to win."

"And," she whispered again, "what if I wanted you to give me a run for my money outside of the Christmas competition?"

His heart kicked his ribs, and a wave of need rolled through him, weakening his legs and prompting him to sag onto the table, closer to her. "I don't understand."

Her hands had slid a bit closer across the table, her fingertips brushing the sleeves of his shirt. He swallowed hard, licked his lips and glanced around the table where the onlookers who'd been interested in their conversation had lost interest and directed their attention elsewhere.

"What if I told you that I'm interested in you?" she asked, her lips brushing the shell of his ear. "That even though we haven't known each other long at all, I've enjoyed every moment I've spent with you so far and would like to be near you more? That I find you intriguing and attractive? And that instead of being friendly enemies, once this Christmas competition is over, I'd very much like to explore being friendly neighbors and maybe something more? What would you say if I asked you that?"

He froze, his breath stalling his lungs.

Every cell in his body urged him to say yes, that he'd welcome the chance to explore a relationship with her. That he wanted to test this chemistry between them thoroughly, to find out exactly how strong these emotions he had for her were and how much more intense they might grow.

But his gaze shifted over Jordyn's shoulder and focused on Roxie, who still stood by Tucker's side, laughing out loud at something he said and taking another bite of her candy apple, an expression of joy enveloping her cute face.

Right now, Roxie was happy, safe and secure in the knowledge that he and Tucker would be there for her every day, all day, for the rest of her life. She didn't fear the future or worry things might change on a whim—things that might occur should he upset the status quo he'd worked so hard to build. Roxie's days at the ranch were fun but predictable and filled with memories of a mother who, even though they'd never had a chance to meet, had loved her more than life itself. And those memories were especially important this time of year.

At the thought of Macy and all she'd lost—all that had been stolen from her, Nate sat back, a wave of guilt and regret rushing through him as he put distance between himself and Jordyn. He looked up reluctantly, barely able to meet her eyes.

"I'm afraid I'd have to say," he whispered, "that I'm not available."

The words he'd chosen were simple—polite and benign—but they had an unexpectedly harsh impact on her.

The rosy color in her cheeks drained, the teasing light in her eyes died and a wounded expression appeared on her pretty face.

"Jordyn . . ." He lifted one hand in appeal. "I only meant—"

"I know what you meant." She smiled, though the act was insincere.

"But I . . ." He floundered for the right words. "You . . . you were joking, right? Just kidding around?" He forced a laugh. "Trying to knock me off my game before the contest?"

He had hoped, on some level, that she'd agree with him. That she'd play off her advance, admit she was trying to rattle him, then wave off his concern.

But she didn't.

"No. I was just trying to be honest and open with you." She laughed nonchalantly but the blazing flush on her face spread down her neck, and she avoided his eyes. "But I understand, and it's okay. Thank you for being honest with me, too."

Her fingertips left the sleeves of his shirt, her hands retreated across the table, and she stood as though to leave.

"Jordyn, wait." He stood, too, but when she looked at him, his throat closed with remorse at having hurt her and he couldn't think of a single thing to say.

She met his gaze then and smiled, sincerely this time, a teasing light entering her eyes. "Don't sweat it, Nate. It really is okay. I'm a risk-taker, took my shot and struck out. That's all. And now, I know where I stand." She left then, pausing a few feet away to turn back and smile. "Good luck fishing, Neighbor Nate. I'll see you around sometime."

Nate watched her walk away, then sat down again.

Eventually, Jordyn chose another table among the many arranged in the town square, sat in a chair and conversed briefly with the man sitting in front of her. Mason Walker, a dashing local cop who was two years closer in age to Jordyn, took advantage of Jordyn's proximity, engaging her in a deep discussion, leaning across the table and saying something that made her laugh.

Nate frowned and refocused on the bucket of candy canes in front of him.

"Get them Stones, man," Tucker drawled from the sidelines, chewing another mouthful of candy apple.

"Yeah," Roxie shouted. "Win this one, Daddy!"

Nate smiled back at them and went through the motions, greeting the next person who sat in the empty chair Jordyn had vacated, listening intently as Noel's Nanas walked onto the stage still positioned in the center of the town square and announced the countdown for the contest. And when the contest began, he clenched his candy cane tightly between his teeth and dove into the task at hand wholeheartedly, using the strange surge of jealous anger within him as extra energy to snatch up candy canes from the bucket in front of him and sling them into a high pile by his side.

But when it was over, even though he won second place and moved a bit higher on the Tree Scoreboard, he had trouble smiling.

Instead, his gaze kept returning to Jordyn where she still sat across from Mason, laughing at his jokes and engaging in conversation. He told himself that he was happy Jordyn was settling in and forming new acquaintances, getting to know everyone. But he couldn't shake the immensely unpleasant thought that even though he'd told Jordyn he wasn't available, it wouldn't be very long before she discovered that other men in Noel were.

Chapter Seven

"We got people for that, you know."

Nate, standing in one of the stables at Frosted Firs Ranch, dragged his forearm over his sweaty forehead and glanced over his shoulder where Tucker stood in the doorway, his fists propped on his hips and one eyebrow lifted, a look of derision in his eyes.

"I'm aware of that," Nate said. Returning to the task at hand, he dug his shovel into the soiled shavings on the stall floor, lifted it and dumped the contents into a wheelbarrow that sat nearby. "But I preferred to get a little exercise today. Anything wrong with that?"

"Not a thing." Tucker sauntered farther inside the stable and leaned on one of the stalls nearby, watching Nate through narrowed eyes as he resumed mucking the stall. "Thing is, I wouldn't question what you're doing except for the fact that it's freezing out here and you haven't taken it upon yourself to muck out a stall in at least six months."

Nate dug his shovel into the soiled shavings again, shook off the clean bits, then dumped the manure that remained into the wheelbarrow with more force than necessary. Metal clanged on metal as the shovel dinged the side of the wheelbarrow, the raucous noise echoing throughout the empty stable.

"So . . ." Tucker sighed. "It's clear something's eating at you. You might as well just come on out with it and tell me what's up."

"I never said anything was bothering me."

Tucker laughed. "And that right there is the problem. For three days now, you've been making yourself scarce and working yourself to the bone. Even Roxie has asked if there's something wrong with you."

Nate lowered his shovel to the floor, propped the handle against the door of the stall, then leaned back against the wall and crossed his arms over his chest. "There's nothing wrong with me. There's just a lot of work to do around here and I don't mind pitching in even when I don't have to."

Tucker made a face and rolled his eyes, then glanced away briefly, looking out the open entrance of the stable. "Whatever. I'm just telling you that you'll feel better if you just get whatever it is that's bugging you off your chest." His attention returned to Nate, his eyes seeming to peer right through him and pick apart his thoughts. "I mean, it's not like I don't already know what's on your mind."

Nate scoffed. "And what exactly do you think that is?"

"Our feisty little neighbor, Jordyn Banks." Tucker grinned, his smile growing even wider as Nate fumed.

"There's nothing going on between me and Jordyn."

Tucker winked. "See, now I never said there was anything going on between you two. I just said she was on your mind, which must be true, seeing as how you jumped to such a conclusion."

Nate smothered a groan and leaned more heavily against the wall behind him. He took his time tugging off his gloves and beating them together to shake off the shavings that clung to the sweaty material. "This isn't something I want to discuss right now. Or . . . possibly ever."

Smile fading, Tucker nodded. "I'm aware of that. But it's hard to ignore the fact that you're having a hard time shaking off your fascination with our new neighbor."

Nate frowned. "What're you talking about? Jordyn just got here barely a week ago—"

"I'm talking about the overarching issue here, brother." Tucker crossed his arms over his chest, too, his mouth flattening into a stubborn line. "It's not like we haven't had this conversation before, so how about you don't play coy with me right now?"

"What do you want me to say?" Nate tensed, holding his breath in his lungs for a moment, then inhaling deeply to tamp down his temper. "Are you wondering if Jordyn has caught my eye? Yes. She did—briefly. You wanna know what she asked me at the Candy Cane Fishing contest? She asked if I'd be interested in dating her and possibly pursuing a romantic relationship, and I gave her the same answer I've given every other woman who's posed a similar question to me over the past six years. My answer didn't seem to go over well with her, but being the mature and understanding woman she is, she accepted it graciously and moved on. As did I."

Tucker, a stoic expression on his face and his burly arms still crossed over his chest, continued staring at him.

"There," Nate said. "You've got the whole juicy story now. Does that make you happy?"

As Tucker continued his silent stare, Nate shifted from one boot to the other uncomfortably, then glanced at the open doorway of the stable, his gaze focusing on the field beyond.

It had been three days since the Candy Cane Fishing contest. The snow had melted along the foothills of the mountains, the sun shined a bit brighter than it had in weeks and the temperature, though frigid, had crept up a few degrees, lending the barest hint of warmth to the air. The combination of cold air, full sun, and a steady breeze made for a perfect winter's day, the kind he would normally enjoy with Tucker and Roxie. In the past, the three of them would bundle up, climb into his truck, and drive to town to spend the afternoon strolling along the busy sidewalks, window shopping, enjoying the holiday decorations and grabbing a sweet snack or two along the way.

But today, he couldn't quite shake the irritation he'd felt when Jordyn had sat opposite Mason Walker at the Candy Cane Fishing contest, laughing as though Mason was the most delightful acquaintance she'd made in her life.

"Mason's got nothing on you, man," Tucker said quietly.

Nate's eyes shot back to his brother, the younger man's uncanny ability to read his thoughts as surprising as ever.

"It wasn't difficult to notice," Tucker added. "I saw her sit with you during the contest, exchange a few words, then move to his table. You barely took your eyes off either of them the entire time. I could practically see and hear the steam whistling out of your ears."

"Oh, Lord." Nate rubbed his forehead. "Was I that obvious?"

Tucker tilted his head, considering this, then nodded. "Yeah. Your grinchy, green-eyed envy was on full display. At least to me."

Nate closed his eyes, his face burning.

"Come on," Tucker said. "It's not like that's a bad thing." His tone changed, gentling on his next words. "It's been six years, Nate. I know you loved Macy something fierce and that y'all had something special, but she's been gone for some time now and I know she wouldn't hold it against you if you were to move on."

Nate clenched his jaw, grinding his teeth together to distract himself from the gnawing ache of grief and guilt that spread through his chest. "I don't want to move on."

"I know," Tucker said softly. "It's much easier to just hide out, isn't it? Dig yourself a hole, pull the dirt in over your head and pretend things are just great the way they are. Tell yourself that you're content with reminiscing over what you had because you don't want or need more than you've got."

Nate looked at him then, his mouth twisting. "I don't expect you to understand. You've never been married, never had a child or—"

"Never been the man you are," Tucker finished for him, a muscle flexing in his jaw.

Nate shook his head. "That's not what I was saying."

"I know. You'd never say it out loud, but you don't have to. It's always been there between us—your disapproval of me and how I behave. Loud and clear."

Nate leaned his head back against the stall and stared at the ceiling of the stable, sweat trickling down the back of his neck. "Can we please not do this now? I don't feel up to arguing at the moment."

"We're not arguing. We're having a conversation. The kind I wish we'd have more often, to be honest with you. You bottle things up so tight, you never give yourself a chance to just relax and breathe."

That, unfortunately, was true.

On more than one occasion, Nate had shut Tucker down, refusing to answer his brother's questions about what he wanted out of life, how he was dealing with the grief of losing Macy, and what he thought the future might hold for him. But he didn't hold back talking with Tucker deliberately. It was just too painful to discuss the loss of his wife and too scary to face his future without her.

"I'm not trying to be difficult, Tucker. I'm just trying to take my time with things. Trying to get my feet under me before I even think about changing my life."

"And how long will that be? It's been six years."

"And Roxie is still a little girl." Nate bit his lower lip to still the tremor in his chin. "Do you know how hard it is to think about bringing another woman into her life? She never even had a chance to meet Macy. Never got the opportunity to know what it would feel like to have a mother or how wonderful a mother Macy would've been. And you want me to think about bringing another woman into her life simply to suit my needs? Potentially involving someone else whose ways might not fit in with the way Roxie likes things? A woman who might not sacrifice her own interests for Roxie the way Macy would have? A woman who might change her mind down the road or—"

"Pass away like Macy?"

Nate froze, absorbing the pain of the words that fell from his brother's lips.

"I'm sorry," Tucker said quietly. "I'm not trying to rub salt in the wound, and I understand what you're saying. I'm just concerned about you. You've had countless opportunities over the past six years to try to move on, but you haven't taken advantage of any of them." An exasperated sound burst from his lips. "Even now, when you're actually interested in a woman, you still aren't willing to even consider trying to build a new relationship. You're not obligated to grieve forever. You're entitled to be happy again."

Nate stared down at his boots, his vision blurring as he said quietly, "Knowing Roxie is happy is enough for me. And that's the way I plan to keep it."

Tucker released a heavy breath and turned away, walking toward the open door of the stable. He stopped short of it though and faced Nate again.

"Speaking of Roxie," he said. "She's been beggin' to see that white quarter horse of Jordyn's. I promised her I'd drive her over there when the sun came out and the snow melted a bit. We're going to Chestnut Ridge now to see if Jordyn's home, drop off another free load of firewood and ask her if she'd be willing to introduce Roxie to Star. It'll just be an innocent, neighborly visit." His mouth twisted, an ironic look in his eyes. "And it'll make Roxie happy. You want to go?"

Nate stared. Did he? Of course, he did. He'd thought of little but Jordyn over the past three days. His mind had fixated on her friendly interactions with Mason at the Candy Cane Fishing contest and he'd kicked himself every time he imagined that he could have been sitting across from her where Mason had sat, making her laugh the same way, had he just answered Jordyn's question differently.

But . . . no matter how much Tucker pushed for him to move on, he wasn't ready to explore a new relationship. And misleading a woman was a sure way to stir up trouble. It was better, overall, to let things stay as they were.

"Thank you," Nate said, "but no."

Even though the snow had melted, Jordyn still couldn't get over how magnificent her backyard was. She stood in the back lot of her property, tilted her head and breathed deeply, drawing in the fresh, cold mountain air. The brisk wind that swept over the landscape put a spring in her step as she walked over to stand next to the impressive tree the Nanas had dubbed Fabio.

Star, who'd been strolling through the back lot, took off, galloping across the field, her thick white mane rippling with each leap. Clearly, the brisk winter wind had put a spring in the mare's step, too.

"She's a beauty, isn't she?" Jordyn glanced up at the

noble evergreen to her left and smiled. "Pretty pitiful, ha? Me standing out here in the middle of my field talking to myself. Well . . . I'm not exactly talking to myself—I'm talking to you. Though . . ." she reconsidered, "that might be even worse, seeing as how I'm talking to a tree."

But she had to admit, Fabio Fraser was a good listener.

She'd woken up early this morning after a fitful night of sleep, made a hot, sweet cup of coffee in the new coffee-maker the Nanas had helped her pick out, bundled up in her warmest jacket and led Star out to the back field to admire the view and the perfect Fraser fir that still stood tall on her property.

Her surroundings had lifted her spirits at first, the rolling foothills and majestic mountain peaks in the distance reminding her of what a gorgeous stretch of property she now owned and how much potential it held for the new business she planned to build. But somehow that particular dream of breeding and training barrel racing horses had taken a back seat to her participation in the Christmas competition—and her preoccupation with Nate Reed.

"Oh, this is ridiculous," she grumbled, kicking the dormant grass with the toe of her boot.

It was absolutely ridiculous to obsess over a man she'd just met and barely knew, much less grieve over what might've been, had he accepted her invitation to explore a relationship. And his rejection shouldn't have disappointed her as much as it had. After all, the Nanas had already warned her that Nate wasn't interested in any type of romantic encounter and that he'd already refused a number of women's advances.

Only, she'd held out hope that Nate would respond differently to her. That perhaps he felt the electric energy sparking between them as deeply as she did.

But, in the end, Nate had rejected her, too. His response had stung her pride . . . and heart.

She supposed she should be grateful he'd been honest and direct with her from the get-go. At least now, she knew exactly where she stood. He wasn't interested in a relationship, so she shouldn't pursue one with him. They would be friendly enemies until the end of the Christmas competition and after that, they'd see each other in passing, as polite acquaintances.

Whatever admiration she still harbored for Nate Reed should be tucked away and only allowed to emerge occasionally as a casual appreciation for her new neighbor. That was all that would ever exist between her and Neighbor Nate, and it was better to know that now rather than later.

Wincing, she slipped her hand under her thick scarf and rubbed her chest. Oh, if only that knowledge didn't sting quite as deeply as it did.

The rumble of an engine sounded at her back and, hand stilling against her sternum, she glanced over her shoulder, her breath catching at the site of Nate's truck.

"Oh . . . kay," she breathed.

Had Nate changed his mind?

Her hand lifted to her hair, her fingers hastily smoothing the windswept strands. Had he, after three days of mulling it over, reconsidered her proposition that they date, decided to drive over, apologize for turning her down, admit he'd made a mistake and beg her to allow him back into her good graces?

But when the doors opened, Tucker and Roxie hopped out instead.

Nate was nowhere in sight.

"Ms. Jordyn!" Roxie, her hair pulled back in her ever-present ponytail, bounded across the back lot toward Jordyn, a huge smile on her face. "We came to visit you!"

Taking a moment to dispel her disappointment at Nate's absence, Jordyn smiled at the excited expression on

Roxie's face, knelt and beckoned the little girl over to her side. "Well, hello! What a wonderful surprise."

Roxie drew to a stop inches from Jordyn's knees, placed her small hands on Jordyn's shoulders and grinned down at her. "Uncle Tucker said if we brought you firewood, you might let me meet Star." She craned her neck, peering over Jordyn's shoulder toward the white mare that frolicked in the back lot. "Is that her? Is that Star running?"

"Yep," Jordyn said. "That's Star, all right. And she's pretty revved up this morning. This cold mountain air has put an extra kick in her step and she's enjoying a good run."

"How's her time?" Tucker drawled as he ambled over to join his niece.

Jordyn shook her head. "I'm not timing her. We're semi-retired now, so Star just runs however far and fast as she likes, whenever she feels like it."

"That's a good life for a retired racehorse," he said. "How long did you two tour the circuit?"

"Oh, I've been at it since I was eighteen, so seven years, give or take a month or two."

"Same here," Tucker said, grinning. "Don't know if Nate told you or not, but I rode bulls for several years. Competed all over the country and placed in a few competitions before I settled back in Noel to help him out at Frosted Firs Ranch."

"Really? I'm impressed." Jordyn winked. "How many buckles did you win?"

"Oh," Tucker drawled, a flirtatious gleam lighting his eyes as he wiggled his eyebrows. "It wasn't actually the buckles I was after."

Jordyn laughed. "I see. I tell you what, you and your brother couldn't be more different if you tried."

Tucker chuckled, but a wry note entered his voice. "Believe me, I'm aware of that."

Oh, boy. The crestfallen look on Tucker's face was enough to prove she'd hit a nerve.

"I . . . I didn't mean anything by that," Jordyn said hastily. "I'm sorry if I—"

"No worries." Tucker's charming grin returned full force and he waved off her concern. "I'm well aware that Nate and I are polar opposites and"—he cast a surreptitious glance at Roxie—"that's the main reason I'm here. Aside from the fact," he added in a louder voice, "that Roxie has been beggin' to get an up-close peek at a famous barrel racer." He reached out and ruffled Roxie's blond bangs. "Haven't you, kid?"

Roxie nodded, her eyes clinging to Star's movements as the mare dashed across the back lot. "Yes, sir." She peeled her attention away from Star and blinked up at Jordyn, a hopeful expression on her face. "Can I see Star up close, please?"

Jordyn tapped Roxie's nose, a wave of affection washing over her at the eager plea in the little girl's eyes. "Of course, you can. Star loves meeting new people and you're always welcome to visit her anytime you feel like it."

Taking Roxie's hand in hers, Jordyn led her further into the back lot and whistled. Star, still galloping across the field, changed direction, then trotted over, slowing to a relaxed walk when she reached Jordyn. Stopping by Jordyn's side, the mare nudged Jordyn's chest with her broad head.

"She comes when you whistle!" Roxie's wide eyes roved over the white mare slowly, a bright smile appearing.

"That she does," Jordyn said. "Took me a while to train her, though. She was pretty ornery when I got her, but she came around eventually."

"Is she fun to ride?" Roxie asked.

"You bet!" Jordyn reached out and tugged the little

girl's ponytail gently. "But it can be dangerous if you don't know what you're doing."

"Do you think I might could ride her someday?"

Jordyn furrowed her brow and touched her finger to her lips as if in thought, then said to Roxie, "I think we might can make that happen. It'd be best if you two got to know each other first, though. That way Star'll be familiar with you before your first ride with her and she'll be much more relaxed."

"When can I start getting to know her?"

"How about now?"

A full-blown smile, full of delight, broke out across Roxie's face. "Yes, please!"

Jordyn reached into the pocket of her jacket, pulled out a small plastic bag of apple slices and handed one to Roxie. "Here." She cupped Roxie's hand in hers and raised it toward Star. "Let's give her a snack, shall we?"

As she picked up the sweet scent of apples, Star's nose worked overtime, searching for her favorite treat. She ducked her head and nibbled at the apple slice in Roxie's hand, making the little girl giggle.

Roxie squealed. "That tickles!"

Jordyn laughed. "Yeah. I have a hard time keeping a straight face when I feed her, too. And you're doing an excellent job, by the way."

Roxie flushed with joy. "Thank you. Can I feed her another one?"

"Oh, she's probably ready to take off again now that she's had a snack. Move a little closer—we'll give her a pet and then she'll probably take off."

Roxie did as Jordyn asked, allowing Jordyn to lift her arm toward the mare, then stroked her neck gently and stepped away.

"All right, girl," Jordyn said to Star. "Go have fun."

Star, satisfied with her snack and a dose of loving attention, moved away then took off, sprinting across the back lot again into the distance.

"Can I follow her, Uncle Tucker?" Roxie pleaded, bouncing excitedly. "And watch her for a while?"

Smiling, Tucker nodded. "Go ahead. But be sure to keep your distance because she doesn't know you well enough yet to feel completely secure."

Roxie ran across the field, shouting over her shoulder, "I will, Uncle Tucker!"

Tucker walked over to Jordyn's side, and they stood there by the Fraser fir tree, watching Roxie skip across the back lot, waving at Star as she galloped in the distance.

Jordyn grinned, the charming delight on Roxie's face warming her heart. "I do believe Roxie is the most well-mannered child I've ever met."

"She gets that from her mama."

The somber tone in Tucker's voice drew Jordyn's eyes. He still stared straight ahead, watching Roxie, leaving only his profile visible, but a muscle clenched in his jaw.

"Her mother, Macy, was a good woman," he continued quietly. "She loved the holidays—any holiday—but especially Christmas." A gentle smile curved his lips. "She was good for Nate, and he was good for her. They grew up together here in Noel. Shared a lot of history between them." He shook his head, his smile fading. "Don't think I've ever seen a couple more in love than they were."

It was nothing Jordyn didn't already know, but hearing the words . . .

Well, that hurt just a little bit more than she'd expected.

Neck heating, she lowered her head, half ashamed. What kind of woman would be jealous of a man's late wife? Of course, Nate had loved Macy. He'd married her and had a child with her. From all accounts, he'd been deeply in love and had every right to miss Macy.

Only, she couldn't quite shake the longing that had

rooted deep inside her. The one that kept her wishing Nate might have had a little room left over in his heart for her, too.

"I'm glad he was happy," she said quietly. "That kind of love can be hard to find nowadays."

"Yes," Tucker said. "It can."

They fell silent, the cold wind whistling between them as Star galloped in the distance, Roxie still watching with avid interest.

"Nate could be happy that way again," Tucker said. "If he allowed himself to, that is."

Her cheeks prickled under the weight of Tucker's scrutiny, and she glanced over at him, the compassionate—somewhat pitying—look in his eyes making her squirm with humiliation.

"I'm sorry, I don't mean to butt into your private life," Tucker said. "Or his, for that matter. He'd kill me if he knew I was talking to you like this. But I know he's pushed you away already. I also know that he took a deep liking to you the moment he met you. And I can tell you firsthand, that doesn't happen for Nate. Not even with Macy. Not ever."

Her heart stumbled as she whispered, "For me, either."

Tucker ducked his head and faced forward again, his blue eyes—so like Nate's—following Star's progress across the field. "I'm sure you know as well as I do that horses are a lot like people. Most of 'em have times when they're afraid of what they don't know and are unsure whether they can trust people they've just met. They feel emotions as deeply as we do and sometimes it scares them . . . especially considering their happiness is dependent upon the actions and goodwill of someone else."

Jordyn fixed her gaze on Roxie, waving back as Roxie, smiling, waved in Jordyn's direction.

"Nate's scared, is all—though he'll never tell you that," Tucker said. "He just needs a nudge from the right woman. One who's fallen for him as deeply as he's fallen for her. One with light hands who's used to throwing her hat in the ring, taking a risk and accepting the possibility of getting hurt." He glanced at her again. "You understand what I'm saying, J?"

Pulse fluttering with a heady surge of excitement and dismay, she nodded.

Tucker grinned. "Good. Because as far as Nate's concerned, if you take him by the bit and nudge him in the right direction, he'll come around eventually."

Chapter Eight

Jordyn had liked Mason Walker well enough when she'd met him five days ago at the Candy Cane Fishing contest, but from the moment she arrived at the Terrible Tinsel Triathlon, Noel's favorite cop stuck to her more than the candy cane syrup she'd just been doused in.

"The secret to winning the triathlon is to start off at a moderate pace, cut corners where you can, and save your last big surge of energy for the final few feet of the race." Mason, hopping from one foot to the other beside her at the south end of Noel's town square to warm up for the race, dragged a hand through his wet, sticky hair, then slung a handful of candy cane syrup onto the dormant grass. "Only thing," he said, "is once you get to running, the syrup starts to melt all over you. It slides right into your eyes and ears. It's enough to trip anybody up."

"That's okay," Jordyn said, smiling. "I know a thing or two about racing. But I do have to admit, I've never raced anyone while covered in red candy cane syrup. Had I known a bucket of syrup was going to be dumped over my head, I would've brought a pair of goggles."

She wiped her face as Mason had, then flicked a handful of candy cane syrup to the ground. Opening her eyes wide, she forced her sticky eyelids apart and surveyed the scene before them.

Noel's Terrible Tinsel Triathlon was about to commence. As usual with each contest, a crowd of residents had gathered in the town square, some standing in line waiting for their turn to be doused with candy cane syrup for their run, others dumping the buckets of syrup over the participants, and a few standing by taking pictures, laughing at their friends' and loved ones' sticky discomfort. It was, indeed, a sight to behold.

Overnight, a fresh burst of frigid air had rolled over the little town, dusting Noel's mountain peaks and valleys with a thin layer of snow. It made for a beautiful sight, but it also made the ground slick and slippery, which would pose an added challenge for participants.

"Are you familiar with the course?" Mason asked, shaking his hands by his sides and bouncing from one foot to the other as he continued warming up for his run.

Jordyn nodded. "Kandy gave me a rundown yesterday. From what she told me, we start over there." She pointed at the starting line, which was marked with a line drawn through the snow several feet in front of them. "Then we take off across the town square, run its entire length, grab the gift box marked with our name that's sitting on the other end, circle around and come back down the middle through the obstacle course. When we reach this end of the town square again, we have to wrap our gift box with one of the ribbons on the ground. The first one to finish beautifying their gift box wins."

And boy, did she need to win this one!

So far, she hadn't placed in any of the competitions she'd participated in, and according to Kandy, only the top three performers prior to the tree contest had a good chance of accumulating enough points to win the Christmas Crown. If Jordyn didn't start accumulating points now, she was certain to be at the bottom of the scoreboard, and she'd lose every chance she had to win the Christmas Crown for Noel's Nanas.

"Ms. Jordyn!"

Wiping away a fresh layer of syrup that had seeped over her eyelids, Jordyn glanced to her right, where Roxie was skipping across the town square toward her. "Hello there, Roxie!"

She craned her neck, glancing past Roxie to the sidelines, but Nate was nowhere to be found.

"Uncle Tucker told me you'd be running against him today." Roxie's eyes grew wide as she drew to a halt in front of Jordyn. "Boy, they really dumped a lot of syrup on you!"

Jordyn laughed. "Yeah, I think they did accidentally go a little bit overboard with me."

Tucker, who'd been strolling leisurely behind Roxie, joined them. His hair, normally styled, was coated with syrup, as were his clothes and shoes. "Nah. That was a deliberate hazing. They always dump an extra bottle of syrup over the newbies."

He nodded in Mason's direction and the two men briefly greeted each other.

Jordyn gave Tucker the once-over. "Well, looks like somebody had it out for you today, too. You look like you've got more syrup on you than I do."

He chuckled. "I probably do." Leaning closer, he wrinkled his nose and whispered, "Seems I've upset a few of the ladies in town over the years and today is the perfect day for their revenge." He rocked back on his heels and rubbed his slick hands together. "But the bigger challenge for us will be when they roll us in all that tinsel."

He pointed at an array of multicolored tinsel that had been layered in high stacks along the edge of the town square. Several participants who'd already been doused in syrup had stretched out on the ground and volunteers were rolling them through the piles of tinsel and laughing uncontrollably.

Jordyn groaned. "Oh, I forgot about that."

"That's the best part," Tucker said. "The syrup itself is hard enough to wash off but once the tinsel sticks to it, you'll be pulling multicolored strings of plastic out of your ears for the next three weeks." He laughed. "But if you win, it's worth it."

"Speaking of tinsel," Mason said, nudging Jordyn's arm. "The line for being rolled in it has shortened. Shall we take our turn?"

Jordyn waved a hand. "You go ahead, Mason. I'm going to visit with Roxie and Tucker for a minute."

Disappointment flickered over Mason's expression, but he quickly hid it with a smile. "No problem. I'll see you at the starting line."

Roxie frowned, then peered up at Jordyn. "Are you and Mr. Mason on the same team now?"

Jordyn shook her head. "Nope. I'm still competing on my own. He's just being nice and showing me the ropes."

Roxie smiled. "Well, even though you're going to be running against my uncle Tucker, I hope you do good, Ms. Jordyn."

Jordyn squatted on her haunches in front of Roxie. "You know, that's really nice of you, Roxie." She winked and tapped her cheek. "But they always say good luck is best served with a kiss on the cheek."

"You mean . . ." Roxie eyed Jordyn's sticky face and shuddered. "You want me to give you a good luck kiss on your cheek?"

Jordyn nodded.

"But . . ." Roxie made a face, her mouth twitching into a smile. "You're all syrupy!"

Jordyn spread her arms out and growled. "That's right! Come here, little girl!"

Jordyn, laughing maniacally, reached for her, but Roxie hopped out of reach, giggling. "No way! I'm not going to kiss you with all that syrup on you. Yuck!" Laughing, she added, "Good luck, Ms. Jordyn!"

With that, she dashed off, running across the field, weaving between people to join Nate, who now stood on the sidewalk outside the town square, watching her.

Standing slowly, Jordyn lifted her arm and waved hesitantly at Nate. He waved back and smiled, though even from this distance, she could tell the gesture was polite and restrained. But despite the guarded expression on his face as he met her eyes, he'd smiled. She'd take it.

After Tucker's and Roxie's visit to Chestnut Ridge two days ago, she'd thought over what Tucker had said about Nate, turning it over in her mind all afternoon. It had given her a bit of hope to think that Nate's hesitancy to explore a relationship with her might be due to the pain he'd experienced in the past rather than a lack of interest in her.

She, of all people, knew how difficult it was to lose one's sense of security in life and how comforting predictability could be. But she'd also had the advantage of experiencing firsthand on the rodeo circuit how rewarding risk could be. How life could hold surprises and enjoyment that she never would've imagined.

"He's pining, you know?"

Jordyn broke eye contact with Nate and faced Tucker, his syrupy, lopsided grin making her smile. "He doesn't look like he's pining."

"Oh, believe me," Tucker said, wiping a handful of syrup from his mouth. "The man's been acting morose ever since he turned your invitation down. And his eyes turned green and burned a hole in Mason Walker the entire time you sat with him at the Candy Cane Fishing contest."

"Well, there's no reason for him to be jealous. There's absolutely nothing between me and Mason Walker. He's a nice guy, but we're just friends."

Tucker shrugged. "I'm not saying it's a bad thing. As a matter fact, speaking as a man, myself," he said, placing a hand on his chest, "I have to admit that sometimes a little bit of jealousy is all it takes for a woman to get our attention."

"That's not how I'd like to get your brother's attention though," Jordyn said quietly. "I don't like games, and I certainly wouldn't like to play someone else."

Tucker dipped his head. "Duly noted. Though in that regard, my brother and I are complete opposites. I'm the only one in the family that tends to play games."

Jordyn winced. "Oh, I didn't mean it that way. I'm sorry if—"

"Don't sweat it." He held up a hand, waving off her concern. "I didn't mean anything by it, either. But it was good to hear because Nate is just as straightforward and honest as you are." He grinned. "Just another reason why I think the two of you would hit it off perfectly if he would just give dating a chance." His brows rose. "You give any thought to what I told you the other day?"

Jordyn narrowed her eyes. "Maybe. But does Nate know you've been talking to me about him?"

Tucker guffawed. "Are you kidding me? If he had any clue that I was talking with you about this kind of thing, I'd be laid up in the hospital with broken limbs about now."

Jordyn laughed. "So, Nate's a private person then?"

"Very private." Tucker glanced over her shoulder at Nate. "He barely opens up to me about his feelings." His eyes returned to her face, a somber note in them. "That's why, this time, I'm nudging a bit." He flashed another wide grin. "But just a very little bit, mind you. One of you two has got to pick up the slack and do some work yourself; otherwise, there's no way y'all will ever hook up. And I can tell you right now that it won't be him that does the chasing. So put your racing shoes on and get after him, woman."

Laughing, Jordyn saluted him. "Yes, sir."

"And don't think for a minute," he said, holding up a finger, "that I'm going to take it easy on you in this race just because I've taken a shine to you as a potential date for my brother." He scowled down at her. "I'm gonna wipe the floor with you, woman."

Jordyn lifted her chin, growling back, "Give it your best shot, dude. I can take it."

"Alright then," he drawled, sauntering away. "It's on!"

She watched him join the others at the tinsel station, then glanced at Nate once more before walking over and joining the tinsel line, too.

A little bit jealous, huh?

The last thing she wanted was to play games with Nate by using another man's presence to make him jealous. But . . . she wouldn't be averse to the idea of him noticing that other men might take an interest in her. Maybe then, he would start contemplating how he felt about her himself, and if Tucker was right—which she really hoped he was—Nate did harbor some affection for her.

A fluttering sensation moved through her chest at the thought and she quickly reminded herself that that's all it was—just a thought. Nate, himself, had done nothing over the past three days to indicate that he had changed his mind about dating her. So for now, she'd do best to focus on the race, give it all she had, and try to cinch a win.

"Whoever's next, please!" one of the volunteers at the

head of the tinsel line shouted as she waved for the next participant to come lie down on the pile of tinsel.

Jordyn hurried over. "That'd be me!"

Ten minutes later, all the triathlon participants had been doused with syrup, rolled in tinsel and lined up at the starting line. Jordyn stood in the middle of the pack, with Tucker to her left and Mason to her right.

"Everyone ready?" Carol Belle, standing on stage in the center of town square, waited for the participants to indicate they were ready, then held up a whistle. "When you hear the whistle, take off. Run to the other end of the town square, retrieve the gift box with your name, race back through the obstacle course, and at the opposite end of the town square, tie the bow on your gift and declare you're finished. All participants are being timed and the competitor with the fastest time wins. Ready, set . . ."

Carol Belle blew the whistle and at the sound, the line of participants shot off from the starting line and dashed across the snow-slicked ground toward the opposite end of the town square.

Jordyn ran as fast as she could, saying a silent word of thanks for her long legs, which enabled her to keep pace with Tucker and Mason. With each step, her skin warmed despite the chill in the air, and the red candy cane syrup began to melt, dripping over her face, clinging to her skin and making every move of her limbs a sticky challenge.

"You're falling behind, cowgirl!" Tucker shouted as he pulled ahead a couple feet.

Jordyn laughed and lurched forward. "Only for a moment! Watch your back!"

Moments later, she surged ahead of the pack, reminding herself to keep her attention straight ahead and not look back to see if others were gaining on her.

When she reached the other end of the town square, she

quickly found her gift box, spun around and headed straight for the obstacle course. She darted through a series of tires that had been lined up on the ground in pairs, sneezing twice when tinsel that clung to the syrup tickled her nose. Next, she climbed a short rock wall, straddled it and slid down the other side, slamming her feet onto the ground and dashing through the last stage of the obstacle course. Volunteers, holding jumbo holiday inflatables such as reindeer, Santa Claus, and gumdrops, battered her and the other contestants as they passed.

An inflatable candy cane smacked into Jordyn's forehead, rocking her off balance momentarily, but she regained her footing, ducked under it and ran faster, mumbling under her breath, "Good grief, these people love their candy canes!"

As she reached the opposite end of the town square, still in the lead, the cheers from the bystanders grew louder and she could hear Roxie's voice among the crowd shouting, "Go, Ms. Jordyn! Go!"

She glanced in Roxie's direction, struggling to see her through a haze of red candy cane syrup and tinsel, then snatched up a length of ribbon from the ground, wrapped it around her gift box and did her best to tie it into a bow despite the goopy syrup and tangled tinsel tangling around her fingers.

Tucker slid past her on his hands and knees and struggled to halt his momentum by digging his heels into the ground. After gaining a firm footing, he crawled across the ground, retrieved a ribbon and began hastily tying it around his own gift box, shooting anxious glances in Jordyn's direction as he worked.

Despite his valiant efforts, Jordyn managed to finish tying her bow moments before his and she took a moment to gloat, running in his direction, jumping over him and shouting, "In the dust, man! I'm leaving you in the dust!"

With that, she took off, sprinting the last few feet to the finish line, lifted her wrapped gift box into the air and did a little dance as the crowd cheered her on. Tucker crossed the finish line mere seconds after her, securing second place.

"First place, sucker!" Jordyn laughed, sticking her tongue out at Tucker. "I got first!"

Slamming her gift box on the ground like a football, she did another dance, laughing louder as the Nanas and by-standers clapped and shouted, cheering her on.

Jordyn tilted her head back and closed her eyes, savoring the raucous sound of approval emanating from Noel's residents as they chanted her name, feeling—for the first time in her life—as though she fit right in.

Finally, a win!

"Feeling a bit left out?"

Nate, standing in front of the stage in the center of the town square, smiled at the sound of Kandy's voice next to him.

"I don't mean to break your solitude," Kandy said, leaning closer to be heard above the cheers of the crowd. "But I thought you looked a bit lonesome over here."

And, Nate admitted reluctantly to himself, he couldn't argue.

At the conclusion of the triathlon thirty minutes ago, Nate stood on the sidelines and applauded with the crowd as Jordyn was cheered for her first-place win. Roxie had left Nate's side to run across the field and congratulate Tucker on his second-place win (a position Nate knew must've hurt his pride). Roxie helped Tucker up from the ground then led him over to the hose-down area where other participants had lined up, raising their arms and laughing as volunteers sprayed them with warm water from several water hoses, washing away as much of the candy cane syrup and tinsel as possible then wrapped them in thick blankets to ward off the chill in the air. The job was undertaken mostly in vain as the candy cane syrup and tinsel were practically glued to each contestant and would require several scrubs of soap and water for complete removal.

Nate had laughed at the sight of the sweaty, sticky participants, but his enjoyment had faded as soon as Mason Walker, having finished third, jogged over to join Jordyn as she left the hosing-off station and walked to the stage for the award ceremony.

The uncomfortable churn in his gut that had first surfaced during the Candy Cane Fishing contest returned with a vengeance. He gritted his teeth and forced himself to focus on Roxie and Tucker instead, trying to smile as Roxie grabbed a hose and vigorously sprayed down his brother.

But that had been in vain, too. Despite his best efforts, his gaze continued to drift back to Jordyn and Mason, his teeth clenching tighter each time Mason made Jordyn laugh.

It wasn't Mason's fault. Nate had no right to be angry with Mason, seeing as how he'd turned down Jordyn's invitation. But the fact was, any man who had the ability to make Jordyn tilt her head back, smile that beautiful smile of hers and laugh wholeheartedly, would make Nate's blood boil.

And that realization shocked him. He'd never experienced such intense emotions for anyone whom he'd known such a short time. At this point, Nate had to admit that he'd felt something very intense for Jordyn from the outset.

He didn't believe in love at first sight, but he couldn't deny Jordyn had a strong claim on his emotions.

"There's room close to her, if you're interested?"

Nate shook his head. "I'm sorry, what?"

Kandy gestured toward the front of the crowd, nearest the stage. "You can get a much better view of Jordyn receiving her award from the foot of the stage than you can from back here." She rose to her toes, craned her neck and smiled. "Roxie's muscled her way up to the front. She's more excited than anyone, I think, to watch Jordyn receive her first-place ribbon."

Despite the awkward tension coursing through him, Nate managed to smile. "I imagine so. But she's up there to support Tucker, too."

"Yes, but as a newcomer, Jordyn's much more intriguing at the moment, don't you think?"

Nate faced her then, searching her expression, his mouth twisting at the mischievous light in her eyes. "You know, Ms. Kandy, you Nanas are always up to something, but you act real subtle-like, as though you think the rest of us won't catch on." He narrowed his eyes. "I think I'd prefer it if you'd just come out and say whatever it is you'd like to say to me."

Kandy at least had the good grace to look suitably chastised. "I know we Nanas are sticking our noses where we shouldn't, but we have concerns."

Nate lifted one eyebrow. "Which would be . . . ?"

"Jordyn hasn't been here long and she hasn't met many people," Kandy said quietly. "But it seems she's taken a liking to you."

Nate faced the stage again, remaining silent.

"The other day," Kandy continued, "she mentioned to us that she was going to talk to you about her interest in you. And judging by how down she's been the past couple days, I'm thinking she had that conversation with you?"

Nate sighed. "I'm aware this is a very tiny town, Ms. Kandy, but I don't see how my personal business is anyone else's concern."

"I agree," she said. "And it shouldn't be. But that kiss Jordyn put on your cheek the other day was witnessed by quite a lot of people, and word of it has made its way around town. I care about Jordyn—so do the rest of the girls—and we're doing everything we can to help her settle comfortably in Noel. That would be quite a lot harder to do if someone were to break her heart right off the bat."

Nate watched Jordyn take her place, center stage, and smile as Tucker and Mason joined her, one man standing on either side of her. Holly announced each winner, starting with Mason and ending with Jordyn, pinning a ribbon on her syrup-stained sweater beneath the thick blanket that was wrapped around her. Jordyn, beaming, lifted her chin and grinned wide as the crowd chanted her name.

"Jordyn is a good person," Nate said softly. "And I'm glad she's my neighbor. I have absolutely no intention of making things difficult for her or misleading her in any way."

Kandy tapped her lips with one finger, issuing a soft sound of discomfort. "Well, see, that's why I wonder if you were completely truthful with her during your talk the other day."

Nate frowned. "I'm not sure I follow?"

"What I mean is," she said, "from what Jordyn told us, you made it rather clear that you aren't interested in pursuing a potential relationship with her. But for someone who supposedly isn't interested, I've noticed you keep quite a lot of your attention on her."

Nate knew better than to give Kandy any more ammunition, so he remained quiet.

"I'm not trying to pry," Kandy said. "And this will be the only time I say this to you. Carol Belle, Eve, and I have known you all your life, Nate. I know you went through a very difficult time losing Macy. Carol Belle and I have suffered the loss of a spouse and know just how painful the experience can be. Life can be terribly cruel—especially when it steals those we love from us. I understand your throwing yourself into this Christmas competition since it was Macy's favorite time of year, but I don't think you enjoy it. To be honest, that's one of the main reasons Carol Belle has tried her best to get you to bow out of the Christmas competition this year."

Nate looked at her in surprise. "But I thought she wanted to increase participation and—"

"Yes." She smiled gently. "That's exactly what Carol Belle would like you to think—that she just doesn't want you to win the Christmas Crown for the tenth year in a row. The truth is, she's spoken to us on many occasions about how seriously you take the contest and the holidays. She's afraid you may be participating for the wrong reasons. We all do."

Nate scoffed. "How could anybody participate in a Christmas competition for the wrong reasons? I didn't realize having fun wasn't a good reason."

"Oh, it is. But are you having fun, Nate?"

Her question, blunt and unexpected, caught him off guard . . . almost as much as the realization that he didn't exactly have a firm answer.

He ducked his head and avoided her eyes.

"I think participating in the Christmas competition has become a period of mourning for you rather than joy," she whispered. "Winning the Christmas Crown in honor of Macy's memory is a very valiant and loving thing to do. But devoting the entire year, every year of your life, to her memory may be depriving you of a new life." She looked at the stage, smiling as her gaze settled on Jordyn. "A new life with new people who might bring more joy to you than you realize."

Nate followed her gaze, focusing on Jordyn as well. She bowed in tandem with Tucker and Mason, then high-fived both of them, all three laughing.

An ache unfurled in his chest and seeped into his veins, making him long to celebrate with her. To smile and laugh with her. To be a part of the cheerful moment.

"Life can be scary and painful," Kandy said quietly next to him. "But I'm beginning to believe that the unexpected gifts it gives us along the way, especially when we're not looking for them . . ." She sighed contentedly, her gaze straying toward someone in the crowd. "Might make it worth it in the end."

Kandy turned then and disappeared into the crowd, leaving Nate standing alone among the cheerful bystanders. He remained motionless for several minutes, watching Roxie climb up onto the stage, wiggle her way in between Jordyn and Tucker, grab their hands and smile, and for the first time in all the years he'd participated in the Christmas competition, he felt as though he were on the outside, looking in.

Chapter Nine

Jordyn learned quickly that falling from grace was a painful experience.

Three days after winning the Terrible Tinsel Triathlon, she stood in the kitchen of her cabin, waving her arms furiously to dispel the black smoke that once again billowed through her home.

"Heavens! How did this happen?" she moaned.

The day had started well enough. She'd gotten up early, drank a hot cup of coffee, fed and petted Star before letting the mare out into the field to stretch her legs, then spent almost half an hour admiring the mountain range behind her cabin. Today was warmer and the sun was bright, casting a golden glow over the rolling foothills of Chestnut Ridge. She had taken a moment to breathe it all in, closing her eyes and inhaling the clean mountain air, standing beside Fabio Frazer, savoring the woodsy aroma of the beautiful tree and reminiscing over her first-place win in the triathlon days before.

It had been surreal hearing the cheers of Noel's residents as she received her first-place ribbon. She hadn't expected the moment to feel so thrilling. The applause, the smiles, and the admiring glances of her neighbors had filled her heart to overflowing and made her eager to tackle a new contest and emerge a winner again. For the first time since arriving in Noel, she'd truly felt as though she belonged.

So, after scrubbing off all the candy cane syrup and tinsel that still clung to her (which had taken a lot longer than she'd expected), she and Kandy had gone on a shopping trip to town that same afternoon, browsing the shelves in several local stores and gathering up various ingredients to create the tastiest—and most beautiful—Christmas cookies known to man.

After all, the Christmas Cookie Crumble was the next contest scheduled, and Jordyn had every intention of winning with the help of Kandy's advice. And boy, did Kandy have a lot of advice—though she'd stopped short of physically helping Jordyn prep the ingredients, as Kandy considered anything more than verbal advice to be an act of cross-conspiring, which was against the rules.

After unloading a pile of ingredients, cookie sheets, and over a dozen recipes onto the countertops in Jordyn's kitchen, Kandy had left her to it, leaving Chestnut Ridge and advising her to bake several test batches of cookies before preparing the final three dozen she would need to enter tomorrow's contest.

"It's simple," Kandy had said. "Just follow the recipes."

Yeah, right!

Jordyn, arms outstretched, coughed as she groped her way through the black smoke toward the window in the living room. Judging from the simple directions, Jordyn had felt sure that baking would be an easy endeavor. But she discovered pretty quickly that it took a lot more than stirring a few ingredients together and punching a button on an oven to create a batch of beautiful—and tasty—Christmas cookies.

Shoving the window open, she stuck her head out into the winter air and inhaled, filling her lungs with clean oxygen as she simultaneously waved clouds of smoke out of the cabin. She tugged her cell phone from the back pocket of her jeans and, once the smoke had cleared enough for her to be able to see, quickly dialed Kandy's number.

"Merry Christmas, Jordyn!" Kandy greeted her over the line. "How're things going?"

"Merry, indeed," Jordyn grumbled, covering the phone with one hand briefly as another round of coughing overtook her. "I'm in a bit of a bind, Kandy."

"What do you mean? Did we forget an ingredient? Or do you not like the recipes?"

"I don't think it has anything to do with the ingredients or the recipes." Jordyn continued waving smoke away furiously. "I think it has to do with me."

"How so?" Kandy asked.

Jordyn sighed. "I told you I had no experience with cooking or baking. In all my twenty-five years of life, I've only cooked twice, and both times involved popping something in the microwave for less than five minutes. I really wanted to win this next contest, too, but I never imagined how difficult it would be to slap together a few dozen cookies. Quite frankly, I'm simply no good in the kitchen!"

"Oh, Jordyn," Kandy said gently. "You mustn't underestimate yourself. It takes practice to perfect a spectacular Christmas cookie—especially when you have little experience cooking. Just continue practicing like I told you and you'll get it. You still have the rest of today to bake before the contest tomorrow."

"If I put any more dough in that oven," Jordyn said, "I'll end up burning the house down!" A second round of coughing overwhelmed her. "As it stands, my cabin is already full of smoke for the second time since I moved in."

Kandy gasped. "Oh, my! Did you forget to put the timer on?"

"No," Jordyn sputtered. "I mixed the dough, kneaded

it, rolled it into little balls on the pan then put it in the oven at exactly the right temperature. Every single batch has only been in that oven for five minutes before the dough bursts into flames. The cookies turn into crispy critters faster than I can haul them back out of the oven!"

A sound of dismay crossed the line, then Kandy said, "Oh, dear. Perhaps there's something wrong with the oven."

Jordyn frowned. "You mean like there was a problem with the fireplace? Oh, sweet Lord! I'm not sure how many more problems I can handle and still put on a decent performance in the rest of the Christmas competition."

"Well, don't panic. Every problem has a solution. We just have to think of one."

"I've got a solution." As the smoke began to clear from inside the cabin, Jordyn leaned her elbows onto the windowsill and inhaled a much-needed lungful of clean mountain air. "How about you come back over here and walk me through baking at least one batch of cookies to see if you can determine where the problem's originating? Or better yet, how about I come over to your place and use your oven?"

Kandy tsked her tongue. "Oh, no. That won't do. Not at all. I'm your mentor, not your teammate. My offering you anything other than advice—especially physical help baking those cookies—would violate the rules of the competition. I promised Carol Belle that I'd only mentor you, not engage in—"

Jordyn groaned. "I know, I know. No cross-conspiring, right?"

"That's right."

"Then what do you suggest I do?"

"I don't know at the moment," Kandy said. "But don't panic. You still have several hours to figure it out and I'm sure—"

The familiar sound of an engine rumbled up the long driveway leading to Jordyn's cabin. She glanced to her left where a truck was pulling to a stop out front.

"I'm sorry, Kandy, I've got to go. I've got guests. Tucker's brought Roxie by again, I think." Jordyn left the window and headed for the front door. "Thank you for helping me get the ingredients and recipes together. I'll give my dilemma some thought and figure it out somehow."

"And please let me know what you decide to do," Kandy asked.

"Yep. Will do." Jordyn said her goodbyes, disconnected the call, returned her cell phone to her back pocket, then opened the front door.

Immediately recognizing the truck parked in front of her cabin, Jordyn smiled as the passenger door opened and Roxie hopped out. But the ripple of joy she felt at the sight of the little girl shifted to nervous tension as instead of Tucker, Nate slid out of the truck and followed Roxie as she ran ahead.

"Hi, Ms. Jordyn!" Roxie skipped up the front steps, threw her arms around Jordyn's waist and pressed her cheek to Jordyn's middle. "Merry Christmas and congratulations again on your first-place win!"

Smiling, Jordyn hugged her back. "Thank you, and Merry Christmas to you, too! I'm so happy to see you. I don't get many visitors other than the Nanas."

"I was hoping you'd be home." Roxie released her and stepped back, smiling up at her with a hopeful expression. "I wanted to see if it would be okay for me to visit Star again."

"Of course! You're more than welcome to visit Star anytime you'd like. She's already had a run for today though, I'm afraid. She's settled snug and comfy in her stall for a nap."

"If she's not asleep, is it okay if I . . ." Roxie's voice

trailed away as her gaze fixed on the open window where black tendrils of smoke still slithered over the windowsill and curled up into the cold winter air. "Ms. Jordyn, something's burning in your house!"

Jordyn winced. "Yeah. I'm afraid I had a little trouble in the kitchen today."

Nate, striding up the front steps to join them on the porch, glanced at the smoke wafting from the window, then swept his gaze over Jordyn from head to toe before meeting her eyes. "Are you okay?"

The concern in his tone warmed her on the inside.

"Yep." She smiled brighter and shoved her hands in the pockets of her jeans, trying to hide the tremors running through her. "I just gave baking a try for the first time in my life and, unfortunately, it didn't turn out so well."

Nate's tense posture relaxed as a slow smile spread across his face. "Getting ready for the Christmas Cookie Crumble, are you?"

Jordyn nodded. "Or, at least, trying to."

Gracious! Even though his rejection of her suggestion that they date still stung, she found him as gorgeous as ever.

Look away. Look away!

She tried desperately to pry her gaze from his, but after three full days of absence, his charismatic appeal was a balm to her senses and . . . she'd missed him. Biting her lip, she ducked her head. Oh, boy. There it was.

She'd missed him.

It'd only been three days since she last saw him, but it felt like a year. And now, face-to-face with him, she felt as though Christmas had arrived early, bringing Nate Reed to his romantic senses—and her front door—on a beautiful winter's morning.

Only, that was a silly fantasy, seeing as how Nate had

told her himself that he wasn't available—and quite possibly not interested in her at all.

"I'm sorry if we disturbed you," Nate said softly, still holding her gaze. "But Roxie was anxious to see Star again, and Tucker said you didn't mind when he brought her by to visit the other day, so I thought . . ."

"Oh, I don't mind at all. Roxie's welcome to visit Star anytime. I mean that," she said, smiling brighter. "Really. As a matter of fact, why don't I take y'all out to the stables now and let her have a visit?" Jordyn leaned back inside the door, grabbed her coat from the coatrack, then joined them on the porch and led the way toward the stable.

As they approached the entrance, Roxie took off, jogging inside, then slowing her steps as she approached Star's stable. The white mare, warm and comfortable beneath her Christmas blanket, lifted her nose in greeting as Roxie strolled over.

"Hello, Star," Roxie whispered, pressing her hands together in front of her middle. "I came to visit you."

Jordyn grinned. "You can pet her if you'd like. She likes being stroked on the neck, especially."

Smiling broadly, Roxie lifted her hand tentatively and stroked Star's thick neck. Star dipped her head and nuzzled Roxie's small hand, making her giggle.

"She likes me!"

"Of course, she does," Jordyn said. "What's not to like?"

"Can I come by and see her tomorrow, too?" Roxie asked, smiling over her shoulder at Jordyn. "And if she's hungry when we get back from the cookie contest, maybe I can feed her some more apple slices?"

"I don't see why n—"

"Roxie, it's not polite to just invite yourself ov—"

Jordyn glanced at Nate as they both stopped talking. As

his face flushed, she smiled, leaned closer and whispered, "Yeah. It's better to just show up, isn't it?"

Nate stared straight ahead but his mouth kicked up. "You got me," he whispered. "A gentleman would've called you before showing up on your front porch—especially after our, er . . . mutually agreed-upon arrangement as friendly enemies. Guess I no longer qualify as a gentleman."

Jordyn laughed. "I wouldn't say that." Raising her voice, she said, "Roxie, you're welcome to visit Star anytime you'd like so long as you have your dad or uncle's permission."

"Thank you, Ms. Jordyn!"

"Speaking of the cookie contest," Nate said, glancing over at her. "You plan on giving baking another shot, or are you hanging up your apron?"

The teasing gleam in his blue eyes stole her breath. "Why? Are you hoping I'll bow out of the contest and lessen the challenge for you, Neighbor Nate?"

He laughed. "No, not at all. Roxie and I are pros at baking and decorating Christmas cookies, and Tucker can pack away more of 'em than an elephant, in one sitting, so I have no doubt that our team will walk away with a first-place win tomorrow."

"Oh, really?" Crossing her arms over her chest, Jordyn narrowed her eyes and asked playfully, "But that'd be so much easier for you if I just happened not to show up with three dozen Christmas cookies and a healthy appetite, wouldn't it?"

Nate grinned. "Possibly."

"Uncle Tucker always eats the most cookies," Roxie said as she continued stroking Star's neck. "He eats so many that no one else can keep up with him and they crumble." She smiled proudly. "Dad says that's why they call it the Christmas Cookie Crumble. Because everyone but the winner crumbles during the eating part of the contest."

Nate chuckled. "Yep. It's a shame you won't get to participate. I'd love to see how many Christmas cookies you could scarf down before folding."

"But she could still play." Roxie stopped petting Star and walked over, slipping her hand in Jordyn's. "Dad makes the best Christmas cookies in Noel, and he could show you how to make 'em, too, couldn't you, Dad?"

Nate tilted his head and pursed his lips, considering this. "I won't argue with you." He winked at Jordyn. "I am the best Christmas cookie cook in Noel."

Jordyn grinned. "Well, I know my lack of baking experience is contributing to my failure, but I think my oven may be the real problem. It's been officially added to Chestnut Ridge's In Need of Repair list."

"If your oven's broken, you can use an oven at our house!" Roxie beamed up at her. "We have two of 'em."

Jordyn glanced at Nate in surprise and the lighthearted expression on his face faded.

"Macy—Roxie's mom—loved to cook," he said. "Especially during the holidays. She insisted on a state-of-the-art kitchen when we built our house."

Jordyn nodded, a bittersweet ache spreading through her belly. The tenderness in his tone as he spoke of his late wife was all too clear. Oh, how much he must've loved her!

Throat tightening, she whispered, "I see."

"So, can she, Dad?" Roxie asked. "Can Ms. Jordyn come cook Christmas cookies with us?"

Jordyn glanced at Nate, noting the hesitancy in his expression. "I don't know about that, Roxie. It's nice of you to offer, but you and your dad are on a different team than me, and it's against the rules for one team to help another in the Christmas competition. It's—"

"Cross-conspiring," Nate said quietly.

Roxie frowned. "But . . . Ms. Jordyn's our friend. And she's our neighbor, Dad. And you said we should always help our neighbors when they're in need." She squeezed Jordyn's hand. "We could help her with her cookies as friends and not as another team."

Nate grinned down at Roxie but remained silent.

Jordyn cringed. Oh, boy. Nate had already made it clear he wasn't interested in spending time with her, yet here they were, standing in her stable while his daughter begged him to invite her into his home. He must truly feel as though he were stuck between a rock and a hard place.

"It's a very sweet idea, Roxie," Jordyn hastened to add, "but—"

"But we'll need to help Jordyn gather her ingredients and load them in the truck before we can take her home and introduce her to our ovens." Nate smiled at Jordyn. "How 'bout Roxie and I help you pack up your sugar and flour? We need to head over to Frosted Firs Ranch and get started soon if we're going to whip up six dozen Christmas cookies before the contest tomorrow."

"Yay!" Roxie released Jordyn's hand and darted out of the stable. "Come on, Ms. Jordyn. We're gonna make Christmas cookies together!"

"But . . ." Jordyn watched Roxie run off, then faced Nate again, the tentative smile on his face surprising her. "Y'all helping me is cross-conspiring. You understand that, right?"

He shrugged. "Only if we make the cookies for you— which we won't. Using someone else's oven to bake your cookies is only a technicality, seeing as how yours is broken. Even the Nanas would understand that."

"But . . ." Jordyn rubbed her forehead, overwhelmed by a mix of excitement, hesitation, and confusion. "You told me that we should only be friendly enemies, neighbors at best. And that we . . . shouldn't spend more time together." She swallowed hard, her lips trembling. "And yet, you show up at my house unannounced, offering—"

"Christmas cookies and an oven," Nate said lightly, his gaze holding hers. But his intent gaze belied his easygoing tone. "That's all."

So much for being forthright and not sending mixed signals.

"And this is the kitchen," Nate said, leading Jordyn into the kitchen of the family house at Frosted Firs Ranch. "We have a single galley, with the island running parallel to the prep, sink, and cooking areas. All appliances—including our two ovens—are banked at eye level, and our pantry is well stocked in the event that you need additional ingredients for your cookies."

Whistling low, Jordyn strode ahead of him, walking to the center of the kitchen. She glanced around, the red waves of her hair rippling over her back as she turned her head, scanning the room. "You told me y'all had a state-of-the-art kitchen, but I don't think I quite knew what that meant." She spun around and faced him, her smile bright. "I may not be a cook, but even I can tell that this is amazing, Nate!"

He smiled. Thirty minutes earlier, after he and Roxie had helped Jordyn gather her baking essentials, they'd loaded Jordyn's cooking materials into his truck and had driven to Frosted Firs Ranch, where he took it upon himself to give Jordyn a formal tour of the family home. He led her from room to room of the three-story house, briefly detailing the high points of interior design in each area and enjoying the delighted expression on her face as she admired the Christmas decorations that he, Roxie, and Tucker had already put up throughout the house.

Her delighted expression had been captivating, but he'd

had just as difficult a time keeping his attention from the rest of her. The soft green sweater and stylish jeans she wore highlighted the curves of her figure. As she moved from one room to the next, she had transformed the space around her, brightening every inch of the spacious house with energy that lifted his spirits.

Having her here, in his home, made him feel less alone somehow. Her physical presence brought home the realization that something very precious had been missing from his life.

The effect Jordyn had on him was nothing short of alarming. Every moment he spent with her, she pulled him in deeper with her optimistic smile, vivacious personality and flirtatious humor.

Christmas cookies and an oven, he reminded himself. That's all. Baking was the only reason he had invited Jordyn over to his home.

But was it?

Already, he could feel himself dreading the moment her visit would end, and his gut hollowed at the thought of driving her back to Chestnut Ridge and watching her walk away from him. The feelings he had for her were so unsettling, the last thing he should do was to throw caution, logic, and common sense to the wind and give in to the urge he felt to spend time with her.

Who knew how long Jordyn planned on staying in Noel? Even though she'd bought Chestnut Ridge, she could, at any moment, decide to return to the rodeo circuit and leave her new domestic life behind. Or she could change her mind about pursuing a romantic relationship with him and decide she'd rather not deal with the potential baggage a widowed single father might bring into her life. And even if he did give in and try dating her, she might find that he wasn't as exciting or interesting as the men she'd known on the circuit. Men like Tucker, who lived on the edge, chasing adventure and enjoying life's challenges, might be better suited to her interests than his predictable, organized existence.

And there was one more very important concern—the most important one. Taking a chance on building a romantic relationship with Jordyn wouldn't just risk his own heart; he'd be risking Roxie's as well. And allowing Roxie's heart to be broken . . . well, that was out of the question.

"I can see why you're such a great Christmas cookie cook," Jordyn said, slipping her hands into the pockets of her jeans. "With a kitchen like this, anyone can be a chef. This is a cook's dream!"

Nate nodded. "Thank you. I wish I could take the credit, but Macy was the one who put it together. She taught me everything I know."

He held Jordyn's gaze, and after a moment, he looked away and shifted from one boot to the other, his mouth going dry. It was a strange feeling to stand in Macy's kitchen, just feet away from a charismatic woman who tugged at his heart more than any other . . . including Macy.

"This is my mom's trophy case!" Roxie, who'd trailed behind them during the tour of the house, slipped past Nate, grabbed Jordyn's hand in hers and led her to the other end of the kitchen, where a large glass trophy case stood in the corner, each shelf filled with glittery Christmas Crowns of various designs. "These are the Christmas Crowns from the competition. There's nine in all. My mom and dad won the first three crowns, and then me, my dad, and Uncle Tucker won the other six. The top three my mom and dad won are my favorite. That first has a reindeer in it, the second an angel, and the third a Christmas tree, see? Aren't they all beautiful?" She looked up at

Jordyn and grinned. "If we win this year, we'll have ten crowns in all! Dad says it's important that we win this year so we can carry on the family tra—ditch—dish—"

"Tradition," Nate corrected quietly, meeting Jordyn's eyes again. "It became a tradition when Macy and I married—winning the crown, I mean."

"And now you win them in honor of her memory?" Jordyn asked.

He nodded, saying softly, "In a way, yes."

She looked away, her eyes moving slowly over the nine crowns in the trophy case, her bright smile dimming.

Nate dragged a hand over his face and stifled a groan. *Oh, man.* Could he possibly be more insensitive? Here he was, having invited Jordyn over to bake Christmas cookies for the contest tomorrow, an event that should be fun and uplifting. A positive activity they could enjoy together as a first, tentative step toward deciding whether he should pursue a relationship with Jordyn. But instead, within less than an hour of entering his home, his focus had returned to Macy and the life—and love—he'd shared with her.

Maybe that was a sign that he should stick with his first decision and keep to the status quo. As it was, he had his hands full running Frosted Firs Ranch and taking care of Roxie. He had no idea whether Jordyn had given any thought to having a child in her life—even one as wonderful as Roxie.

But the last thing he'd ever want to do was to unintentionally hurt Jordyn more than he already had.

"Look." He clapped his hands together and rubbed them briskly. "Why don't we get started on these cookies? We've got six batches to make and decorate in one evening. The sooner we start, the sooner we'll finish, and the better chance we'll have at winning the cookie contest tomorrow."

Jordyn's grin returned.

"Before we start," she said, "I need to make absolutely certain that this isn't a sabotage attempt." She lifted one eyebrow as she looked at Roxie. "Is your dad planning to teach me the wrong way to bake cookies so I'll lose the contest tomorrow?"

Roxie giggled. "No way! He wouldn't do something like that, and even if he tried, I wouldn't let him. But I can show you myself how to decorate them, and you'll have the best cookies ever in the contest tomorrow."

Jordyn tapped Roxie's chin with one fingertip, affection in her eyes. "Thank you, sweet Roxie. I feel better about my chances already having you on my team—even if it's just for a few hours."

The tenderness in her touch and tone stole Nate's breath as Roxie beamed with joy, basking in her attention. He was caught off guard by the wave of gratitude that washed through him at the sight of them together. Sometimes, he forgot how much his little girl had missed, having never known what it would be like to have a mother.

"You'll teach Ms. Jordyn the right way, won't you, Dad?" Roxie was looking at him now, pride in her eyes. "My dad's the best cookie decorator in Noel. Everyone says it."

Nate grinned. "I don't know about all that, but I'll be happy to teach Ms. Jordyn everything I know about baking and decorating Christmas cookies."

Three hours later, with all three of them covered in flour, sugar, colorful sprinkles, and specks of icing, Nate sampled the first of Jordyn's meticulously decorated Christmas cookies.

"Here goes nothing." Standing opposite Jordyn at the kitchen island, he broke off a piece of a sugar cookie that had been shaped into a reindeer, and popped it in his mouth, moaning with pleasure as the confection melted on his tongue. "Mercy!" he garbled out around the mouthful of cookie. "That's what I call a Christmas cookie."

Jordyn, flour dusting her red hair and coating her left cheek, beamed. "Hot dog! I guess the fifth batch is the charm."

Roxie, sitting on a stool beside Nate, pinched off a piece of the cookie and popped it into her mouth, too. "Mmm. I told you that you could do it, Ms. Jordyn! These taste even better than Dad's."

"Whoa there!" Nate held up his hands as Jordyn and Roxie laughed. "That's taking the praise a bit too far. It's impossible for the student to beat the teacher on the first day."

Jordyn propped her elbows on the island, cradled her chin in her hands and flashed a teasing grin. "I can't help it if you're a great teacher. And you should be proud. My accomplishment is your accomplishment."

He chuckled. "And you winning tomorrow is the same as me winning, is that it?"

"Nah." Jordyn stuck out her tongue. "If I win, you lose, and that's that."

"Who's losing?" Tucker strolled into the kitchen, holding Roxie's winter coat in one hand. "You two? Because all I see is a couple of co-conspirators. Y'all got the whole house smelling like a sugar cookie. I oughta turn y'all in to Ms. Carol Belle, but I won't, seeing as how that would toss me out of the running, too." He walked over to the island, took a piece of Jordyn's cookie and sampled it as well. "Whoo! That's what I'm talkin' 'bout!" He glanced at Nate. "She's got you beat, brother."

"I highly doubt that," Nate drawled. "I saved my secret ingredient for my last batch of cookies, and it's bound to knock the Nanas' socks off."

"Well then, I'll leave you to it. But I'll go ahead and

warn you, Jordyn, that half tomorrow's contest is about how many cookies you can pack away in ten minutes, and ain't no way you can beat me at that." As she laughed, he motioned for Roxie to join him. "Come on, kid. Help me round up the horses for the evening while these two finish up in here, okay?"

Nate looked at Tucker, the mischievous sparkle in his brother's eyes making him narrow his own. Tucker, it seemed, was all too eager to do some matchmaking.

"What?" Tucker spread his arms in a futile gesture of innocence. "You and Jordyn have been entertaining Roxie for hours, so now it's my turn." He grinned at Roxie. "You can't hog my niece all day. Besides, that will give you and Jordyn a chance to talk while you bake."

Nate cleared his throat. "That's considerate of you, but unnecess—"

"No sweat." Tucker held out Roxie's coat.

Roxie hopped off her barstool and skipped over to Tucker, holding her arms out so he could slide the coat on. "Thanks for baking cookies with us, Ms. Jordyn. You'll come over again soon, won't you? We could bake something else together. Maybe the gingerbread for the gingerbread house contest?"

Jordyn smiled but glanced at Nate, apprehension in her gaze. "I'd love that, Roxie, but that's up to your dad. He might want to keep y'all's gingerbread baking secret to get a leg up in the competition."

"No, he won't." Roxie frowned at Nate. "You don't mind if Ms. Jordyn cooks her gingerbread with us, do you?"

Nate stood between Jordyn and Roxie, the weight of their scrutiny making his hands tremble with nervous tension. "We'll see."

"Let's take care of the horses, Roxie," Tucker said quickly. "Your dad and Ms. Jordyn have earned some time to themselves." He looked at Nate and winked. "Drink some coffee, relax, sample a few more cookies. Try having a little fun for a change—it'll do you good."

With that, Tucker led Roxie out of the kitchen, leaving a heavy silence in his wake.

Nate looked down at the pan of cookies before him, removed the lid from a container sitting nearby and began carefully stacking the cookies inside. "Sorry about that," he said. "Tucker has a habit of sticking his nose into other people's business."

Jordyn laughed softly. "Yeah, I've noticed that. But . . ."

He reached for another cookie, but her hand covered his, her soft fingertips resting lightly over his knuckles as she stilled his movements.

"He has a point," she continued. "I don't mean to put you on the spot again, Nate. But I have to admit, you're confusing me, and I thought you intended to be honest, seeing as how you were so upfront when I asked if you were interested in me." Hesitating, she asked softly, "Why did you really come to Chestnut Ridge today? And why did you ask me over? You made it clear to me you aren't available, so I don't understand why—"

"Because . . ." Nate turned his hand over, weaving his fingers between hers and squeezing gently before his mind could talk his heart out of it. "I've reconsidered my answer."

Chapter Ten

How anyone could be expected to look sexy the night after eating three dozen Christmas cookies was a mystery to Jordyn, but as she stood in front of the full-length mirror in her bedroom, scrutinizing her appearance, she had to admit that she'd given it her best shot.

"Jordyn, darling?" Holly called through the closed bedroom door. "How does it fit?"

"Tight." Jordyn eyed the hooded Santa dress with fuzzy white trim, a wide black belt and shin-high boots. "And short." She frowned at how much of her bare legs the miniskirt exposed. "I'm gonna freeze my butt off!"

But she supposed baring her legs in twenty-degree weather was a small price to pay in order to win Sexy Santa's Eggnog Nod contest. Even though, she thought, tapping her chin, she still wasn't exactly sure what the contest entailed. From what the Nanas had told her, she needed to look her very sexy best.

Stomach rumbling uncomfortably, she placed her hand over her belly and grimaced.

The cookies Nate had taught her how to bake had turned out beautifully and were even tastier than she'd hoped they would be. Only problem was that presenting beautiful, tasty Christmas cookies had been only half of the Christmas Cookie Crumble contest. The second half entailed participating in a cookie-eating contest in which the participants sat at a long table loaded down with the fresh-baked Christmas cookies, which they were expected to stuff into their mouths as fast as they could.

Having been seated directly next to Tucker, Jordyn had struggled to be on her A-game. No matter how fast she had shoved cookies into her mouth, Tucker continued to beat her, scooping up multiple cookies at a time with one hand and downing them in almost one go.

Jordyn scowled at her reflection, her lips twitching with humor as she recalled her loss and subsequent fitful night of stomach upset.

At least Tucker had been honest when he'd warned her he'd win. Turned out, Nate's brother was a piggish, bottomless pit! Not only had he devoured all of his cookies and eaten half of hers, but he'd also started on a third pile of cookies the participant beside him had baked. It hadn't taken long for everyone to realize that Tucker had that win in the bag. By the time the timer dinged, signaling the end of the eating competition, Jordyn had already over-indulged, her stomach straining the buttons on her jeans.

And today—oh, gracious! Today was even worse. From the moment she had rolled out of bed this morning until an hour ago when she'd begun prepping for tonight's contest, her stomach had been growling angrily. She had barely been able to down her morning cup of coffee and had not been able to even entertain the thought of consuming anything else all day. Even now, her stomach roiled, begging her to crawl back into bed, pull the covers over her head, and sleep.

"Jordyn?" Holly knocked on the door. "I don't mean to rush you, but you need to come on out. The contest is starting in half an hour and it'll take at least ten minutes to get to the town square. You need to leave soon."

"You don't want to be late, do you?" Kandy asked on the other side of the door. "You really need this win."

Stifling a groan, Jordyn rubbed her aching belly once more. She could just see the Nanas now, huddled on the other side of the closed bedroom door, wringing their hands, hoping she had it in her to pull off one more win. And they were right—she desperately needed one. As it stood, she was in fifth place on the Tree Scoreboard, directly below Nate and far below the Stone family. If she wanted to have any hope of winning the Christmas Crown for the Nanas, she had to do well in tonight's contest.

"Okay." She sucked in a strong, cleansing breath, squared her shoulders, and opened the door. "How do I look?"

The Nanas stared back at her. Eve gasped, Kandy grinned, Holly squealed, and Carol Belle nodded with satisfaction.

"Good golly, girl!" Carol Belle said. "You've got this one in the bag."

"Well, now," Eve said, holding up one finger. "She is gorgeous—no doubt about that—but we can't underestimate the competition. Sandy Simmons wins the sexy portion of the contest just about every Christmas, and I've already heard that she's chosen a killer outfit for this year."

"Oh, fiddlesticks," Carol Belle said, frowning. "That gal's got nothing on our Jordyn." Smiling, she reached out and brushed a fuzzy piece of lint from Jordyn's sleeve. "You're gonna knock 'em dead. I know you will!"

"You look stunning!" Kandy clapped her hands together. "Absolutely stunning."

"But you're missing one thing," Holly chimed, digging into the little red handbag she carried. "You need a hint of Raunchy Red," she said, holding up a small tube of lipstick. "My beautician, Patty Dalton, told me this is the trendiest color of the season. Here"—she nudged it toward Jordyn—"slather some on."

"Oh, there's no need for that." Kandy pushed Holly's hand away from Jordyn. "She looks beautiful just as she is."

"Well, it couldn't hurt. It can only help. Don used to love it when I wore red lipstick! He'd be all over me in . . ."

Jordyn frowned as Holly's voice trailed away, her expression changing to one full of regret. "Who's Don, Holly?"

"A boyfriend of mine," Holly whispered. "Well, an ex-boyfriend. And nowadays, not even a friend. Not after the way I behaved. It seems our bad romance ruined any chance of us remaining friends, and our friendship is what I miss the most lately."

Jordyn winced at the sorrow in Holly's voice. She touched Holly's arm. "I'm sorry. Would you like to talk about it?" Hesitating, she smiled. "After being fortunate enough to meet the four of you, I've learned it helps to talk things through with a friend."

Holly shook her head. "Sometime, maybe. But not tonight." Her grin returned. "Tonight is all about you and this trendy Raunchy Red, darling!" Holly lifted the lipstick closer to Jordyn. "Why not just give it a shot? It'll give your mouth a little pop. I'll even put it on for you."

"Can't do that, Holly," Carol Belle said, frowning. "That's cross-conspiring."

"Oh, no, it's not." Holly dismissed Carol Belle's chastisement with a careless wave. "And if it is, then I won't put it on for her, I'll just strongly suggest she utilize it to enhance her appearance."

"Besides, Carol Belle," Eve said, "if you think no one else in this competition has ever cross-conspired, you're a bit naïve, don't you think? I can assure you that many people have done so. We simply haven't caught them in the act."

Carol Belle scowled. "Well, they ought not to. Ain't no fun in breaking the rules. It's not a true win, in my opinion, if it's not achieved fair and square."

Jordyn smiled. "That's why I need your help, Carol Belle. Speaking of playing fair, would you please give me a rundown on tonight's contest again? How is this thing supposed to work?"

Carol Belle's frown melted away, an excited expression taking its place. "You're going to have the time of your life, Jordyn! The contest is held in Drake Stone's bar in downtown Noel—right across from the town square. This event happens behind closed doors with no children allowed. The first half of the contest is the Sexy Santa competition."

"That's when you make your grand entrance," Kandy said with a shimmy. "The men will be on one side of the bar and the women will gather on the other side. The men are going to be dressed in their sexiest outfits, too, and they'll be the ones who get to choose a Mrs. Claus for the Eggnog Nod part of the competition."

"That's right," Eve said. "Ladies chose first last year."

"Anyway," Kandy continued. "Whichever lady a man chooses is who he'll end up competing against in the Eggnog Nod."

"And that's when the real competition begins," Eve said, nudging her glasses up higher on the bridge of her nose. "There's a stage in Drake's bar, and after the couples are paired off, you and your Sexy Santa partner have to strut your stuff across it for the crowd's approval."

"Whichever one of you earns the loudest applause from the audience," Kandy said, "wins the points for the Sexy Santa portion of the contest."

"After which," Carol Belle said, "comes the Eggnog

Nod portion of the contest. You and your Santa partner will be pitted against each other at the bar, and whoever drinks the most eggnog without giving in"—she made a face—"either physically or mentally, wins the second half the contest."

"And that's where you've got to be careful," Holly said, leaning closer. "Very careful. Drake puts rye whiskey *and* Jamaican rum in his eggnog—lots of it! I've seen more than one person fall off a barstool after overindulging in that stuff."

Despite the churn of her stomach at the mention of liquor, Jordyn laughed. "If there's one contest I should be able to excel at, it's holding my liquor." She grinned. "I had to learn real quick when touring the circuit how to put away my liquor and drink the guys under the table. It's hard keeping up with the boys sometimes, but I did it occasionally on the circuit to hustle up a few extra dollars when I was running short after a loss in the arena. Not my proudest moment—but it beat going hungry." She frowned. "Only, back then I was basically living in my truck and all I had to do was walk to the parking lot and crawl in the back of the extended cab to sleep it off. How am I supposed to get back home to Chestnut Ridge after all that drinking?"

"No worries," Holly said. "Those who come to watch the contest draw numbers on the way into the bar and certain numbers are assigned designated driver responsibilities for the contestants. Knowing that, you still think you can handle your liquor well enough to place?"

Jordyn smiled. "Believe me when I say that I'm well prepared for that part of the contest."

Holly grinned. "Which is why I think you should put on the Raunchy Red lipstick. That'll add to your sexy outfit and ensure that you win the Sexy Santa part of the contest, too. If you want to win the Christmas Crown, you need all the winning points you can get."

"Who do you think will choose her?" Kandy asked, a wistful note in her voice. "I bet all the men will be clamoring to have Jordyn as their partner."

"Oh, you know who'll choose her." Carol Belle crossed her arms over her chest and waggled her eyebrows. "In that outfit, Mason Walker will make a beeline for her before I have a chance to say go."

"Oh, but what about Nate?" Eve blushed as everyone's attention turned to her. "I mean, he's bound to choose Jordyn as his partner."

Carol Belle frowned. "That's only if he competes—which, sadly, he never does." She sighed. "Nate can be such a stick-in-the-mud."

"But this year is different," Kandy said quietly. "He might change his mind. Don't you think so, Jordyn?"

Face heating, Jordyn looked down at her shiny, black boots. "I wouldn't really know since this is my first year competing. But I hope Nate decides to compete tonight."

"And there's a good chance of that," Holly said. "You did tell us that he said he'd reconsidered."

"Yes," Carol Belle said. "But did he say exactly what he had reconsidered? Spending time with you? Dating? Cross-conspiring with you by helping you bake gingerbread?"

Jordyn winced. She really shouldn't have shared Nate's comment with the Nanas this morning, but ever since he'd smiled at her across the island in his kitchen over perfectly baked, sweetly aromatic Christmas cookies and revealed that he'd reconsidered his answer, she'd been fit to burst to tell someone.

But even she had to admit that she wasn't sure exactly what Nate had meant by the comment. All she knew was that his soft words and the warm looks he'd tossed her way during the Christmas Cookie Crumble contest had given her hope. Hope that he might reciprocate her feelings. After all, he had to feel some sort of strong attraction to her to be able to cheer her on as she forgot good manners and stuffed her face yesterday in an eating contest against his brother.

"I don't know," Jordyn said. "But I'll take his comment as encouragement." She looked up then, smiling at the Nanas and thinking of all the romantic possibilities, then held out her hand to Holly. "You know what? I think I'll take you up on that Raunchy Red lipstick."

"Wow!" Tucker shouted over the loud chatter of patrons gathered in Drake Stone's bar. "I don't believe this place has ever seen the likes of that Scintillatin' Santa before."

Nate, sitting on a bar stool beside Tucker, glanced at the open entrance of the bar, his eyes doing a quick double take at the curvy redheaded vision across the room.

There Jordyn stood, the long red waves of her hair tucked underneath a festive red hood trimmed with fuzzy white fur. Her green eyes sparkled beneath lush lashes and her soft mouth had been painted a tempting shade of red that matched the Santa dress she wore. Her long ivory legs, toned beneath satiny skin, were bare beneath the mini skirt of the dress, and black Santa boots rose almost to her knees, completing the ensemble.

The warm, shapely vision contrasted with the soft snow falling beyond her outside the bar, lending her the sexy but vulnerable air of a Christmastime Red Riding Hood.

A wolf whistle pierced the hazy air of the bar and echoed across the stage. At the bar, the group of men surrounding Nate and Tucker, all dressed in Sexy Santa outfits, fell silent for a moment, then clapped their hands in a raucous round of approval.

EVERGREEN CHRISTMAS   179

Nate scowled and raised his voice to speak to Tucker over the roar of the crowd at his back. "That's just wrong. It's crude and rude to leer at a woman like that. I mean, every one of these women could be someone's daughter, sister, wife, niece, or cousin. In twenty years, Roxie might even be one of the women walking through those doors on a night like tonight. It's disrespectful! Don't you think this is a chauvinistic tradition?"

This was the main reason Nate had never participated in the Sexy Santa Eggnog Nod. Normally, he would sit quietly in the background, watching the festivities, and at the end of the drinking portion of the contest, he'd stay after all the contestants had left and help a small group of volunteers clean up Drake Stone's bar. This year, however, after hearing that Jordyn planned to participate, he'd arrived early along with Tucker, who'd donned his annual Sexy Santa outfit and fully planned to participate in the night's contest as he had every year—with gusto!

"Chauvinistic?" Tucker made a face as he paused his clapping. "Of course, it's chauvinistic. But don't for one moment think it's one-sided. Some women can be just as rude and lewd as men if they choose to be. You heard the way those women howled at me when I walked through the door." A mocking look of affront showed in his expression as he crossed his arms over his chest protectively. "Like I was a piece of meat or something." He issued a long-suffering sigh. "But the thing is, we're all consenting adults, partaking in a bit of harmless—albeit, raunchy—Christmas fun. And far be it from me to put a damper on the Christmas cheer. I'm doing my part by participating, and if I only bring a smile to one woman's face tonight, I've done some good." As Nate, incredulous, stared back at him, Tucker shrugged. "What? You think I dress like this every day?"

Nate glanced down, his mouth twitching at the sight of

Tucker's bare chest, covered only by a pair of thin suspenders in a candy cane pattern, which were hooked to a pair of red Santa pants with a wide belt buckle. The pants were tight—so tight they clung to every inch of his brother's frame. The only parts of him that were modestly covered were his feet, which were encased in big black Santa boots, and the top of his head, which was covered by a Santa hat.

"I gotta say, that's a hard question to answer," Nate drawled. "There've been quite a few mornings in the past when you've shown up at the house in the wee hours of the morning, looking just about like you do now."

Tucker, somehow, managed to look offended. "What do you mean? I've only shown up at the house half naked once in my life, and that was after Buffy Taylor"—he leaned closer and whispered—"kicked me out of her bed on account of the fact that I forgot her name."

Nate shook his head and chuckled softly. "Serves you right, you mutt."

"Heck no, it don't! It only happened because I was slightly inebriated from pulling my weight in the Eggnog contest. That was two Christmases ago—why, this very night!" He shuddered. "You have any idea how cold it is outside the door at three in the morning? And there I was, half naked and exposed to the elements, having to walk all the way from Buffy's place back to Frosted Firs Ranch in the snow. It was painful and humiliating."

And well deserved.

Nate, however, did not repeat himself. He'd learned not to voice too many criticisms around Tucker. His brother might be a rambunctious scoundrel, but Tucker was a good man who had a good heart, and at least he was always upfront with the women he dated, letting them know he wasn't interested in anything that might involve a long-term commitment.

He could learn a thing or two from his brother, Nate thought ruefully. He should have done the same with Jordyn and stuck to his answer of not being available, as he'd set out to do initially. But as he'd told her two nights ago, he'd reconsidered. Mostly due to what Kandy had said to him during the award ceremony for the Terrible Tinsel Triathlon.

Life can be scary and painful—but the unexpected gifts it gives us along the way, especially when we're not looking for them, make it all worth it in the end.

He'd had difficulty getting those words out of his head.

He wasn't naïve. He'd loved deeply before and had truly enjoyed his life with Macy—what little time they'd been given. He'd also dated briefly prior to getting married. He was well aware the emotions he felt for Jordyn and the connection they'd shared, almost from the moment of meeting, were rare and sometimes never found. That realization, coupled with his gnawing jealousy at the thought of Jordyn taking an interest in another man, had compelled him to take a chance and open his heart again.

Only, he still had reservations.

The applause died down as Jordyn entered the bar and Sandy Simmons walked in behind her, drawing new attention. But despite Sandy Simmons's allure, several pairs of male eyes still followed Jordyn's every move, and one pair in particular made Nate's temper flare.

"You might want to consider playing it cool," Tucker said above the holiday music blaring through the bar as he leaned closer to Nate. "You keep staring at Mason like you are, you're gonna burn a hole through that man's skull."

Heeding Tucker's advice, Nate tore his attention away from the other man and refocused his eyes on Jordyn. He couldn't hold it against Mason for admiring her. In his opinion, she was always the most beautiful woman in the room, but tonight, she was downright sensational.

The thought, however, did little to tamp down the flare of his jealous temper. In less than five minutes, the Sexy Santa's Eggnog Nod contest would commence, Carol Belle would kick off the choosing of partners and Mason, no doubt, would make a beeline straight for Jordyn. Nate was afraid his self-control might wear thin by that time.

He glanced at Tucker and narrowed his eyes. "Give me your suit. You've been demoted."

Tucker reared back, his mouth falling open in shock. "You're joking, right?"

"No. Take it off."

Tucker crossed his arms over his bare chest and looked around sheepishly. "Right here? Right now? You could at least buy me a drink first."

Nate rolled his eyes as Tucker doubled over and burst out laughing.

"Forget it," Tucker said, catching his breath and wiping a tear from his eye. "You're too much of a prude to pull something like this off, and we need a win."

Nate stood. "Just for tonight, I will lower myself and participate in this humiliating display—even you will be proud." He snapped his fingers. "Now, I mean it. Get up and come to the bathroom. We're swapping clothes . . . or scraps of clothing."

It took Nate two minutes to drag Tucker through the crowd to the small bathroom at the back of the bar. It took another minute for Tucker to strip out of his skimpy outfit, grumbling all the while about missing out on a chance to spend time with his dream woman. Two more minutes later, Nate had successfully swapped outfits with Tucker and stood in front of the small bathroom mirror over the sink, eyeing his exposed chest with discomfort.

Good Lord, what if Roxie heard about this? What kind

of example was this to set for his young, impressionable daughter—especially when he'd already worked so hard to help her see the value of a person's character rather than their appearance.

Yet, here he was, half naked, about to shake his butt for a bunch of screaming women.

He winced. "This is the most distasteful, sexist display I've ever—"

"Oh, shove it, Nate!" Tucker pushed him out of the bathroom and back into the noisy, crowded bar. "You're getting your shot with Jordyn and depriving me of the opportunity to let a woman take advantage of my spectacular physique for the night. Just enjoy the evening, Casanova."

That was easy for Tucker to say. He was now dressed warmly and respectably in Nate's jeans and flannel button-down shirt, whereas Nate was walking half naked through a pack of leering women.

"Oh, my!" a female voice shouted in the crowd. "Nate Reed is jumping into the mix this year! Have you ever seen such magnificent pecs? Nate, honey, you've got my vote!"

Heat snaked up Nate's neck as applause broke out from the women who stood opposite the men in the small bar. He ducked his head and soldiered on, returning to the bar and sitting on a barstool beside Tucker.

Jordyn, standing on the opposite side of the room among the other women, met Nate's eyes, a surprised grin spreading across her face. She held his gaze as her brows rose in question.

Face now burning, too, he shrugged sheepishly and ducked his head.

"Okay, ladies and gentlemen," Carol Belle announced from the stage at the other end of the bar. "It's that time. The rules are the same as last year"—she smiled—"namely, there aren't any, other than whoever's left standing—however unsteadily—in the drinking contest, wins. And men will have first choice of Sexy Santa partner this year since the ladies had first choice last year. To kick off the choosing of partners, Nate Reed will have first choice tonight since this is the first year he's participated in Sexy Santa's Eggnog Nod contest." She glanced across the room and gestured toward Nate. "Go ahead, Nate—choose your partner!"

Nate stood, rubbing his bare arms to ward off the cold as applause broke out. One person shouted, "About time you joined us, Nate!" as he walked to the center of the small room. He kept walking, weaving past several women before he stopped in front of Jordyn and held out his hand. "Jordyn, would you do me the honor of being my Sexy Santa partner for the evening?"

Good Lord! No matter how much respectful dignity he tried to infuse into the invitation, it still sounded ridiculous as the words left his lips.

Jordyn laughed, the soft, flirty sound sending a delicious shiver over his skin that dispelled the cold and left a streak of heat. "I'd be honored."

She slipped her hand in his and it fit perfectly. He led her toward the stage, where they took their place at the front of the line, waiting for the rest of the participants to choose their partners and join them.

"Have you really never participated in this contest before?" Jordyn asked, smiling at him.

Nate crossed his arms over his bare chest, deeply aware of the attention they were attracting. "Nope. It's not exactly my kind of thing."

Jordyn laughed. "I can tell." Her gaze swept over him from head to toe and she winked. "But the look sure suits you."

Her flirtatious amusement made him smile. "Oh, you

like this getup, do you?" Uncrossing his arms, he lowered them to his sides and flexed his pectorals. "You're not the only one. I have it on good authority that my pecs are well appreciated."

She threw her head back and laughed, the rich joyful sound music to his ears.

Take that, Mason Walker!

"So long as you give it your all on that stage, Neighbor Nate," she teased. "I assure you that I'm just as uncomfortable as you are, but we both need this win."

"Agreed." He looked down at her, admiring her long lashes, bright eyes, creamy skin and soft, red mouth. "With you on my arm, I can guarantee a win. If I forget to tell you later . . ." He hesitated, then whispered, "You're the most beautiful woman in this room, Jordyn Banks."

Her lips parted as her eyes roved over his face, the pretty blush on her cheeks deepening. "Thank you. And thank you, too, for choosing me as your partner—even though I'm going to drink you under the eggnog table later." She rose to her toes, her warm mouth brushing his temple as she whispered in his ear, "There's not another man in the world I'd rather spend tonight with."

Lord help him! He could swear his heart actually stopped beating as his brain absorbed her words. His mind reeled as his pulse raced, searching for a suitably flattering reply. "I . . . I—uh, me, too."

Oh, man. Way to sweep her off her feet!

She didn't seem to mind though. She looped her arm around his and grinned as Carol Belle called them to the stage to strut their stuff. "Let's give this crowd a glimpse of what a Sexy Santa should look like."

And they did. He and Jordyn sashayed across the stage, arm in arm, to a particularly sexy Christmas tune, delighting in the applause of the crowd. They danced to the pulsing beat, and he spun Jordyn gently in his arms, then dipped her for the crowd. During the upbeat chorus, she cradled his biceps, showing them off, then, at the pleading of the crowd, she even spun him around and lightly smacked his backside for good measure.

Surprisingly, Nate enjoyed himself. Perhaps a little too much, considering that two hours later, well into the Eggnog Nod portion of the contest, Drake Stone's liquor-infused eggnog had lost its burn as it coursed down his throat, and he'd grown rather fond of the fuzzy, cotton-wool feel of inebriation pulsing through his veins.

"Hit me!" He slapped the slightly damp countertop of the bar and narrowed his eyes at Jordyn, who sat across from him. "I'm good for another."

A collective cackle rose from the amused crowd of onlookers surrounding them.

Jordyn bit her lip, concern in her eyes. "Are you sure, Nate?" She leaned across the counter, eyeing him closely. "You can admit defeat, you know. I've already ousted the rest of the competition and you're all that's left. You've lasted a lot longer than I thought, but you're about to fall off that barstool."

Man, was she gorgeous! Those emerald eyes, those ruby-red lips, those beautiful, bountiful curves beneath that skimpy Santa suit and those gorgeous legs . . .

"You're maleficent," he breathed.

She frowned.

"No," he hastened, waving a clumsy hand in the air. "That ain't right. You . . . you're maj-a-ficent. No—magnificent!"

All three of her beautiful faces smiled. Laughter rippled across the crowd surrounding them.

"Thank you for that," she whispered. "But I really do

think you should fold while you're ahead and call it a night."

A heavy hand settled on Nate's back. "I second that, brother. You've held a lot more liquor than I thought you could in that old, stuffy, straitlaced body of yours."

It took considerable effort, but Nate managed to swivel his head to the side and peer up at Tucker. "Fuh-get it. Not giving up."

"Take your hand off his back and step back, Tucker," Carol Belle said from her position beside Drake Stone behind the bar. "You're not allowed to touch or physically support contestants during the Eggnog competition."

Tucker laughed. "Trust me, Ms. Carol Belle, when Nate falls off this barstool, it's gonna take a lot more than my hand to keep him from hitting the floor." He removed his palm from Nate's back and raised both hands. "But I'm happy to comply." He grinned. "It's not every day I get to see Nate half naked and plastered."

Jordyn laughed, the glorious sound coaxing his attention back to her. "Make it a double, please, Drake. I hate to do it but I need this win, and I think that's all it'll take to do him in."

"Uh-uh." Nate patted his chest, and the feel of bare skin meeting his fingers prompted him to look down in confusion. "Lost my shirt."

"Here you go." Drake Stone set two tumblers on the bar between Nate and Jordyn, both filled to the rim with liquor-laden eggnog. "Throw 'em down the hatch on the count of three. One . . ."

Jordyn picked up her tumbler and Nate, a bit clumsily, picked his up, too.

"Two . . ." The crowd joined Drake, counting down. "Three!"

Four hefty swallows of eggnog, three slow blinks, and

two moments later, Nate came to, lying on his back, blearily gazing up at Jordyn's anxious face.

"Nate?" She tugged the Santa hat off his head and cradled his jaw. Her palms were soft and warm against his chilled cheeks. "Are you okay?"

He shoved himself onto his elbows and squinted at the crowd of smiling faces behind Jordyn. "Wh—what happened?"

"You passed out, that's what!" Tucker, hunched over behind Jordyn's left shoulder, guffawed. "Then you lost." He straightened and lifted his arms over his head. "Long live Jordyn—Noel's Eggnog Nod Queen!"

Cheers erupted around the bar as the crowd of onlookers dispersed, some returning to the bar for another round, others making their way to the stage to dance to the holiday music still blaring from the surrounding speakers, while a few exited the bar, shrugging on their coats and walking out into the cold, snowy night.

"Nate," Jordyn prompted, her fingertips lightly tapping his cheeks. "Are you sure you're okay?"

Lying down? With her hands on him? "I'm in heaven," he whispered, tugging her hands from his face and kissing each of her fingertips. "You know what I wanna do?"

Her lips twitched as she stared down at him. "What?"

His gaze, though blurry, homed in on her delectable mouth, an overwhelming surge of need moving through him. "I wanna kiss you. A lot."

She grinned. "Oh, really?" Leaning down closer, she asked. "Are you wanting—*a lot*—to kiss me just once? Or are you wanting to give me *a lot* of kisses?"

"Wh . . . what?" As he tried to comprehend her words, his mind whirled right along with the room, so he focused on her mouth again instead, refusing to think. "Either. Both." He reached up and trailed his thumb over the curve of her lower lip. "Just kiss me, please?"

She glanced around, her cheeks reddening. "Right here? Our first kiss? On a barroom floor in front of God and everyone?"

Oh. She had a point. That wasn't something a gentleman would do. "Okay. Maybe not such a good i—"

Her soft mouth touched his and everything disappeared—the bar, the people . . . the world. All that existed was the gentle press of her lips and the sweet-smelling waves of her hair spilling down around him. He cupped the back of her head, weaving his fingers through the long strands as her chest lowered against his. Then he parted her lips with his, kissing her deeply, tasting her, savoring the feel of her against him.

"Hey!" A throat cleared. "Get off him, woman. My brother's in a vulnerable state."

And just like that, she was gone.

Nate reached out but only cold air hit his hands. "Jordyn—"

Then her warm hand curled around one of his arms and a stronger one grabbed hold of the other one, tugging him off the floor and to his feet.

"Tucker's right," Jordyn said near his ear as she helped him gain his balance. "You need to get home and into bed."

He smiled, finally focusing on her face—just one of them this time. "Yep. That's exactly what I wanna do. But with you."

Jordyn flushed.

Tucker cackled. "Oh, man. I'm never gonna let him live this one down."

"Another time, maybe," Jordyn said, leaning over and kissing his cheek. "When you're good and sober."

"But . . ." Her hands left him, and he watched her walk away, her red Santa suit and long red hair disappearing into the throng of people still milling about the bar.

"Come on, brother." Tucker, grinning ear to ear, threw his arm around Nate's waist and hauled him toward the door. "I'm gonna drive your chauvinistic butt home and put you to bed. You need a good night's sleep, 'cuz you're dang well gonna regret every second of this in the morning."

Chapter Eleven

Jordyn should be embarrassed—thoroughly embarrassed—for showing up at Nate's front door the next afternoon, but a call from Roxie early that morning, inviting Jordyn to come to Frosted Firs Ranch and bake gingerbread had been impossible to resist.

So, at two o'clock the next afternoon, Jordyn stood at the front door of the main house at Frosted Firs Ranch, cradling a basket stocked full of cooking supplies in her arms while her heart beat rapidly in her ears.

"Just stay cool," she whispered to herself quietly. "You don't even get this worked up in the arena."

Okay, so she'd kissed Nate on the floor of the bar the night before. So what? He'd asked her to, and when she'd hovered over him, looking into his deep blue eyes as he pleaded with her, she hadn't had the heart to deny him. In fact, she had longed for the moment for quite some time, hoping he'd come to his senses and decide to take a chance on her. But her secret fantasies of Nate finally succumbing to his attraction to her had not involved copious amounts of alcohol.

That, she could have done without.

It wasn't that she didn't think he could fall for her when sober. She knew how to turn on the charm when she needed to, and she had a sneaking suspicion that Nate was just as strongly attracted to her as she was to him—especially if his words the night before were anything to go by.

I want to kiss you. A lot.

That's what he had said as he had stared up at her with a yearning expression.

Her blood rushed at the thought. Even now, she'd give in to him again in a split second if he extended the invitation for her to kiss him a second time. And oh, how she hoped he would!

The remembered feel of his lips against hers had stayed on her mind—and heart—all last night and through the morning and afternoon. There was nothing in the world she wanted more than to feel Nate's arms around her again, his mouth on hers and his—

The front door opened and Nate stood in front of her, a carefully guarded expression on his handsome face.

"Oh!" The basket slipped in her grip, and she hefted it higher against her chest, her cheeks burning. "I . . . good morning—er, afternoon, I mean."

Boy, did he look wonderful! Despite the dark circles under his eyes and his stubble-lined jaw (possibly small signs of a hangover that still clung to him), he looked as gorgeous as ever. His blond hair was tousled adorably and unlike last night, today, he was dressed in jeans and a long-sleeved flannel shirt suitable for the winter wind that swept over the porch and rustled through their hair.

"Hi." He stared back at her for a moment, his mouth opening and closing silently before he stepped back and opened the door wider. "Please, come in, out of the wind. You must be freezing."

"Oh, it's not that bad," she said, walking past him into the foyer. "A little windy, I guess. But I'll take it. The weatherman said the cold front coming through is going to bring another round of snow." She smiled, just the thought of a white Christmas making her giddy. "Wouldn't that be wonderful? Seeing snow fall on Christmas morning?"

He issued a small smile. "Yeah. But that doesn't happen too often—even up here in the mountains. It's kind of a guessing game as to when we'll get snow and how much of it."

"But the thought of it's nice, just the same," she said, hefting the basket higher in her arms again, the weight of it digging into the soft skin of her forearms.

"Here." He reached out, grabbed the basket and lifted it from her arms. "Why don't we go put this down and give your arms a break?"

"Thank you. I appreciate that."

How formal they were being, considering that less than twenty-four hours before, they'd been kissing on the floor of a barroom.

Oh, for heaven's sake! Stop thinking about the kiss, girl. Focus on being calm and collected.

"I was pleasantly surprised when Roxie called me this morning." She followed him into the kitchen, watching as he set the basket of gingerbread ingredients on the island. "When we spoke, I didn't think to ask if it was okay with you if I came over. I was just so excited at her invitation, considering the gingerbread contest is tomorrow and my oven's still broken and all." She picked at the hem of her sweater. "Do you mind? That I came here today, I mean?"

"No." He faced her then, his gaze clinging to hers, his blue eyes intense. "Not at all."

"Good." She sighed. "Because I was hoping—"

"I wanted to—"

They both fell silent, staring at each other. After a moment, Jordyn gestured for him to continue.

"I'm glad you came today," he said. "I wanted to . . ." His chest lifted on a deep inhale. "I wanted to apologize to you for my behavior last night."

Oh, no. No, no, no! She didn't want an apology from him; she wanted—

"I shouldn't have . . ." His cheeks flushed a deep scarlet red. "I shouldn't have done a lot of things, I suppose. But I especially shouldn't have done them in the middle of the contest or on the floor of a bar in front of everyone."

"Do you . . ." She glanced around, taking in the empty kitchen and hallway nearby, then continued in a low voice, "Do you regret kissing me?"

He moved closer, his tan hand sliding across the counter-top of the island, stopping inches from her arm. After what seemed like a silent eternity, he said softly, "No. Of all the things I do regret about last night, that's the one thing I don't." He grimaced. "I just wish I'd chosen a more suitable location and time."

She ducked her head, trying to hide her smile, but the pleasure that bubbled up from her middle at his words was difficult to contain. "Good. Because I don't regret it either." She looked up then, holding his gaze as she smiled. "I rather enjoyed it."

He smiled back. "I did, too. Very much." But then, his smile faded and he looked away, his fingers moving nervously against the edge of the countertop. "But I don't want you to think I don't still have reservations—because I do." His eyes returned to hers and a muscle in his jaw ticked. "You see, there's more to this than just you and me. I have a daughter. A daughter I need to consider in all my choices. And what I did last night . . ." He closed his eyes and shook his head. "That's not exactly the example I'd like to set for her."

"I understand," she whispered. "You're a good father, Nate. No one can dispute that."

"Thank you. But I'm not as good a one as I could be." His hand lifted toward her, then stopped briefly in midair before continuing its journey, his fingers trailing through the long waves of her hair as he said softly, "I won't lie to you, Jordyn. I do feel very strongly for you." He moved even closer, his palms cupping her face. "And I do still want to kiss you." One corner of his mouth lifted. "A lot . . . in every way."

A soft sigh of relief escaped her lips, and she stepped closer to him, lifting her own hands and curling them around his forearms. "And I still want you to kiss me."

He fell silent, his thumbs drifting over her cheeks. Then he looked down at her hands, which were still curled around his forearms, released her and stepped away. "I just don't know that I'm ready for this."

Jordyn stilled, her heart hammering against her chest. "You're not ready? Or your heart isn't ready?"

He held her gaze, a guarded expression crossing his face. "Both." A groan escaped him as he rubbed his forehead. "I loved Macy very much—I still do. I don't know that I'm truly ready to let her go yet."

Even when I can love you? As much as she did? Jordyn froze, the thoughts flitting through her mind making her breath stall in her lungs. Love? Was that really how she felt about him?

She stood there before him in the silence, considering it. And then, her pulse slowing and breath returning, she could admit it . . . at least to herself.

Yes. She loved him. She loved Nate Reed. From the moment she'd met him, it seemed.

Not that she was sentimental or believed this kind of thing was common. But she couldn't deny how she felt about him. And she didn't want to.

Yet he was standing right in front of her, telling her he wasn't sure if he was ready for a relationship. Or if he was even ready to let his late wife go.

So . . . where did that leave her?

"Please understand," Nate said softly. "I'm trying here.

I'm really trying. I just don't know how much of my heart I have left to give. Or how much of it I'm willing to risk, considering that every decision I make regarding my life directly affects my daughter in some way."

Jordyn lowered her head and looked down at her hands. Then she threaded her fingers together and squeezed her palms tightly against each other, buying a few more silent moments to collect her thoughts.

"Thank you for telling me," she said softly. "And I do understand." She glanced up and managed to smile. "Truly, I do."

She just hoped, with all her heart, that he'd change his mind.

"I'm not saying never," he whispered urgently, searching her expression. "I'm just saying—"

"Ms. Jordyn!"

They sprang apart as Roxie barreled into the room, ran across the kitchen and threw her arms around Jordyn's waist.

"I'm so glad you're here." Roxie propped her chin on Jordyn's middle and looked up, smiling brightly. "We're gonna have so much fun! I already took the butter out so it'll be soft for mixing and I have the brown sugar and the molasses and cinnamon and ginger and flour and—"

"Roxie, don't jump all over Jordyn the moment she arrives," Nate said, smiling.

Grinning, Jordyn waved away his concern. "Oh, I don't mind. I'm just as excited as she is, actually." She looked down at Roxie, cupped the little girl's face in her hands and lifted her chin. "Go ahead. Tell me all about it, sweet girl."

Roxie's eyes sparkled with excitement. "I don't know what you like to put on your gingerbread houses, but I like gumdrops and peppermint on mine. And I got some white icing and some pink icing and some yellow icing and—"

"Every color icing there is," Nate finished for her, laughing.

"How perfect," Jordyn said. "You can never have too much icing."

"Hey, Jordyn." Tucker strolled into the kitchen, an urgent look on his face.

Jordyn greeted him, then asked, "Everything okay?"

"Yeah." Tucker motioned toward Nate. "But the gift shop's packed full. I could really use a hand checking people out."

Nate hesitated, glancing from Roxie to Jordyn then back again. "But—"

"Go ahead," Jordyn said. "Roxie and I can handle the ovens on our own."

"We sure can!" Roxie shouted. "And I'll show Ms. Jordyn how to make the gingerbread."

"But you didn't come over here to babysit," Nate said. "You shouldn't have to—"

"I'm not *having* to do anything," Jordyn said softly. She looked down at Roxie and tugged the little girl's blond ponytail gently. "Besides, I'm not babysitting. I'm spending time with a new friend and learning how to make gingerbread. How awesome is that?"

Roxie smiled from ear to ear. "Really awesome! And I promise I'm going to help you make the best gingerbread in the world so you'll win the Gingerbread Architect contest tomorrow."

"Hold up, there," Tucker said, his mouth twitching. "Don't be giving away all our secrets, kid. Ms. Jordyn here has already taken several wins from us already."

Roxie made a face and planted her hands on her hips. "You're supposed to share, Uncle Tucker. Ms. Jordyn has just as much right to win the gingerbread contest as we do."

"Good girl," Nate said, bending down and kissing

Roxie's forehead. "I'm proud of you for displaying such good sportsmanship. That's a vital quality in a good competitor."

Tucker groaned. "Whatever. Just get the lead out and come help me in the gift shop. You have no idea how long that line is. We'll be lucky if we're able to close it down by midnight tonight."

"Alright, I'm coming." Nate followed Tucker as he exited the room, but he paused on the threshold and glanced back at Jordyn. "You sure this is okay with you?"

"Of course." Jordyn waved him on. "Go ahead. Take care of business. Roxie and I will have all the fun to ourselves."

"That's right, Daddy. You're gonna miss all the fun, and our gingerbread houses are gonna be the best gingerbread houses in Noel."

Nate grinned. "With you in charge, I have no doubt about that."

After Nate left, Jordyn and Roxie gathered all the ingredients and organized them in neat rows on the island. Roxie laid out paper patterns in the shape of rectangles in different sizes for the gingerbread houses they were going to make. Next, they mixed the dough by beating together butter, brown sugar, molasses, cinnamon, ginger and several other ingredients, humming Christmas tunes over the bang of the mixer.

After chilling the dough for thirty minutes, they rolled it out on a large cookie sheet, placed the patterns on top of the dough and cut out each of the shapes. After that, they baked the gingerbread and removed it from the oven, placing it on the counter to cool.

"That's all there is to it?" Jordyn asked, sitting on the barstool next to Roxie.

Roxie laughed. "No! That's the easy part. Now, we have

to decide which decorations we're gonna use to pretty up the house."

"And then we can put our house together?" Jordyn teased.

"Nope." Roxie grinned back. "You can't put your gingerbread house together until the actual contest. You have to do that in the town square in front of the judges." Her smile faded a bit. "That's the part I'm scared of."

"What do you mean?"

Roxie sighed. "I told Daddy and Uncle Tucker that I wanted to be the one to make the gingerbread house this year." She looked up at Jordyn and lifted her chin. "I'm old enough now. And I make really good gingerbread houses. It's just that . . . well, I get nervous in front of people."

Jordyn smiled and smoothed the child's bangs gently away from her forehead. "I think everyone gets nervous in front of people, sweetheart. But if you just focus on the task in front of you rather than the crowd, you'll do a wonderful job."

Roxie looked up at her, uncertainty in her eyes. "Do you think so? You think I can do it?"

Jordyn nodded. "I know you can."

Roxie stared up at her for a moment, her eyes roving over Jordyn's face as she remained silent. Then, she took one of Jordyn's hands between her own and turned it over, drawing a gentle line with her finger from Jordyn's wrist to the tips of her fingers.

"Your hand's a lot bigger than mine," Roxie said quietly.

Jordyn laughed softly. "Well, that's because I'm a lot older."

"You're twenty-five, right?"

Jordyn frowned. "How do you know that?"

Roxie glanced up, her cheeks blushing. "Daddy and Uncle Tucker talked about it when you first moved in next door."

Interesting. Jordyn hid a smile. So, Nate had discussed her with Tucker? That could be interpreted as a good sign, she supposed.

"Dad said my mom was twenty-four when she . . ." Roxie fell silent, then continued quietly, "When she had me."

The somber note of grief in Roxie's voice was unmistakable.

Heart aching, Jordyn eased her elbows onto the counter, then laid her free arm on the counter, palm turned up in invitation.

Roxie accepted, placing her other hand on top of Jordyn's palm and pressing it against Jordyn's. "You're older than she was."

Jordyn nodded.

"Did you . . ." Roxie glanced at Jordyn beneath her lashes. "Have you ever thought about having a little girl one day?"

Throat tightening painfully, Jordyn met the little girl's direct gaze. "Yes," she whispered. "I've thought about it before. That's one of the reasons I moved to Noel. I wanted to make a home for myself. Maybe even a family."

Roxie lifted her head, biting her lip before she asked, "So you want one? A daughter, I mean?"

Jordyn smiled gently. "Yes. One day. I suppose I've always wanted to be a mom at some point in the future."

Roxie looked back down at their hands, considering this. "What's it like to have a mom?"

Jordyn curled her thumbs over the little girl's hands, sweeping them gently across her delicate skin. "I don't know. I've never had one."

Roxie looked up in surprise. "Really? You've never had a mother?"

Jordyn shook her head. "Or a dad. Or a home really." She smiled. "Until now. Chestnut Ridge is the first place I've ever had that's all my own. And as for your other question about a mother, well, I think the Nanas are really close to what a mother would be like."

Roxie's brows rose. "The Nanas?"

"Yeah." Smiling, Jordyn shrugged. "The Nanas care about people. They help them when they're in need, look for ways to make other people's lives better. They fuss over you, bring welcome baskets if you're new to town and"— she winked—"knit wool caps for your head so your ears don't get cold."

Roxie giggled.

"So yeah," Jordyn said. "I think the Nanas are probably a lot like a mother would be."

Roxie hesitated, then squeezed Jordyn's hands gently. "I think you'd be a good mom."

Unexpectedly, tears coated Jordyn's lower lashes, threatening to fall. She blinked rapidly and smiled brightly instead. "And you know what?" she asked Roxie softly. "I think any mother would be proud to have you as her daughter."

Smiling brightly, Roxie hopped up higher on her barstool, threw her arms around Jordyn's neck and squeezed.

Jordyn hugged her back as a fresh wave of tears gathered on her lashes. It was no wonder to her now, that Nate had reservations about opening his heart, his home, and his family to her. Because how in the world could anyone risk breaking this little girl's precious heart?

"Welcome to Noel's annual Christmas Gingerbread Architect contest!"

Nate, standing in the center of the town square the next

afternoon with Roxie by his side, clapped along with the rest of the crowd that had gathered together below the stage as Carol Belle commenced the day's contest.

It was a beautiful day for building gingerbread houses outdoors. There was an arctic chill in the air, but the sun was bright and warm if you stood beneath it. With this in mind, Nate had directed Roxie toward the south end of the tables that had been lined up. The sunlight was strong in that spot and would help keep Roxie's cold fingers slightly warmer and, hopefully, a bit more limber as she constructed her gingerbread house.

"This year," Carol Belle continued, speaking into the mic on the stage, "we had an overwhelming response to the Gingerbread Architect contest. Today, we have the privilege of hosting the largest number of Gingerbread Architects in the history of Noel's Christmas competition. Give yourselves a hand for making today's contest a success before it's even begun!"

The crowd applauded and Carol Belle clapped with them, the bright smile on her face indicative of her pleasure at the increase in participation.

"Daddy?" Roxie tugged urgently at the belt loop on Nate's jeans.

He looked down, smiling. "Yeah, sweetie?"

Her big blue eyes, worried and intense, clung to his. "There are so many people here."

"I know." He bent closer to her ear to be heard over the applause of the crowd. "Isn't it great? That means a lot more people will get to see your beautiful gingerbread house when you finish it."

Roxie nibbled on her lower lip, her gaze darting across the throng of people behind them. "I guess."

Noting the worry that flickered through her expression, Nate sank to his knees in front of her, took her hands in his and squeezed gently. "What's worrying you, sweet-heart?"

She eased closer to him, saying softly, "I don't like get-ting up in front of all these people."

"I know," Nate said. "And you don't have to do it if you don't want to. But I think if you give it a shot, you'll find you enjoy it."

"Maybe, but . . ."

"But what?" He tapped the tip of her nose. "You're well prepared. You and Ms. Jordyn baked the perfect gingerbread sheets for your houses. You showed them off to me last night, remember? You were so excited to get here today so you could build your house."

And he'd been surprised—very surprised, in fact—at how well she and Jordyn had gotten along on their own.

After leaving Jordyn and Roxie alone in the kitchen last night and joining Tucker in the gift shop, he'd thought of little else but the two of them as he rang up customers and wrapped gifts for the next several hours. During the holi-days, Frosted Firs Ranch's gift shop was always busy but this year it seemed it was especially crowded.

Noel's Christmas competition had, as always, infused even more excitement into the coming holiday, and most of the town's residents were out and about, enjoying the sights and sounds of Christmas downtown and sweeping eagerly through each shop, excited to find the next Christ-mas gift on their list.

Nate was grateful for the patronage—every dollar the ranch earned was another dollar he could put away for Roxie's college education or perhaps a car for her six-teenth birthday, or even a savings account that he could set aside for her when she was ready to buy a house of her own, far into the future.

He was grateful for the extra business, and normally he

would even have enjoyed ringing up customers to the tune of holiday music and a cheerful atmosphere.

But yesterday evening had been different. He had wanted to apologize to Jordyn for his behavior at the Eggnog Nod—and he had—but he hadn't planned on having to leave her directly after that. And he certainly hadn't planned on imposing upon her as a babysitter for hours on end while he worked in the gift shop.

What must she think of him? Caring for his daughter was an imposition to say the least, especially when she'd only come over to use the oven.

When the line in the gift shop had finally shortened and Tucker had things well in hand again, Nate had returned to the main house, expecting to find Jordyn polite, but possibly weary of entertaining his daughter for several hours alone.

Instead, when he'd entered the kitchen, Jordyn and Roxie had been huddled at the island in the center of the kitchen, sipping hot chocolate from Christmas mugs, sorting through gumdrops, peppermints, sprinkles, and other edible decorations and arranging them into piles, giggling and whispering all the while.

They'd been so engrossed in the activity that neither of them had looked up when he'd arrived, and he'd stood on the threshold and leaned against the doorjamb, smiling softly as he watched them enjoy each other's company.

There was something about it—the sight of Jordyn sitting with his daughter, sharing soft whispers and giggles, sipping hot cocoa and anticipating the excitement of the next day's Christmas contest. He had on many occasions over the years tried to imagine what life would've been like had Macy survived Roxie's birth. How Macy and Roxie would've looked together, smiling and talking, much as Roxie and Jordyn were now.

The image in his mind had been surprisingly like the one before him, full of patient kindness and shared delight. But the sight of Jordyn, sitting with Roxie in his kitchen, in his home, felt different somehow.

For a moment, he allowed himself to imagine what it might feel like to have Jordyn in his home on a daily basis. To be standing here, in the doorway of his kitchen, watching Jordyn and Roxie enjoy baking gingerbread together and delighting in each other's company, sharing a joyful moment as a mother and daughter would.

A desperate longing took hold of him then, and he found it difficult to let go of the moment, wincing slightly as Roxie glanced up and finally noticed him.

"The gingerbread Ms. Jordyn and I baked turned out perfect," Roxie said now, squeezing his hands and coaxing his attention back to the present. "It's not the gingerbread I'm worried about, Daddy. It's that I have to put it all together in front of everyone."

The applause of the crowd died down as Carol Belle began listing guidelines for the day's contest from her position center stage.

Nate lifted his hands and squeezed Roxie's shoulders. "You'll be great, sweetheart. You don't have anything to worry about. There's no right or wrong in this. Just do your best."

Roxie glanced at the long tables lined up in the center of town square. "I know. But there's so many people. What if I drop something? Or break it?"

"That's okay," Nate said, smiling. "You don't have to be perfect, Roxie. The only thing that's important today is that you have fun."

"Really?" Roxie asked.

"Really. But I don't want you to force yourself to participate. If you really and truly don't want to take part in the contest, you don't have to."

"No." Roxie lifted her chin and firmed her mouth. "I want to. I want to win for you and Uncle Tucker."

Nate smiled. "That's my girl. And win or lose, we'll still be proud of you."

"All right, everyone," Carol Belle announced from the stage. "Please take your places, and when you hear the whistle, begin building your gingerbread houses."

The crowds parted and several people hurried over to the tables. Each participant began unloading sheets of gingerbread, bags of icing, and baskets of edible decorations.

"It's time," Nate said, standing. "You need to carry over your things and get set up if you're going to take part."

Roxie lifted her chin higher, took a deep breath, then nodded. "Yes, sir."

With that, she picked up her bags and walked over to the tables, choosing the one Nate had pointed out to her. She placed her gingerbread on the table and glanced down at the other contestants who'd lined up along the tables to her right, each one of them busily arranging their ingredients. Her eyes widened at the sight of the elaborate designs others had brought.

"How's she doing?" Tucker, who'd sauntered off minutes earlier in search of a candy apple, joined Nate on the sidelines, pausing between biting chunks of his apple to ask, "She decided to go through with it?"

Nate nodded. "But she's not exactly thrilled about putting together a gingerbread house in front of everyone." He smiled gently. "She's got a bit of stage fright."

"That's to be expected," Tucker said. "No one likes to be in front of a crowd of people."

"Except for you?" Nate asked with a grin.

Tucker lifted one eyebrow. "Only when I'm on a bull. Then I don't mind it."

"Well, she's not on a bull." Nate sighed. "And she's on her own up there. Her hands are shaking. See?"

Sure enough, when Roxie placed her bags of icing on top of the table, her hands trembled.

Just then, a familiar black-haired girl strutted in front of Roxie's table, pausing briefly to eye the sheets of gingerbread on the table in front of Roxie with disdain.

"Oh, no," Nate groaned.

"What?" Tucker craned his neck, glancing at Roxie's table. "Is that mean old Angelina Stone bugging her?"

"Tucker," Nate chastised. "You shouldn't talk about a little girl that way."

"That little girl," Tucker said, pointing at Angelina Stone, "tripped me, then kicked me in the gut two years ago during the Terrible Tinsel Triathlon. And she was only six years old back then—same age as Roxie is now. If that don't warrant being called mean, I don't know what does!"

Nate watched as Angelina Stone rolled her eyes and plopped her ingredients on a table near Roxie. "Looks like Angelina's trying to psych our baby girl out a little bit."

"Wouldn't surprise me." Tucker chewed a bit of apple. "That kid right there," he said around the apple in his mouth, "she's a little hellion."

Roxie looked up from her gingerbread then, her eyes searching the crowd frantically, widening with fear as they met Nate's.

"Oh, man," he said. "Looks like she's about to cave. I might have to—"

But then, Jordyn strolled up, set a few bags on the table next to Roxie and smiled down at her.

Roxie perked up immediately, spinning toward Jordyn,

throwing her arms around her waist and hugging her tight. Jordyn hugged her back, squatted down beside Roxie and whispered in her ear. Moments later, Roxie, smiling, nodded and returned her attention to her own table, unpacking the rest of her ingredients with a steady, confident hand.

"Would you look at that?" Tucker laughed. "Ms. Jordyn to the rescue!"

Nate smiled, his eyes meeting Jordyn's across the crowd. Recalling her words to him when he'd helped her during the Snowman Fight, he lifted his chin and mouthed *thank you.*

Her smile widened and she winked at him before turning her attention back to the table in front of her.

Soon after, the contest officially began at the peal of Carol Belle's whistle.

Participants began frantically assembling their gingerbread houses, standing up sheets of gingerbread and gluing walls together with icing. Roofs were added next, then decorative doors and shutters made of icing, then more decorations to make each house unique.

Five minutes before time was called, over three-quarters of the contestants' houses had broken, one or more sheets of gingerbread crumbling beneath their hands or accidentally snapping under the pressure of their movements. Most participants took it in stride, laughing at the destruction, breaking off pieces of their broken houses and popping them into their mouths, enjoying the spicy sweet gingerbread.

By the time the last sixty seconds of the contest arrived, there were only three gingerbread houses left standing: Angelina Stone's, Jordyn's, and Roxie's. All three were well constructed and each had impressive decorations, but Jordyn's stood out—the complex decorations she'd added with icing outmatching the skill of the two little girls on either side of her. It was clear she was in position to take the win.

Chuckling, Tucker clapped a hand on Nate's back. "Looks like our new neighbor's gonna win again. Just another loss we can chalk up for the team."

Nate grinned. "She earned it, fair and square. And Roxie still did a fantastic job."

And she had. Even Jordyn seemed to notice how well Roxie had done as she eyed the gingerbread house sitting in front of the little girl. Then Jordyn returned her attention to her own gingerbread house, picked up a gumdrop, placed it on the seam of the roof, and at the last second before time was called, pressed it down hard, causing the entire gingerbread house to split into pieces and crumble onto the table.

Groans and shouts of disappointment rose from the onlookers in the crowd, but Jordyn just smiled and shrugged, picked up a broken piece of gingerbread and took a bite, issuing a sound of enjoyment as she sampled it.

"Well, how about that?" Tucker drawled, having seen exactly what Nate had.

"She wanted Roxie to have a shot at the win," Nate said softly, his gaze finding Jordyn's again.

Smiling back at him, she wiggled her eyebrows flirtatiously and popped another piece of gingerbread in her mouth.

Carol Belle's whistle echoed across the town square again.

"All right, folks!" she shouted. "Time's up. Step away from your gingerbread houses."

Roxie and Angelina Stone, the only two contestants with gingerbread houses still standing, stepped back from their tables and waited anxiously as a pair of judges sauntered over, bent close to each house and scribbled notes on a piece of paper they held.

Shortly thereafter, the judges returned to the stage and

handed the papers to Carol Belle, who returned to the microphone and smiled.

"We have a unanimous winner for this year's Gingerbread Architect contest," Carol Belle announced. "Noel's newest Gingerbread Architect is Roxanna Reed!"

Roxie, surprised by her name being called, squealed then jumped with joy. Her whole expression lit up at the energetic applause from the crowd and she spun around and hugged Jordyn again, a look of pure bliss crossing her face.

Nate stood there, watching as Jordyn hugged Roxie closer and smiled down at her affectionately. Even as the crowd began milling around him, Nate remained perfectly still, savoring the beautiful—and unexpected—moment.

Chapter Twelve

One week later, on a frigid, frosty morning, Jordyn, bundled up in a thick coat, scarf, and the green wool hat the Nanas had gifted her, stood at the top of a twenty-two-foot ladder and looped a string of colorful Christmas lights around the top of the Fraser fir tree in the back lot of Chestnut Ridge. Decorating the most perfect Christmas tree in all of Noel was a difficult task for one person with an aloof quarter horse as a supervisor, but Jordyn was determined to get it done right.

"You know," she said, leaning on the top rung of the ladder and eyeing the white mare standing on the ground below her, "you could help out a bit more. Maybe come over here, brace your belly against the ladder and hold it steady for me? Or," she said, smiling, "I could stick a string of lights between your teeth and you can just walk around the tree a few times. That would cut my work in half!"

Star lifted her nose in the air and sniffed, then walked away, her long white tail swishing from side to side as she moseyed further across the back lot toward the mountain range in the distance.

"Well!" Jordyn clamped a hand to her chest and pretended to be offended. "I never! You'd think if someone puts a roof over your head, tasty food in your belly, and brushes you down every night, you'd be a bit more accommodating. So, what? You're not gonna stay and help me out at all?"

Star kept walking.

"Looks like you lost your help."

Balancing carefully on the ladder, Jordyn glanced over her shoulder and grinned at the sight of the four Nanas, wrapped up tightly in warm coats, scarves, and mittens, strolling across the back lot toward her, bright smiles on each of their faces.

"I can't imagine that horse of yours would've been much help, anyway, decorating that tree," Carol Belle continued as they drew to a stop at the base of the Fraser fir. She looked up at Jordyn and laughed. "That's probably for the best though. Fabio Fraser's right particular about who he lets give him attention. It takes a tender, loving hand to bring out the best in him."

Holly grinned. "And, dear me, you'll need to use the absolute best decorations if you want a shot at winning the Christmas tree competition tonight."

"Not that Fabio Fraser needs decoration," Eve said matter-of-factly. "He's the best-looking tree in the entire state."

Kandy nodded, her eyes sparkling with excitement as she eyed the boxes of decorations Jordyn had lined up near the base of the tree. "No matter how you choose to decorate Fabio, I know he'll look wonderful. He's bound to win the contest by a mile!"

"I don't know," Carol Belle said, scowling at the white fence that bordered Chestnut Ridge, marking the property line of Frosted Firs Ranch. "I swung by Nate's place this morning on the way to pick y'all up. He's got a mighty fine-looking tree. It's growing right at the front of his biggest Christmas tree lot, standing proud and tall.

It's the first tree that greets you when you round the drive-way to the tree lot. I hate to admit it, but that tree of his is going to give our Fabio some competition this year—something I didn't think was possible given how perfect our Fraser fir is."

At the mention of Nate, Jordyn's excitement dwindled.

Over the past week since she'd thrown a potential win in the Gingerbread Architect contest, she'd decided to stick strictly to the Nanas' rules for the Christmas competition, which meant absolutely, unequivocally, no cross-conspiring of any kind! So, instead of seeking out Nate and Roxie for advice regarding each contest, she'd turned to Kandy instead, asking for singing and dancing lessons prior to the Christmas Karaoke and Christmas Dance Craze contests. She'd also asked for Kandy's opinion as to which of the ugly sweaters she'd purchased in the town square would have the best chance of winning the Ugly Sweater Wrapping Pretty contest.

Heeding Kandy's help and advice, Jordyn had done well in each competition, if she did say so herself. Despite her less than stellar singing voice, she'd managed to snag third place in the Christmas Karaoke contest, choosing to sing "Blue Christmas" in her best Elvis Presley impersonation. For the Christmas Dance Craze, she'd fared even better, placing second after rocking out solo to Springsteen's version of "Santa Claus Is Coming to Town."

And, oh boy, had that been a blast! It had been years since she'd let loose, given herself over to the music and just enjoyed the excitement of the moment, and she had earned much-needed points at the same time.

The Ugly Sweater Wrapping Pretty contest didn't go quite as well though. She scored points for her fabulously ugly sweater, which featured an evil squirrel, dressed as Santa, stealing gifts from underneath a Christmas tree. But the gift-wrapping portion of the contest proved to be too much of a challenge for her. Because she'd spent Christmas on her own for most of her life, she lacked the gift-wrapping skills Noel's other participants had honed over the years, and her fingers had fumbled their way through the task, mangling the pretty red bow she'd failed to tie attractively around the gift.

But in the end, she'd done well enough, and her name had moved up to second position on the Tree Scoreboard. She was now directly below Nate and right above the Stone family.

All that remained was the Christmas Light Delight contest, which would be coupled with the Christmas tree judging that would take place later tonight. During the contest, Noel's residents and a trio of judges were scheduled to tour the top three participants' homes, taking notes and scoring the outdoor Christmas lights. Then they'd inspect each participant's Christmas tree entry, evaluating the ornaments, lights, health of tree, and overall impression.

Considering the Fraser fir at Chestnut Ridge was as perfect as a Christmas tree could be, she was sure she'd have a really good shot at winning the Christmas tree contest and the competition overall.

But though the thought of winning the Christmas Crown had delighted her before, it didn't sit quite as well with her now. For one thing, if she did win the competition, it would mean Roxie wouldn't have a tenth crown to put in her mother's trophy case. Also rather concerning was the fact that Jordyn's tree would have to knock Nate's out of the running, which would end his tradition of winning the Christmas competition and possibly decrease the attention Frosted Firs Ranch would get for its Christmas trees this year.

And then . . . there were the Nanas.

The four women had so graciously welcomed Jordyn

into their group and hometown weeks ago, opening their arms and hearts to her, leading her through the Christmas competition and welcoming her as part of their community. And all they had asked in return was for her to enter Fabio Fraser into the Christmas tree contest and walk away a winner. It was a small price to pay for all they'd done for her . . . but, somehow, her heart just wasn't in it anymore.

"Speaking of Nate," Carol Belle said quietly as she scrutinized Jordyn's expression. "We've been meaning to tell you how proud we were of you the other night."

Jordyn raised her brows in question.

"The way you helped our precious Roxie in the gingerbread contest?" Holly prompted. "We all saw what you did."

"Everyone saw it," Eve added. "It was obvious to everyone who was watching that you purposely blew your chance at winning so that the little girls would have a better shot at placing in the contest."

"And our sweet Roxie," Kandy said, clutching her hands to her chest in an affectionate gesture. "She was so happy when she won first place. She'd worked so hard, and the win was well deserved. There's no way she would've earned it had your gingerbread house remained in the competition."

Jordyn shrugged nonchalantly, but her mouth curved into a gentle smile as she recalled the surprised but excited cheers that had burst from Roxie upon hearing her name called as the winner.

Deliberately breaking her own gingerbread house had been worth it just to see the sheer delight on Roxie's face.

"It wasn't that big a deal," Jordyn said. "I knew how nervous Roxie was and how much she wanted to do well in the contest. Her success was more important than winning a few more points."

The Nanas blinked, staring up at her silently.

"What?" Jordyn asked. "What is it? You're looking at me like I sprouted another head."

"What we're thinking of," Carol Belle said softly, "has nothing to do with your head and everything to do with your heart . . . and Nate."

Face heating, Jordyn looked down at the string of Christmas lights in her hands and turned her attention to straightening them, putting more effort into untangling the strands than the task necessitated. "Yes, well, not a whole lot matters where my heart is concerned, seeing as how Nate's heart is unavailable."

"Oh, Jordyn." Kandy stepped forward, placing her hand gently on a low branch of the tree as she gazed up at Jordyn. "Did he say that? Did he really say he wasn't interested in you at all?"

"Not really," Jordyn said. "But he does have reservations. Ones that have everything to do with Roxie's happiness and well-being, and I completely understand."

"But you're so wonderful with Roxie," Eve said. "We all saw how well you two got on together at the gingerbread contest. The two of you were having a great time and no one can doubt that you care about her. You can say what you did was a little thing, but your sacrifice meant the world to that little girl."

Jordyn smiled. "I guess it did. And I'm glad I could help her." She bit her lip, hesitating. "But I got to thinking this past week that Nate might be right about a lot of things. And that he might be especially right about protecting Roxie's heart." She looked down at the Nanas then, her chest aching at the memory of the grief in Roxie's tone the night she'd spoken of Macy in the kitchen at Frosted Firs. "Roxie has already suffered the loss of one mother. She should never be put into a position where she might end up losing another parent she loves."

"But who says she's going to lose if you and Nate commit to each other?" Carol Belle asked, stepping forward and joining Kandy at the base of the tree. "You enjoy spending time with Roxie and she with you—you told us so yourself. And Nate has really broken out of his shell since you arrived in town. I mean, he's taken part in the Christmas competition for a decade now, but in all those years, he never entered the Sexy Santa contest. He did that for you because he wanted to spend time with you." Her mouth firmed. "Having you in their lives would be good for both of them."

"If it worked out," Jordyn said softly. "But I'm not sure it would, long term." She issued a sound of self-derision. "Well, I know it would work for me, considering the way I feel about Nate. But he told me himself that he didn't think he was ready for a relationship. And that he wasn't sure he would ever be ready to let Macy go." She sighed. "That doesn't bode well for a new romance, and the last thing I'd ever want to do would be to enter Roxie's life just to turn around and leave again." She shook her head, her stomach dropping as she voiced the words she knew she should accept. "If Nate isn't ready for a romantic relationship, I don't know that I want to take the risk of ruining any friendship we might have. I just can't see pursuing a relationship with him unless he's truly ready to move on from Macy."

"But there must be a chance that he'll change his mind." Holly gazed up at her with wide, pleading eyes. "I mean, he could change his mind. Men do that occasionally. Women, too! Sometimes I think if Don could ever get over the grudge he has against me and catch me at the right time, I might be willing to change my mind about commitment, too. Please don't give up on Nate yet."

Smiling, Jordyn nodded. "I'm still holding on to a little hope that he will change his mind. But I'd have to see some sign that he was ready and that he truly wanted to move forward. Otherwise, I just don't think it's worth the risk to his or my heart—and, most especially, to Roxie's."

The Nanas fell silent, continuing to stare up at her with concerned expressions.

"Anyway," Jordyn said, summoning a bright smile. "As you said, Nate may very well change his mind. So, if it will please you, I'll continue holding on to my last bit of hope for the rest of the week. Christmas is one of the most romantic seasons of the year," she said softly as she gazed at the beautiful Fraser fir in front of her. "So, there's still a chance that Nate will come around. But in the meantime, Fabio Fraser needs our attention. After all, we have a Christmas tree contest to win!"

Standing in the back lot of Chestnut Ridge among the crowd of townsfolk, Nate hugged Roxie closer to his side, rubbing her arms briskly as she shivered in the cold night air, waiting for Jordyn to introduce her perfect Fraser fir to the trio of judges. At half past seven in the evening, it was dark outside, but the distant glow of lights from Frosted Firs Ranch and the starry sky overhead brightened the shadowy figures that comprised the crowd of onlookers.

But despite the darkness and the frigid temperatures, it was a gorgeous night for judging a Christmas tree contest as the snow-capped mountain ranges, velvet sky, and sparkling stars overhead lent a festive atmosphere to the event.

"I can't wait to see Ms. Jordyn's tree," Roxie said, bouncing against him with excitement. "I bet she has the most beautiful tree in the world! When will she turn the lights on so we can see?"

"Soon, sweetheart. Any minute now, she'll flip the power and that tree will come to life for the judges."

And the moment couldn't come too soon.

For over two hours, Nate, Roxie, Tucker, and a large group of Noel's residents, including the trio of judges, had toured Noel's town square, admiring the Christmas lights and enjoying hot cocoa and warm apple cider. Then they'd piled into their cars and driven in a Christmas convoy of sorts to view the Stone family's entry in the tree competition.

The Stones, currently ranked third in Noel's Christmas competition, had done well for their entry. Their tree was a fifteen-foot Leyland cypress with full branches and a rich green hue. They'd decorated their tree with red and gold poinsettias of all different sizes and had topped it off with a beautiful bouquet of poinsettia blooms woven together with red and green Christmas lights that sparkled brightly against the night sky above.

The crowd, clearly impressed, had oohed and aahed, strolling around the large tree, taking group pictures, posing for selfies, and getting a closer look at the bountiful poinsettia blooms decorating each limb.

Drake Stone and his family had gathered beside the tree, explaining as they introduced their entry that the theme they'd chosen for their tree was meant to reflect the poinsettia blooms that lined the streets of downtown Noel. He explained that his family wanted to capture a bit of the Christmas magic of the town square and bring it home to enjoy as they celebrated the holidays as a family.

The three judges in attendance had smiled during the introduction, then circled the tree multiple times, jotting down notes on the notepads they held in their hands.

Then it was time to move on to the next contestant's entry, Jordyn's famous Fraser fir.

With her name listed in second place on the Tree Scoreboard, Jordyn had a great shot at winning the Christmas Crown, but her potential win all hinged on this one contest.

Nate glanced around him, noting the eager and excited expressions on other people's faces as they squinted into the darkness, straining for a better glimpse of the unlit tree that loomed over them in the empty lot.

"Boy," Tucker said as he stood beside Nate. "She's pulling out all the stops, isn't she? It's real theatrical—and smart—of her to give the tree a grand entrance." He shoved his hands in his pockets and shivered. "Only thing is, she could've taken into consideration that we'd have to freeze our butts off waiting for her to turn the lights on."

Nate frowned. "Tucker, you—"

"That's not nice, Uncle Tucker." Roxie beat Nate to it, poking her head around Nate's midsection and sticking her tongue out at Tucker. "Ms. Jordyn can have all the time she wants. Now, take it back."

Tucker held up his hands, palms out, and grinned. "I know, kid. I'm well aware of how much you like Ms. Jordyn—I like her, too! And I know you want Ms. Jordyn to do well, so I'll cheer her on . . . no matter how cold I get." He made a face. "How about that? You forgive me?"

Roxie smiled. "Yeah. I forgive you."

A flurry of movement near the back of Jordyn's cabin caught Nate's attention and he glanced over, peering into the darkness as Jordyn's voice rang out across the clearing.

"Thank you for coming, everyone," Jordyn called out through the darkness. "I'm sorry to have kept you waiting but I wanted to make sure everything was in order before I introduced you to my fabulous Fraser fir." She fell silent for a moment, then, in a proud tone, announced, "Ladies and gentlemen of Noel, North Carolina, it's my pleasure to introduce you to the spectacular Fabio Fraser fir!"

A click echoed across the clearing, an electrical buzz filled the frigid air, then a burst of multicolored light shined from the almost twenty-foot-tall tree, sending a festive glow across the back lot.

Every lush, emerald branch of the perfect Fraser fir was graced with lights and colorful round ornaments. And the brightest of the lights was saved for the very top of the tree, where a five-point star blazed bright white high above them, standing out among the blanket of stars that sparkled in the night sky.

A collective gasp arose from the crowd as the perfectly formed tree towered above them in dazzling holiday splendor, a mesmerizing glow of color, rising high before the snow-capped mountains in the distance.

"Please come closer." Jordyn walked into the dazzling pool of light that emanated from the tree and waved everyone over, smiling brightly at their pleased expressions. "If you look closely at the ornaments, you'll see that each one has a unique design that represents the things I love most about Noel." She glanced up at the tree, her pretty features highlighted by the glow of the Christmas lights, her expression tender as she spoke. "You'll find a red ornament etched with a glittery cupcake, which represents the delicious red velvet cupcakes Kringle's Café bakes every year. They were my first treat when I arrived in Noel."

"And on this side," she continued, walking a few feet to the left, "there's a blue ornament hanging from one of the branches that has a snowman painted on it to represent the Snowman Fight at First Snow."

Leading the crowd of onlookers further around the impressive Fraser fir, she said, "You'll find dozens of other ornaments with designs that represent all of Noel's Christmas contests, each of the Christmas stores in Noel's town square, and"—she continued walking around the tree, waiting as the crowd joined her for a better look—"over here, you'll find a series of ornaments that bear the names of people I've met so far, all of whom have helped me in some way and brightened the season for everyone in Noel."

Roxie, her eyes wide with delight, tugged Nate's sleeve. "Come on, Daddy. Let's look at the names. Do you think ours are on one of the ornaments?"

Nate smiled, his chest warming as he studied the tender smile on Jordyn's face. "I don't know, but we can take a look."

He led Roxie closer to the tree and forged a path to the front of the crowd so Roxie could search the thick branches. She carefully studied the colorful ornaments, narrowing her eyes as she read the names painted in glitter on each one.

Jordyn, standing nearby, walked over, bent close to Roxie's ear and whispered, "To your left, three branches down."

Nate met Jordyn's eyes over Roxie's head. She smiled at him, her cheeks flushing, then turned away and walked to the other side of the tree.

"Here we are, Daddy!" Roxie tugged at his sleeve again. "Look! It's all of our names. Yours, Uncle Tucker's, and mine." She looked up at him, grinning from ear to ear. "And she drew hearts underneath every one of them."

Nate stilled as he studied the ornaments that bore his and Roxie's names and the heart Jordyn had painted in glitter beneath each one. The gesture, though seemingly small to some, left a warm glow in his chest.

"Chestnut Ridge is the first real home I've ever known," Jordyn told the crowd. "And this Fraser fir is my first true Christmas tree." She smiled, the pretty blush deepening across her cheeks. "Whether my tree wins this contest or not, it's perfect to me. Because every branch holds something—or a reminder of someone—that's dear to me." She looked up then, her eyes finding Nate's. "And so"—her gaze left him as she refocused on the crowd and the judges—"even though I've only been here a few weeks, I couldn't be prouder that I've chosen Noel as my new home."

A collective sound of approval murmured through the crowd and applause followed. The judges, as meticulous as ever, strolled slowly around the tree, examining the ornaments closely, whispering to each other and making notes on their notepads.

Nate nudged Tucker, who stood beside him, with his elbow. "You mind staying here with Roxie for a minute while I speak with Jordyn?"

Tucker shook his head, still shivering. "No problem. But don't interrupt the judges or anything. It's cold out here and we still gotta trek over to the ranch and show them our tree."

Nate chuckled. Tucker might be the most musclebound bull rider he'd ever come across, but his brother sure couldn't handle the cold.

Nate weaved his way through the crowd and joined Jordyn on the other side of the tree. Up close, she was just as gorgeous as the Fraser fir, her beautiful green eyes sparkling in the glow of the Christmas lights.

"The tree turned out beautiful," he said quietly. "It looks absolutely magnificent the way you've decorated it."

"Magnificent?" She grinned and tapped her chin thoughtfully as she studied him. "I seem to recall hearing that word somewhere before . . ."

Nate ducked his head and laughed. "Oh, Lord. Let's not relive that night at this moment. It's too perfect to ruin."

"You think so?" she asked softly, looking up at him. "You think the moment's perfect?" Her gaze lowered to his mouth, her lips parting on a soft breath. "Perfect for what?"

He stood still as she searched his expression, an expectant look in her eyes. There was so much he wanted to say. So many things he wanted to share with her—including his gratitude for the concern she'd showed for Roxie's feelings during the gingerbread contest.

As they stood there in the glow of the tree nearby, the crowd milling around them seemed to melt away and he leaned closer to her, longing to wrap his arms around her, hold her close and prolong the magic of the moment.

But . . . this wasn't the right time.

"Well," he said, clearing his throat and stepping back. "The tree certainly couldn't be more perfect."

His response disappointed her. Some of the joy faded from her smile and she stepped away as well, rubbing her hands together briskly to ward off the cold.

"You know . . ." he said softly. "I haven't had the chance to thank you properly for what you did for Roxie."

Her smile returned as she waved away his thanks. "It wasn't a big deal. I just knew how hard she'd worked on her gingerbread house. Besides, a grown woman, competing against two little girls?" She shook her head and shrugged. "Well, it wasn't exactly fair play, was it? Dropping out of the competition was the only right thing to do."

"Maybe," he said quietly. "But not everyone would do it."

She shrugged again then looked away, her gaze straying to the crowd.

"Looks like the judges are done," she said, gesturing at the trio of judges, who'd tucked their notepads back in their coats and had begun their walk across the back lot toward the white fence that bordered his ranch. "You should probably get going." She met his eyes again, her smile sincere this time. "You don't want to be late introducing your own tree, do you?"

"That's a good point," he said, backing away reluctantly but offering a teasing smile. "I have a contest to win. And, woman, perfect Fraser fir or not, you and your tree are in for some competition."

She laughed as he walked way, calling after him, "Good luck with that!"

He glanced over his shoulder, his stomach dipping as the distance increased between them. "Thanks! After what I've seen here, I'm gonna need it."

But twenty minutes later, as he stood with Roxie and Tucker beside the nineteen-foot Fraser fir in the front Christmas tree lot of his ranch, he had to admit that their tree was still in the running.

He, Roxie, and Tucker had worked hard over the past few days, adding lights and decorations to the tree during every minute of their spare time, hoping to put their best foot forward in tonight's contest. Overall, he thought they'd done a good job. Their Fraser fir might not be as perfect as Jordyn's, but the attention and care that had gone into the decorations were evident.

"Welcome to Frosted Firs Ranch," Nate announced as the crowd, along with the three judges, gathered in front of the impressive tree.

Just beyond the first line of onlookers, he spotted Jordyn's red hair and pretty features. She smiled up at him and he smiled back, then said, "I planned to introduce the entry for our team, but someone else wanted the honor." He glanced down at Roxie, who stood beside him, smiling brightly. "My daughter, Roxanna—or Roxie, as we call her—has asked to explain the theme of our tree this year. It seems she's had some recent practice at standing in front of a crowd, and after considering the advice of someone she admires very much, she wanted to give it another try." He held out his arm in invitation. "Roxie, would you please introduce our tree?"

Smiling, Roxie followed his lead and moved to the front of the tree.

Nate stole another glance at Jordyn, who looked back at him, her eyebrows raised and surprise in her eyes as Roxie took his place in front of the tree. He winked at her, mouthing the same words he'd spoken to her the day she ensured Roxie would win the gingerbread contest: *Thank you.*

The two words were simple and small—not nearly expressive enough for the encouragement Jordyn had given Roxie—but he hoped she knew how much her gesture had meant to him.

Jordyn smiled, her eyes glistening as she mouthed back, *You're welcome.*

A brief flash of fear moved through Roxie's expression as she cleared her throat to speak, but she glanced over at Nate, then Jordyn, studied their encouraging smiles, took a deep breath and spoke. "This year, we decorated our Fraser fir tree in honor of my mama's memory."

A soft hush fell over the crowd. Many of the onlookers who'd known Macy smiled gently as Roxie moved closer to the tree and began her explanation.

"My mom was Macy Reed," Roxie said. "And she loved Christmas. She liked white lights the best, so we used white Christmas lights to decorate our tree."

Nate smiled. The white lights on the Fraser fir contrasted beautifully with the dark green branches. Macy, no doubt, would've been pleased with the sight.

"My Dad tied a big, white bow at the top of the tree," Roxie continued, "and my uncle Tucker wound white ribbon around the tree all the way to the bottom. The bow and ribbons are made of white silk—the kind my dad said my mama's wedding dress was made out of."

Nate's smile faltered, his throat closing at the memory

of Macy, dressed in her wedding gown, walking down the aisle toward him.

The day they'd married, there'd been so much hope in her eyes. So much love. And so much certainty. Macy had been confident that they would have a long, happy life together.

Only things hadn't turned out that way.

"And over here," Roxie said, pointing to a small silver crown that hung from one branch, "there's a crown hanging from one of the branches and eight others on other limbs. There's nine in all. One for each year my mom or my dad has won Noel's Christmas competition. If we win this year, we will be able to add the tenth, and that would make a whole decade of winning the Christmas Crown for my mom." She turned and faced the crowd again, smiling brightly, a sheen of moisture glistening in her eyes as she spoke. "My dad said we would put the brightest lights on our tree so that Mama can see them from heaven and know we still love her." Lips trembling, Roxie—his beautiful, brave girl—managed to smile. "Dad said he knows she can see it. And he knows she'd be proud of us, too."

Nate studied Roxie, her gentle voice and long blond hair so reminiscent of Macy. An ache stirred in his chest as the crowd applauded and circled the tree, gazing up at the bright lights and sparkling Christmas Crowns that hung from the branches.

It was unavoidable then—the knowledge that Macy was no longer physically with them. And that she never would be again.

But instead of the grief, pain, and regret that had weighed Nate's heart down for years, something shifted inside of him in that moment and broke free, releasing the tension in his shoulders and the heaviness in his chest.

And then, something small but strong unfurled within

him, streaming through his veins, coaxing his mouth into a smile and dissolving the tears that coated his lashes. He'd loved Macy . . . so very much. But he'd lost her. Though things would never be the same for him or Roxie, they could be different. They might even be . . . better.

All he had to do was summon the courage to reach out.

His attention returned to the crowd, his gaze sifting urgently through the crowd of onlookers, searching for Jordyn's face, hoping to share another smile, to catch a glimpse of the joy the future might hold for him.

But she was no longer there.

Chapter Thirteen

"Nervous?"

Nate stilled in the act of lifting the cup he held to his mouth and glanced to his left, where Tucker sat in the chair beside him on the stage in Noel's town square.

"Why?" Nate frowned.

Smiling, Tucker gestured toward the cup in his hand. "Because you've been tipping that cup back every five minutes for the past ten minutes and it's been empty for over half an hour."

Nate glanced down at the empty cup in his hand and grimaced. Even he had to admit that he had been somewhat preoccupied during the initial proceedings of Noel's Christmas Crowning. But that wasn't totally his fault. He had good reason to be distracted and even more reason to be worried.

Last night, after Roxie had finished introducing their Fraser fir tree to the judges, he had searched for Jordyn in the crowd, hoping to catch her attention and speak with her. But she was gone, disappearing into the darkness that engulfed the outskirts of his ranch.

He'd wanted to go after her, but people still milled about the Christmas tree lots on his ranch, their interest apparently piqued by the viewing of the Christmas tree entries. Over the next two hours, he and Tucker had sold, cut down, and loaded more trees into trucks and vans than they had over the past two days combined.

Win or lose, the Christmas tree contest had boosted sales at Frosted Firs Ranch and made the night a resounding success. Well, except where Jordyn was concerned.

He couldn't blame her though. For weeks, he'd been giving her mixed signals about his true intentions, and even now he wasn't completely sure how he planned to proceed with their relationship. But, for the first time in years, he knew without a doubt that he did want to pursue something new—a new romance, love, and family . . . with Jordyn.

Rather than frightening him, the revelation excited him and he'd picked up his cell phone multiple times last night, wanting to call her and tell her how he felt. But the evening's Christmas tree contest had made for a long day and the late hour had certainly not been the best time to broach a subject of such importance—especially over the phone.

So, he'd tucked Roxie into bed, sprawled out on his own, and stared at the ceiling for hours, wondering what the future held and how inviting Jordyn into his life might affect Roxie. But somehow, he eventually slept—deeply and soundly—and had awoken this morning refreshed and energetic, eager to tackle the day.

He'd gone to work with plans of leaving early in the afternoon to drive over to Chestnut Ridge and visit Jordyn, but the crowds had grown even bigger at the gift shop than in recent days, and he had been unable to escape from the cash register. He'd ended up spending the majority of his day ringing up customers, wrapping gifts, and carrying large purchases out to vehicles.

He'd wanted to see Jordyn before tonight's Christmas

ceremony, to speak to her and tell her what he was thinking and feeling. But as had been the case for them since the day they'd met, it seemed the time hadn't been right. And from the guarded expression Jordyn had sported when she'd arrived moments ago, the time might not be right tonight either.

Nate glanced to his right, where Jordyn sat in a chair on the other side of the Stone family. She wore a beautiful green dress that contrasted appealingly with her ivory skin and highlighted the warm red waves of her hair. He studied her face, his gaze lingering on her mouth, and he had an almost overwhelming urge to stand, cross the stage, pull her into his arms and share with her, openly and honestly, all of his fears and dreams and hopes for the future that he hoped to build with her.

It had taken so long for him to see things clearly and finally let go of his grief over losing Macy. Last night, hearing Roxie's loving words about her mother had driven home the truth that though Macy was gone, her memory had not faded and would never completely disappear from their lives. Now Roxie treasured it in her heart, and that was what Nate had wanted most of all—for Roxie to know and love the mother she'd never had the opportunity to meet.

But now, a different kind of opportunity waited right in front of him as it had for weeks. He'd just been too afraid to take a chance and reach out.

Sensing his scrutiny, Jordyn turned her head, her eyes meeting his, holding his gaze. He smiled tentatively and after a moment, she smiled back, though the movement was small and restrained.

"Good evening, ladies and gentlemen!"

Carol Belle, flanked by the three other Nanas, walked to the microphone in the center of the stage and greeted the crowd.

"We've reached the moment you've all been waiting for," she continued. "Tonight, we're going to announce the winner of Noel's Christmas tree contest. After the winner is announced, a crew will visit the owner's property tomorrow afternoon, chop down the tree, wrap it carefully, and transport it to the town square, where it will be put on display for the entire town to enjoy. We extend our best wishes and good luck to the participants."

There was a brief round of applause.

"Also," Kandy said into the mic, "after the winner of the tree competition is announced and celebrated, we will also announce the winner of the Christmas Crown. As you know, the winner of the crown is the individual or team who has earned the most points over the course of the twelve contests. The crown will be presented tonight, and the recipient will be the guest of honor at Noel's annual Christmas Eve celebration!"

The crowd applauded again, smiles and cheerful chatter echoing all around the town square.

"Now," Carol Belle said, "without further ado, Eve will announce this year's Christmas tree winner."

Eve, standing to the left of Carol Belle, smiled and made her way to the microphone. She adjusted the height, the mic squealed briefly, then she tapped it with one finger and smiled.

"The judges just handed me the name of the owner of the winning Christmas tree," Eve said, lifting a small piece of paper in her hand. She tucked her finger under one edge and dragged it across the fold, unsealing it. She unfolded it, read it, and, a wide smile spreading across her face, shouted, "This year's winner of the Christmas tree contest is Jordyn Banks!"

The crowd gathered below the stage erupted in applause, yelling and shouting its approval.

"We're all very proud of Jordyn," Holly said, sweeping

an arm in Jordyn's direction. "As a newcomer, she's thrown herself into our Christmas competition and given her all in every contest. The judges also wrote that they were impressed with the theme of her tree as it reflects the most important values of Noel, which include appreciating the beauty of our town, helping each other, and finding joy in the simple things in life." She waved her hand, motioning for Jordyn to join her. "Come on, Jordyn. Accept your award, step up to the mic and say a few words."

Nate glanced at Jordyn, who rose unsteadily to her feet. Instead of the exuberance he expected to see on her face, she seemed hesitant, unsure and a bit . . . regretful.

"Ms. Jordyn won!" Roxie shouted from her seat beside him. Watching Jordyn approach the microphone, she clapped her hands and smiled brighter. "Isn't that wonderful, Daddy?"

Nate nodded and despite the uncertainty coursing through him at Jordyn's anxious expression, he said, "Yes, it is. I'm very happy she won. She deserves it."

And he truly meant it. He was thrilled Jordyn's perfect Fraser fir had won, and didn't feel the least bit disappointed that his tree had lost. But Jordyn didn't seem to share the same excitement he and Roxie felt over her win.

The crowd continued applauding, but the clapping died down as Jordyn arrived at the microphone. Each of the Nanas hugged Jordyn, then stepped back, giving her room to speak.

"I, um . . ." Jordyn lifted one hand and tucked a wavy strand of her red hair behind her ear. Her fingers trembled. "Thank you for this award." Her voice shook slightly. "And thank you for welcoming me to your town. Everyone has been so wonderful and kind." Slowly, she turned her head, glancing in Nate and Roxie's direction. "You've truly made this Christmas the most special it's ever been for me."

Despite her affectionate words, her gaze held resignation. The sight of it sent a wave of dread through Nate.

Jordyn faced the crowd again, lifted her chin and said, "But I'm afraid I can't accept this award. I'm officially withdrawing my Fraser fir from the Christmas Tree competition."

"Jordyn, what's going on?" Eve asked. "What do you mean, you can't accept the award?"

Jordyn winced as Eve, standing beside her at the microphone in the center of the stage, stared at her with a shocked expression. "I'm sorry, Eve. I know how much a new Christmas tree contest winner meant to you and the rest of the Nanas and how much you wanted Fabio Fraser in the town square."

"Then, why?" Carol Belle walked across the stage and placed her hand on Jordyn's arm.

"Give her a moment, Carol Belle," Kandy said. Her gaze held Jordyn's, sorrow and understanding in her eyes. "She knows what she's doing."

"But she worked so hard in the Christmas competition, and she decorated that tree so beautifully." Carol Belle took Jordyn's hands in hers and shook her head. "You've earned this!"

The crowd of onlookers standing below the stage clapped encouragingly and a few shouted for Jordyn to accept the award.

Jordyn glanced out at the crowd, her gaze scanning the familiar faces that looked up at her. Many of the people encouraging her to accept the award she recognized as having competed against her in several of the Christmas contests. Others, she remembered cheering her on during the Terrible Tinsel Triathlon and celebrating her first-place win with as much excitement as she felt.

She hated to disappoint all of them by turning down

the award, but in her heart, she knew it was the right thing to do.

"I know how much winning the Christmas tree competition mattered to everyone competing this year," she said as the encouraging cheers of the crowd died down. "And I feel awful about taking one of the top three spots on the stage that could have been given to someone else and then turning down the award, but . . ."

Inhaling deeply, she glanced over her shoulder at Nate and Roxie, the confused expressions on their faces sending a new wave of regret through her.

She forced herself to face the crowd again and continue. "I just don't have the heart to cut down the Fraser fir at Chestnut Ridge. You see, that tree might be just another Christmas tree to some of you, but for me, it's the first real Christmas tree I've ever had." She smiled gently. "And even better, it's growing right in the backyard of my new home! A home that I've truly grown to love." She looked down and sighed. "It just doesn't seem right to cut down that tree, put it on display in the town square for a few days and then toss it away at the end of the holiday."

All eyes were on her, and she squirmed uncomfortably, twisting her hands together at her waist.

"I just think," she stated firmly, "that a tree as perfect as that should be left right where it is and allowed to grow. That tree grew perfectly beautiful all on its own. It's the most perfect Christmas tree I've ever seen, and it should be celebrated all year long. Not for just a short month or two at the end of the year."

A hush settled over the crowd and Jordyn stepped away from the microphone as she said softly, "I'm sorry to disappoint you and disrupt the Christmas ceremony." She walked away, pausing at the edge of the stage to turn and whisper to the Nanas, "I'm so sorry."

Disgruntled groans and voices peppered the air as people in the crowd began discussing the new development.

Jordyn, however, didn't stick around to take stock of the damage she'd caused to the little town's annual Christmas holiday celebration. Instead, she exited the stage and walked across the town square to the parking lot as quickly as her high-heeled shoes would allow. She had every intention of going home, stuffing her face full of sugar-laden holiday treats, crawling into her warm bed, pulling the covers over her head and licking her wounds.

She'd lie low for the rest of the Christmas season, then, hopefully, the Nanas and Noel's residents might forgive her.

But just as she reached her truck, which was parked on the far side of the parking lot, she heard Nate call her name.

Her hand stilled on the door handle, and she closed her eyes for a moment, wishing she'd chosen a less dramatic exit from the Christmas competition. But last night, after Roxie's beautiful presentation of the Christmas tree at Frosted Firs, she hadn't anticipated winning the Christmas tree contest and had hoped that tonight she would be congratulating Nate, Roxie, and Tucker on their victory rather than accepting a win of her own.

Instead, her name had been called and there she was, sitting on stage in front of all of Noel's residents, forced to make a decision on the spot.

"Jordyn?" Nate's deep voice sounded close at her back. "Would you please slow down for a minute and talk to me?"

Reluctantly, she opened her eyes and faced him, wincing at the hurt and confusion in his eyes. "I'm sorry, Nate. I truly didn't mean to cause such a scene. But I didn't expect to win, so I didn't think I'd be put in that position to begin with."

Nate shook his head. "What do you mean you didn't

think you would win? Your tree was perfect. You have to know that. It's—hands-down—the best tree we've ever had in the competition."

The warm approval in his tone made her smile—a real one that warmed her chest and broke her heart all at the same time.

"That means a lot to me," she said, smiling wider. "I mean, considering it's coming from a bona fide expert in Christmas trees and all."

Nate smiled back and a soft chuckle escaped his lips. "I don't know that I'm an expert, but I do know a thing or two about Christmas trees and I have to say, the love and attention you put into decorating yours made it outshine the others."

Her smile faded. "I don't think so. I think there was more love and affection in Roxie's tree than could have ever been in mine."

Nate held her gaze, his grin fading, too. "Roxie wanted to do something special for her mother this year. She asked me to help her incorporate the things Macy liked most and I—"

"You don't have to explain," she said quickly. "You had every right to dedicate your tree to Macy. I know you and Roxie both love her very much and still miss her."

"Yes," he said softly. "But—"

"I've thought it over and I think you're right."

He fell silent for a moment, staring back at her with a guarded expression, then asked, "Right about what?"

"You were right about thinking it wasn't a good time to explore a relationship." It hurt to say the words out loud. She could almost feel her heart breaking into a million pieces. "You told me you weren't ready in the very beginning, and I should've listened. I never should have pushed you into something you weren't ready for. And then there's Roxie . . ."

Nate remained silent, his eyes searching her expression intently.

"It wasn't until I spent some time alone with her, baking gingerbread"—she smiled gently at the memory—"that I realized how much she misses having a mother. And then I thought that if you and I started a relationship and somewhere down the road, you realized you weren't really ready to let Macy go and didn't have a place for me in your heart, I wouldn't be able to bear the thought of walking away from her. And I couldn't bear knowing that I'd been the cause of breaking her heart." Her throat tightened and she swallowed past the knot forming in her throat, trying to keep her voice steady. "What I'm trying to say is that if I had to choose, I'd rather have you and Roxie in my life as good neighbors and friends rather than risk losing you both for good."

Nate continued staring at her, his jaw clenching as he looked away, glancing back at the lights of the town square, where holiday music had begun playing and cheerful voices filled the air.

"Are you sure that's the best way to avoid the risk?" he asked softly.

She frowned. "What do you mean?"

He faced her then, saying softly, "The Nanas—Kandy, in particular—told me during one of the Christmas contests that no matter what we might do to avoid it, life brings risk all the same."

The wounded look in his blue eyes sent a wave of pain through her.

"Yes," she whispered. "I think I agree with that. So, you see, I'm faced with a pretty tough dilemma. Either I risk loving and losing you and Roxie, or we remain neighbors and friends, and I keep you both in my life in some way."

Something tickled her cheek and she brushed her hand over her face, wiping away a tear.

"I won't cut my Fraser fir down," she whispered, holding his gaze. "And I won't risk losing you and Roxie. I plan to put roots down here in Noel. It already feels like home. Star and I will continue settling in at Chestnut Ridge, I'll work on starting up my business, and every now and then I'll pop over to Frosted Firs Ranch to use your oven and ask for advice." She smiled, a real one this time. "We'll be good friends. And maybe, down the road, when you're truly ready, we can have this conversation again."

Before she could change her mind, she rose to her toes, kissed his cheek, and whispered, "I wish, with all my heart, that you and Roxie have a very Merry Christmas."

She returned to her truck, climbed into the driver's seat and cranked the engine. As she drove away, she glanced in the rearview mirror, a fresh wave of tears flowing freely down her face as Nate stood motionless in the dark and watched her leave.

Chapter Fourteen

Later that night, the drive home from Noel's town square to Frosted Firs Ranch seemed to take longer than it ever had before as Nate, Tucker and Roxie made their way home.

"But I don't understand," Roxie said from the back seat of the extended cab. "Why wouldn't Ms. Jordyn take the Christmas tree award?"

Nate, sitting in the driver's seat, guided his truck around a sharp mountain curve. "She had her reasons, sweetheart."

"But what were they?" Roxie insisted.

Nate focused on the road and clenched his jaw, trying to hold back the warring emotions within him.

After Jordyn had driven off into the cold, dark night over an hour ago, he'd stood in the parking lot beside the town square, his mind and heart reeling over the idea of having Jordyn in his life solely as a neighbor and friend.

It was a nice thought, he supposed. After all, a neighborly friendship was all he had wanted with Jordyn initially, but now, he felt very differently. As a matter of fact, he wanted . . .

Wanted what?

The intensity of emotions that had taken hold of him as he'd stood in the parking lot had overwhelmed him at first, but after a moment, everything was all too clear.

He didn't want to be just Jordyn's neighbor and friend. He wanted to be more than that. He wanted Jordyn to be in his life on a daily basis and he wanted to be in hers. He wanted Jordyn's face to be the first he saw every morning and he wanted to know that every day, she would be a part of his and Roxie's life and home. He wanted Jordyn by his side, tucking Roxie into bed at night, kissing his daughter's cheek with him, wishing her sweet dreams and knowing, in their hearts, that they would do everything possible to make Roxie's life a safe, fulfilling, and happy one.

And every night, he wanted to end the day with Jordyn in his arms, grateful that he'd been blessed to spend another day with her. He wanted Jordyn in his heart, in his home, and in his life. He wanted . . .

He wanted everything!

"Her tree was so beautiful," Roxie said softly from the back seat. "It would've looked so great in the town square, and on Christmas Eve, we could've all stood around it drinking hot chocolate and having a good time." Her voice broke. "And she didn't even tell me goodbye before she left."

"She was upset," Nate said softly. "Otherwise, she would have."

After he had followed her into the parking lot, he'd noticed right away that she was struggling with her decision. The tears in her eyes and slight tremor in her voice were clear indications that she didn't want to walk away from Roxie or from him. And that perhaps she still wanted to explore the intense emotions between them despite what she was saying.

In his heart, he knew that she did, in fact, want more. But given the reservations he'd voiced, she had gracefully bowed out and chosen to walk away rather than take a chance on his fickle heart and risk breaking Roxie's.

She'd chosen to sacrifice her own interests because she loved his daughter . . . as much as she loved him, he hoped.

"Jordyn would've said goodbye," Nate whispered, staring straight ahead as the road curved before them. "But she didn't because she didn't want to leave you to begin with."

Roxie was quiet for a moment, then sniffed and said, her voice trembling, "I don't understand, Daddy."

Nate turned onto the driveway leading to Frosted Firs Ranch, drove slowly along the paved path to the first Christmas tree lot and parked the truck in front of Macy's tree. He stared at the Fraser fir in front of him, studied the white silk ribbon that curved around the thick branches and the bright white lights that sparkled among the lush limbs of the evergreen.

Tucker, who had been uncharacteristically quiet as he sat in the passenger seat during the drive home, sighed heavily. He swiveled in his seat, reached into the back seat, unbuckled Roxie's seat belt, and lifted her into the front seat of the truck, placing her on his knee and hugging her briefly.

"It's all right, baby girl," Tucker said, kissing Roxie's forehead. "What happened tonight wasn't exactly a bad thing. Actually, it was good in a way."

Roxie, tears rolling down her cheeks, frowned up at Tucker. "Why?"

Tucker smiled gently, his eyes meeting Nate's briefly before he returned his attention to Roxie. "Well, because there's a reason people do the kinds of things that Jordyn has done."

Roxie frowned. "What things? You mean, not taking the Christmas tree award?"

Tucker nodded. "That . . . and other things." He tilted his head and made a face, thinking hard, then said, "You know, there's something else she did, too. At the gingerbread contest, maybe? Do you remember what she did?"

Nate cleared his throat in warning. Tonight had been rough enough without telling Roxie that she hadn't won the gingerbread contest on her own. "Tucker, it's not a good idea for you to—"

"It's okay." Tucker held up a hand, sending Nate a pointed look, then smiled down gently at Roxie. "Roxie knows what's up, don't you, baby girl?"

Nate glanced down at Roxie, who shifted into a more comfortable position on Tucker's knee and avoided his eyes. "Roxie?" he prompted.

She looked up then, her big blue eyes meeting Nate's. "I know Ms. Jordyn helped me win the gingerbread contest, Daddy. And that I didn't win first place all on my own. But Uncle Tucker told me—"

"Did you tell her what Jordyn did?" Nate asked, narrowing his eyes at Tucker.

Tucker made a face. "Really? You think I'd do that?"

"He didn't do it, Daddy," Roxie said softly. "I saw Ms. Jordyn do it on my own. I told her when we made gingerbread that you should never push down on the top of your house or it'll fall apart." She lifted her chin and sniffed, talking through the tears. "I know Ms. Jordyn helped me win. But Uncle Tucker told me that she didn't win the contest for me. He said my gingerbread house was really good and that in the end, the contest was between me and Angelina Stone and that I won fair and square at that point." Roxie looked up at Tucker. "Isn't that right, Uncle Tucker?"

244 Janet Dailey

Smiling, Tucker nodded. "That's right, baby girl. Ms. Jordyn might have bowed out of the competition to help you out, but you're the one that closed the deal. Your hard work paid off."

Nate smiled at Tucker, who smiled back at him, then made an *I told you so* face.

Chuckling softly, Nate lowered his head back against the head rest and rubbed his forehead, stifling a groan. Tucker might not be the most responsible or dependable man when it came to romantic relationships, but one thing Nate would never doubt about him was that he was a wonderful brother and fantastic uncle.

"Now don't you feel bad about doubting me?" Tucker asked, raising one eyebrow.

Nate rolled his head to the side and smiled. "Yeah. You got me this time."

"Every time," Tucker said, smiling wider. "And don't forget it. Which brings me back to my original point," he said, returning his attention to Roxie. "There's a reason Ms. Jordyn did the things she did, Roxie. And now, I'm gonna let your dad tell you all about it while I go inside, grab a hot cup of coffee and warm up. It's too dang cold to sit out here!"

With that, he opened the passenger-side door, slid out of the truck, then lowered Roxie into the seat he vacated.

After he left, Roxie, her cheeks still wet with tears, looked up at Nate, her eyes full of questions. "What did Uncle Tucker mean, Daddy?"

Nate smiled gently and reached out, wiping her wet cheek with his thumb. "Well, let's see. Why do you think Ms. Jordyn broke her gingerbread house to give you a chance to win first place in that contest?"

Roxie blinked, then issued a small smile at the memory of her win. "Because she wanted me to win."

"And why was that?" Nate asked.

Her expression brightened. "Because she likes me. And she wanted me to be happy."

"Yeah," Nate said softly. "People make sacrifices for those they care about."

And for those they love. He bit his lip at the thought, a wave of longing rolling through him.

Nate tipped Roxie's chin up gently with one knuckle, searching her expression intently as her eyes met his. "And how do you feel about Ms. Jordyn? Do you care about her, too?"

She smiled wide, her whole expression brightening. "I love Ms. Jordyn! She's nice and pretty and fun and she likes spending time with me."

Nate laughed softly. Jordyn, it seemed, had already won over Roxie's heart, too. "And," he asked slowly, "how would you feel if Ms. Jordyn spent more time with us?"

Roxie fell silent, her brow furrowing as she considered this. "You mean, like if she came over to visit every day? And maybe joined our Christmas team next year?"

"Yeah," he said quietly. "But maybe more than that. Maybe we could invite her to join us more often for things other than just the Christmas competition."

Roxie scrambled up onto her knees and reached across the front seat, her small hands curling around Nate's forearm and her eyes lighting up with excitement. "Like, maybe we could have her over for Thanksgiving, too? And for my birthday? And for Uncle Tucker's birthday and yours?"

Nate chuckled and ruffled her blond hair. "Yes. We could invite her to spend all our important days with us. And we could help celebrate hers as well."

Roxie nodded eagerly. "I'd really like that, Daddy."

Nate grinned, the pleasurable swell of excitement and anticipation blooming in his chest, making him want to shout with joy. He looked out the windshield, his eyes refocusing on Macy's tree, and he was able, for the first time in years, to smile softly at the memory of her and the life they'd shared. The grief and regret were gone now, and something else had taken their place.

He smiled wider. He was free. Free to love again. And free to offer his heart to Jordyn.

Roxie scooted across the driver's seat, laid her head on his shoulder and smiled at Macy's tree, too. "It's beautiful, isn't it, Daddy?"

"That it is, sweetheart."

"But Ms. Jordyn's tree is even more beautiful," she added softly. "I wish we were there at Chestnut Ridge now with Ms. Jordyn and Star." She looked up, propping her chin on his shoulder and meeting his eyes. "And I wish we could do something nice for her, like she did for me. She really should've kept the Christmas tree award, you know?"

Nate nodded, a slow grin making its way to his lips. "Yeah. And I know just what we can do to make it up to her."

The crowd had left the town square, and cold night air settled over Noel as the Nanas trudged to the parking lot where Carol Belle's car was parked.

"I can't believe it," Carol Belle said, her expression dazed as she rubbed her forehead. "I can't believe Jordyn actually withdrew Fabio Fraser and refused the Christmas Crown."

"I know." Eve groaned. "Trees as perfect as hers don't come along often, and since Nate's tree had the second highest score, he'll win the Christmas Crown by default. Not to mention the uproar and disappointment it caused the other participants." She shook her head and sighed. "This is a tragedy for our competition! Just unbelievable."

"Not really." Kandy, trailing behind the other women, stopped in the center of the empty parking lot and shoved her hands in her pockets. "I don't think this is a tragedy at all. As a matter of fact, I think it's the best thing to ever happen to our Christmas competition in all the years we've hosted it."

Carol Belle and Eve halted mid-step, turned and stared at Kandy, their mouths agape.

Kandy smiled. "Don't you agree?"

Carol Belle scoffed. "No! I don't agree at all."

"How could any of this possibly be a good thing?" Eve asked, propping her hands on her hips.

"For three reasons." Kandy lifted her hand and counted off each reason on her fingertips. "One, tonight's turn of events was dramatic and unexpected. Nothing fuels gossip better than unexpected drama and nothing spreads interest in an event as well as gossip does." She winked. "I guarantee participation will increase next year. Two, Jordyn took our advice—our best advice—and chose to live her life the way she wanted. Not only that, but she did so in front of everyone without hesitation, knowing how much her decision would disappoint the town. She's making her own choices and doing what makes her feel happy and secure regardless of what others think or say."

"She's right," Holly said, nodding at Eve and Carol Belle. "On both counts."

Carol Belle crossed her arms over her chest. "Well, what about the third reason?"

Kandy glanced at Holly, then Eve, and finally, Carol

Belle. "What Jordyn did tonight has inspired me to do the same. I'm going to pursue what makes me happy no matter what others think."

With that, Kandy spun on her heel and walked to the sidewalk, following Noel's festive Christmas decorations toward the town square shops.

"But Kandy . . . wait!" Carol Belle bellowed across the parking lot.

"Where are you going?" Eve called.

"It's cold," Holly yelled. "You'll freeze your buns off!"

Kandy smiled, picked up her pace and shouted over her shoulder, "I'm going where I should have months ago, and I'm warmer than I've been in a long time!"

And it was true. The surge of excitement pulsing through her veins heated her cheeks and made her smile wider.

It wasn't long before she reached the string of shops lining the road in downtown Noel and, thankfully, the sign was still on in front of the business she planned to visit. A bell over the entrance chimed as she opened the door and walked inside.

Immediately, the sweet aroma of chocolate and baked goods enveloped her, stirring a sense of nostalgia within her.

"Kandy." Max Reynolds emerged from his back office and strolled toward her behind a counter stocked with goodies. He smiled, his eyes full of surprise. "After the long day you've had wrapping up the Christmas competition, I expected you to be at home with your feet up by now."

"No." She smiled. "I had something important to do. And you told me I could stop by anytime." Hesitating, she glanced around at the empty café, then bit her lip. "Have you closed for the night? Am I too late?"

He studied her for a moment, remaining silent. Then he opened a wooden door at the back end of the counter and walked over, stopping as he reached her. "No," he said. "You're not too late."

The affection in his blue eyes as he stared down at her made her breath catch. He was so close she could feel the warmth emanating from his broad chest. She longed to place her palms against it and feel his heart throb beneath her touch.

The tender attraction surging through her was thrilling and unexpected and she wondered where it might lead if she allowed herself to . . .

"Do you have time for a cup of hot cocoa?" she asked softly.

He grinned. "With a tablespoon of espresso, five mini-marshmallows and crushed peppermint on the rim?"

She laughed. "You know me so well. But I don't want to keep you from closing if you—"

"I always have time for you. And I'm glad you came. I've been waiting for you to decide to stop by for a long time." He smiled and held out his hand. "Shall we sit by the front window?"

Kandy slipped her hand into his, but her smile faded as she studied her flesh against his. At fifty-eight, his skin was still smooth and youthful whereas hers—

"Kandy?" The tenderness in his tone coaxed her eyes back to his. His handsome expression was almost pleading. "There's a perfect view of the Christmas decorations in the town square from the window. There's nothing I'd love more than for you to join me."

She lifted her gaze to his and spoke before she could change her mind. "Okay."

Chapter Fifteen

Later that week, on Christmas Eve, Jordyn carried an ornate silver tray full of red velvet cupcakes baked fresh by Kringle's Café across the kitchen of her cabin and set it on her newly purchased dining table.

All four Nanas, each decked out in her Christmas best and seated around the beautiful dining table they'd helped Jordyn pick out, clapped their hands together and squealed with delight.

"Oh, what a wonderful Christmas treat!" Eve said, smiling up at Jordyn. "What made you think of ordering these for tonight??"

"It wasn't my doing," Jordyn said. "The owner of Kringle's Café—er, Max Reynolds was his name, I think—dropped them off earlier this afternoon. He said Kandy had mentioned I liked them and that I should consider them a housewarming gift for our Christmas Eve dinner tonight."

Carol Belle, seated at the end of the table, narrowed her eyes at Kandy. "And how did he know we were having Christmas Eve dinner with Jordyn?"

Kandy shrugged, her cheeks flushing. "I might've mentioned it when I stopped by the café for a hot cocoa. I also mentioned how fond we all were of Jordyn and how much she liked his cupcakes, and I suppose he decided to take it upon himself to formally welcome her to Noel." When Carol Belle continued staring at her, Kandy continued, "I do stop by the café on my own from time to time, and Max's red velvet cupcakes are the most delicious Christmas treat Noel has to offer."

"I don't know about that," Holly said, shimmying her shoulders and smiling slyly. "Have you ladies gotten a glimpse of the handsome man that just moved into the house two doors down from me?" She leaned forward, glancing at each of the other women, an excited gleam in her eyes. "Every woman on my block has knocked on his door and tried to get the inside scoop on him. But from what I've been told, he's very private and very mysterious."

Kandy ran a hand through her pink curls and grinned. "He sounds intriguing. Do you know his name? Names can tell you a lot about a person, you know."

Holly shook her head. "I know nothing, except for the fact that he's very easy on the eyes."

Eve shook her head. "Y'all are the absolute worst. Can't you let people have their privacy? Not everyone is looking for a romantic entanglement."

And just like that, the tone in the room shifted.

All four Nanas, avoiding Jordyn's eyes, lowered their gaze and fidgeted with the Christmas tablecloth Jordyn had spread over the new dining table just hours before.

Jordyn turned away and returned to the other side of the kitchen, then busied herself with carefully placing five Christmas mugs on another decorative tray along with a carafe of freshly brewed coffee. Hands trembling, she slowed her movements, taking care not to damage the delicate Christmas mugs she'd purchased two days ago just for tonight's occasion.

Hold it together, girl. Just get through tonight.

And tomorrow. And the next day . . .

When she allowed herself to think about it, the future seemed long and lonely without Nate and Roxie in her life on a regular basis. But, hopefully, with time the pain of having to walk away from them would recede and she'd be able to do as she'd promised and form a new relationship with Nate. One that consisted solely of friendship and neighborly concern.

In the future, whenever he drove his truck past her house, she'd wave, and when they bumped into each other in the town square, she would casually say hello, smile politely and asked how Roxie was doing.

That would be the extent of their friendship, and it was for the best. Really. She'd made the right decision.

She took a deep breath, picked up the tray of mugs and coffee and carried it carefully across the room to the dining table, then set it down and took her seat at the head of the table.

The Nanas stared at her now, scrutinizing her expression.

"It's okay," Jordyn said, forcing a smile. "I know what all of you are thinking and I promise you, it's okay."

The Nanas continued staring and remained silent.

"I mean it." Jordyn tried to inject a bit of cheer into her voice and expression, but it was more difficult than she'd expected. "I told you that Nate and I have decided to remain friends and neighbors—nothing more. And I'm okay with that. Really."

"Oh, but Jordyn." Kandy was the first to break her

silent scrutiny. "I thought for sure that the two of you could work things out and that Nate would come around. I've never seen him have as much fun in the Christmas competition as he did this year."

"Me either," Eve said softly. "After all, he even dressed up for the Sexy Santa contest and drank himself under the table in the Eggnog Nod."

Holly smiled, her tone bittersweet. "And wasn't that just a wonderful sight? Not the part where he passed out," she hastened, "but the part where he strutted across the stage and danced with Jordyn. He was so happy that night and seemed to have such a wonderful time. It was so refreshing to see him enjoy himself for once. I just thought for sure he'd changed his mind."

"It's my fault," Carol Belle said, looking down and picking at the Christmas tablecloth with a fingernail. "I shouldn't have dragged you into this to begin with, Jordyn. I knew Nate hadn't gotten over Macy, and even though my intentions were good, I shouldn't have stuck my nose in, much less dragged you into the middle of everything."

"It wasn't your fault," Jordyn said quietly. "If anything, you helped me enjoy Christmas all the more by participating in the competition and meeting new people. And Nate did have fun during the contests he participated in, too. So, you see, it was the right thing to do in the end."

"But it wasn't." Carol Belle's normally stiff demeanor crumbled, and her chin quivered as tears filled her eyes. "You've had your heart broken and that was the very thing we were trying to avoid."

At that, Jordyn did smile. "No, I didn't. As a matter of fact," she said, "I found one of the best loves a girl can find."

Carol Belle looked up, her tearful eyes meeting Jordyn's in question.

Smiling wider, Jordyn reached out, curling her hands around one of Kandy's and one of Holly's. "I fell head over heels for four of the most wonderful women I've ever met. And now I have the great fortune of calling them my friends."

Holly and Kandy, tears in their eyes, too, squeezed Jordyn's hands in return.

"And," Jordyn continued gently, "I'm the luckiest woman in the world because my wonderful friends have joined me on Christmas Eve to celebrate the holiday. I can't think of anything better than spending Christmas Eve with the four of you, and my heart isn't broken at all. How could it be when I have you here with me?"

A broken sob burst from Carol Belle's lips and she straightened in her chair, dragged her hand across her wet cheeks, then reached out, covering Eve and Holly's hands with her own as she smiled back at Jordyn. "Friends?" she asked in a gruff voice. "We are not friends, ladies." She smiled at Jordyn. "We're family!"

"And that's the best gift the four of you could have ever given me!" Heart overflowing, Jordyn exchanged smiles with the other women, then burst out laughing. "So, seeing as how we're now family and all, I don't have to be on my best behavior tonight, do I?" She looked down at the silver tray full of red velvet cupcakes and lifted one eyebrow, asking in a teasing tone, "The four of you won't mind if I stuff my face full of cupcakes tonight, will you?"

Kandy laughed. "Not at all! As a matter of fact, I plan on doing exactly the same."

On that note, they all shared a good laugh, grabbed a cupcake from the tray, placed it on their plates, then passed around the carafe of hot coffee, filling their Christmas mugs to the brim, then dug into their sweet Christmas treats.

As the delicious taste of cream cheese icing melted on her tongue, Jordyn eased back into her chair and savored the moment. She glanced slowly around the table, listening to the Nanas chatter cheerfully and smile as they ate, then looked toward the living room, where a warm fire popped and crackled in the newly repaired fireplace, lending a comforting glow to the hardwood floor, walls and ceiling of her cabin. Then, her gaze drifted to the window at the front of her cabin, where, beyond the glass pane, something small and white drifted on the wind.

"Oh, how wonderful!" Jordyn pushed her chair back and stood, smiling down at the four other women. "It's snowing. It's Christmas Eve and it's snowing!"

Carol Belle chuckled. "Well, my dear Jordyn, that does happen from time to time around here."

"But it's a first for me," Jordyn said, rushing over to the coatrack by the front door, grabbing her coat and shrugging it on. "So? Are y'all going to join me or what? I thought family was supposed to stay together."

Kandy shot to her feet and hurried over, grabbing her coat, too. "Of course, we are! How can anyone not dance in the snow on Christmas Eve? Ladies, it's time for celebration."

Carol Belle stood, too. "Who needs a Christmas tree in the town square when we've got Fabio Fraser and snow on Christmas Eve right in Jordyn's backyard?" She tapped the table with her knuckles, grabbed her coat from where it hung on the back of her chair, and shrugged it on. "Come on, Eve and Holly. Let's show Jordyn what a real Noel Christmas looks like!"

After everyone had bundled up warmly in their jackets, scarves, and hats, they walked out onto the front porch and leaned on the porch railing, tipping their heads back and smiling as big snowflakes drifted softly to the ground.

"It's more beautiful than I imagined," Jordyn said quietly. "It's perfect. Absolutely perfect."

Except for one thing.

Her smile dimmed as her eyes traced the path of the snowflakes dancing and twirling their way to the ground. If only she were able to share this moment with Nate and Roxie. If only Nate had truly been ready to move on and embrace something new. What a wonderful night this would've been and what a wonderful future they might have had!

But then she glanced at the Nanas, who stood huddled together beside her, smiling, laughing, and chattering cheerfully as they watched the snow fall, and her heart warmed again with gratitude for having found these new friends, her beautiful home at Chestnut Ridge, and the nostalgic charm of Noel.

This Christmas, even though she might not have the love she wanted most, she still had so very much to be thankful for.

"Jordyn," Carol Belle said. "Are you expecting more company?"

Jordyn frowned and shook her head. "No. Why?"

Carol Belle pointed at something in the distance. "Because you have a stream of lanterns approaching Fabio in the back lot."

"Say what?" Clutching her coat tighter around her chest to ward off the cold, Jordyn eased past the Nanas and walked to the other end of the porch for a better look.

Sure enough, there were dozens upon dozens of lanterns

glowing in the distance, each bobbing slightly in the snowy dark as the procession made its way toward the brightly lit tree.

"What in heaven's name?" Eve's voice trailed away as she scooted closer to Jordyn, narrowing her eyes at the sight before them. "Carol Belle, did you have a hand in this?"

Carol Belle scoffed. "Absolutely not. I have no clue what's going on here, but we're about to find out."

With that, Carol Belle tugged her hat lower on her head, walked across the porch and down the front steps, then charged across the grounds, following the procession of lanterns as they surrounded the festively decorated tree.

Jordyn and the other Nanas followed her, jogging to catch up, then jerking to a stop as they reached the crowd of people who'd encircled the tree.

The crowd parted as they approached, and Noel's residents lifted the lanterns they held higher in the air, smiling at Jordyn and the Nanas as they called out in a cheery chorus, "Merry Christmas!"

Kandy, walking beside Jordyn as they made their way through the crowd toward the tree, squeezed Jordyn's hand. "What in the world is going on?"

Jordyn shook her head, her eyes roving over the familiar faces surrounding them. "I have no idea," she whispered.

But then, as they reached a small clearing in front of the tree, Jordyn noticed Nate and Roxie standing in front of her perfect Fraser fir, broad smiles on their faces and an elegant silver crown cradled in Roxie's hands.

"Seeing as how Noel's winning Christmas tree isn't in the town square this year," Nate said, smiling, "we, as a community, discussed it and decided we would bring the party to Chestnut Ridge instead."

Heart pounding, Jordyn drank in the sight of him. He looked as handsome and dashing as ever, dressed in a stylish pair of jeans, long-sleeved, white dress shirt and sherpa-lined jacket. But it was the look in his blue eyes that captured her attention as he strode across the distance separating them, lowered his head and whispered in her ear, "Merry Christmas, Jordyn with a *y*."

She placed her hands on his arms to steady herself, then looked up at him, searching his expression. "What are you doing here?" She glanced around, her gaze roving over the dozens and dozens of people who smiled back at her expectantly. "What is everyone doing here?"

Nate smiled down at her. "We have discussed it and decided that we are going to refuse to accept your withdrawal from the Christmas tree contest."

Jordyn, confused, shook her head. "What do you mean?"

"I mean," he said, a teasing note in his voice, "we've decided to officially designate Fabio as Noel's permanent town Christmas tree." At her stunned silence, he continued, "You were right about one thing. This tree should remain exactly where it is and be allowed to grow. And every year, instead of cutting a tree down and bringing it to the town square, we're going to undertake the trip to this tree at Chestnut Ridge and celebrate its beauty right where it grows."

Excited murmurs arose from the Nanas, who stood several feet behind Jordyn, tears in their eyes as they smiled at the townsfolk and issued words of thanks.

Nate glanced past Jordyn to the Nanas and asked softly, "That is, if it's okay with you, Nanas?"

Carol Belle shook her head, a smile brightening her expression. "It's not okay. It's absolutely wonderful!"

Nate chuckled. "And seeing as how I've brought you

just about the whole town to celebrate this year's Christmas competition, Ms. Carol Belle, does that mean you forgive me for hogging the Christmas Crown all these years?"

Carol Belle laughed, too. "I suppose so. You are officially forgiven, Nate Reed."

"Then there's just one thing left to do," Nate said, glancing over his shoulder and smiling at Roxie.

Roxie, wearing a beautiful white Christmas dress and elegant red coat with her long blond curls flowing loosely around her shoulders, walked over and smiled as she lifted the crown in her hands toward Jordyn. "Congratulations on winning the Christmas Crown this year, Ms. Jordyn!"

Jordyn placed a hand on her chest, right over her heart, trying to calm its frantic beating. She sank to her knees in front of Roxie and smiled hesitantly. "But . . . this was supposed to be your tenth crown, Roxie."

Roxie, smiling, shook her head. "No, ma'am. This is our first crown." She glanced up at Nate and winked. "Yours, mine, and Daddy's."

Jordyn's eyes shot to Nate's, the tenderness in his expression bringing fresh tears of joy to her eyes.

"The first crown of many," he whispered softly. He reached out, lifted the crown from Roxie's hands and placed it on Jordyn's head. Then he took Jordyn's hand in his, tugged her gently to her feet and pulled her close, wrapping his arms tightly around her.

She looked up at him, barely able to catch her breath as she struggled to focus on his handsome face.

He lowered his forehead against hers and whispered tenderly, "I love you, Jordyn. Almost from the moment we first met. I'm just sorry it took so long for me to take the chance and reach out."

She traced the curve of his strong jaw with her fingertip. "What made you change your mind?"

"The sacrifice you made for Roxie and for me." He smiled gently. "It takes someone in love to be willing to walk away from what they want, to serve the needs of someone else. And when we spoke the other night in the town square parking lot, you mentioned that you were worried Roxie's heart might break if I changed my mind about our relationship down the road, but you never mentioned anything about changing yours." He cradled her face with his palms, his skin warm against her cheeks. "It occurred to me then that you might already love me, too. Otherwise, you wouldn't be so certain that your feelings for me wouldn't change later on."

She grinned, her heart overflowing. "And you're quite certain that I love you?"

He grinned back. "Yes, that's one thing I'm absolutely sure of. And that's all that matters because my love for you will never change either. No matter what challenge we might face in the future, we'll work our way through it together." He pulled her closer, his chest pressing against hers, their hearts beating in tandem. "There's nothing I want more than to spend this Christmas—and every one that comes after—with you."

Heart full to bursting, Jordyn smiled and cupped his face in her hands. "I really do love you, Neighbor Nate."

"Is it okay if I kiss you?" he teased, his eyes sparkling with mischief.

Jordyn glanced around, then leaned closer and whispered, "I don't know. That would stir up a bit of trouble in little Noel, wouldn't it? I've heard people like to talk around here."

Nate grinned, a roguish look in his eyes as he cupped the back of her head with one hand, slid his free arm around her waist and whispered, "Then let's give them something to talk about, shall we?"

With that, he dipped her over his arm, covered her

mouth with his and kissed her properly and tenderly right there in front of the most perfect Christmas tree Noel had ever seen.

The Nanas, standing nearby in the crowd among the falling snowflakes, sighed wistfully as they watched Nate cradle Jordyn in his arms and kiss her soundly.

"Oh, how wonderful!" Kandy, smiling, dabbed a tear from the corner of her eye. "Could you ever, in a million years, have imagined that our Christmas ceremony would have such a beautiful ending this year?"

Eve removed her glasses and dabbed at her own eyes, smiling through her tears. "No. After the past few weeks, I definitely didn't see this coming."

"And they make a stunning couple," Holly said, excitement in her voice. "Can you imagine how beautiful their wedding will be?"

Eve paused in the midst of dabbing her tears but continued smiling as she looked at Holly and said, "I'd say that's jumping the gun a bit, don't you think? I haven't heard a proposal yet."

Kandy smoothed one hand over her pink curls and grinned. "Oh, but do you see the way they're kissing? There most certainly will be a wedding—without a doubt!"

Carol Belle, glancing at Jordyn and Nate as they continued kissing in front of the tree, turned this over in her mind, already making plans for next year. "Kandy's right," she said softly, her mouth lifting in a broad smile. "There most definitely will be a wedding. A Christmas wedding, if I have anything to do with it! A beautiful Christmas wedding. I wonder if there's some way we can incorporate it into our next Christmas competition and make everyone in Noel a part of the celebration."

Clapping her hands together, Carol Belle admired Nate and Jordyn as they embraced once more, and she giggled with excitement. "Ladies, we have one year to put together the most romantic Christmas celebration Noel has ever seen! And with all the single men and women in town, we have plenty of options for matchmaking."

The Nanas' eyes roved over the large crowd of townsfolk who milled around the Christmas tree, then narrowed on Tucker Reed, who was smiling at his brother and Jordyn as they embraced Roxie. He stood alone, just waiting for the right woman to steal his wild heart and give him a taste of his own medicine.

A slow smile curved all four of the women's mouths as Carol Belle whispered, "Just imagine the possibilities . . ."

HIDDEN VALLEY

The New Americana Series

In the heart of North Carolina's beautiful Wine Country lies a unique vineyard, passed down through generations of one family's women, and bearing a very special mission—to fill empty glasses and hearts. But can it survive the challenges of a changing world?

Life hasn't turned out quite the way twenty-eight-year-old single mom Mia Anderson expected. But she's always been able to count on the sanctuary of her family's Hidden Valley Vineyard, now operated by her two aunts and herself. Like the Anderson women before them, they've all had bad luck with men and the vineyard has been home and provider. Yet now, inflation and changes in spending habits are challenging them as never before. So, the women embark on a bold plan. . . .

Mia and her aunts take jobs at a local shipping warehouse, putting every extra cent toward throwing an extravagant retreat for a VIP and guest. A glowing, high-profile review will surely breathe new life into their business. And it does—until a scathing post derails everything. Determined to turn things around, Mia makes the critic an offer she's certain will change his mind. . . .

Cynical wine banker Jackson Hall prides himself on his brutally honest assessments. He never expected his negative review to prompt the vintner to invite him back so she could pair him with "his perfect wine." Most of all, he didn't anticipate he'd fall for the valley—and the beautiful, defiant vintner herself. . . . Nor did Mia expect to find a world-weary, heartbroken man beneath Jackson's gruff exterior. A man whose desire to love again is as strong as hers. Business and pleasure may not mix, yet Mia and Jackson long to take a chance again, if only they can find a way to trust each other. . . .

LIE FOR A MILLION

The Rivalries Series

from *New York Times* bestselling author

Janet Dailey

Everything is bigger in Texas, from the vast stretch of sky to the rattlesnakes—and for one prestigious family, that means outsized drama, passions, and scandal following the murder of the wealthy patriarch . . .

Lila Culhane's life is in turmoil. As if coping with the murder of her husband isn't enough, now the glamorous young widow has Frank's even younger mistress to contend with. His *pregnant* mistress, Crystal. But Lila hasn't got time for more heartache. With everyone grasping to profit from Frank's death, including fighting for possession of her beloved ranch, she needs leverage for the battle.

As it turns out, Crystal may be carrying just the edge Lila requires: an heir. Crystal offers to let Lila adopt Frank's baby—for a price. Lila is willing to consider it—pending a paternity test. Until then, she'll focus on her role in the upcoming high-stakes Run for a Million reining competition, and her ranch manager—and lover—Roper McKenna.

Rugged, hardworking, and talented, Roper is finally getting his dream to ride in the prized competition. Lila expects he'll choose the Culhanes' legendary stallion, One in a Million, as his mount but when he considers other offers, she finds herself questioning his loyalty . . .

Meanwhile, Detective Sam Rafferty's list of suspects in Frank's murder is growing. Besides Roper and Lila, Frank's bitter first wife and his sparring extended family, there are adversarial neighbors, ex-lovers, and perhaps even the woman he loves, Frank's own pampered daughter, Jasmine. And as the surprises multiply, a killer remains free to strike again—if these rivals don't kill each other first . . .

Chapter One

"*I need help. I'm pregnant, Mrs. Culhane. The baby is Frank's.*"

The words replayed against the throbbing beat in Lila Culhane's head as she hung up the office phone and sank into the leather banker's chair that had been her late husband's.

Raking her blonde hair back from her face, she muttered a string of unladylike swearwords. Wasn't it enough that Frank was dead—murdered in the stable with the unknown killer still at large? Wasn't it enough that Frank's grown children and ex-wife were scheming to evict her from the house and ranch that had been her home for eleven years—the home she had rightfully inherited?

Evidently it wasn't enough. Fate had just thrown Frank's pregnant mistress into the mess—a young woman Lila had learned about only the day before Frank was discovered dead from a massive injection of fentanyl.

What now?

She leaned back in the chair and closed her eyes. The house was quiet with the recent visitors gone. She could hear a trapped horsefly buzzing against the window. From the upstairs hallway came the sound of a vacuum cleaner as Mariah, the cook and housekeeper, went about her work.

Lila needed a drink. But this wasn't the time to dull her senses with alcohol. She needed a clear head to examine her options.

Crystal—that was the young woman's name. Against her better judgment, Lila had agreed to meet with her to-morrow at the Trail's End restaurant in nearby Willow Bend. It might have been smarter to hang up the phone and have nothing to do with her claim. But she needed to know, at least, whether Crystal was really carrying Frank's child or lying as a way to get money.

The manila envelope, holding the photos Lila had paid for, was taped to the underside of the center desk drawer. Not that there was a need for hiding it. Frank's infidelities were no longer a secret.

But that didn't mean she would share what she'd just learned—especially if Crystal was telling the truth.

Lila's hand shook slightly as she slid the photos out of the envelope and spread them on the desktop. Without a doubt, the handsome, graying man in the motel room doorway was Frank. With his distinguished looks and air of wealth, he'd never had any trouble attracting women. Lila should have realized long ago that his cheating wouldn't stop with his second marriage. After all, he'd cheated on his first wife, Madeleine, with *her*.

As the wronged and angry wife, Lila knew she was a prime suspect in the ongoing investigation of Frank's mur-der. But right now, she had even more urgent concerns.

She'd studied the photos before. But now that she'd spoken with the mystery woman in Frank's arms, she saw the details with different eyes. Crystal had been pho-tographed from behind. Her face didn't appear in any of the photos—just her long black hair and one of her hands, which rested on Frank's shoulder. The hand told a story of its own—the drugstore nails and the gaudy rings on three fingers. Lila knew good jewelry when she saw it. The rings were cheap fakes. Crystal was poor and undoubtedly after money. The only question was how desperate was she?

Paying her to go away might be the simplest solution. Of course, Crystal would have to consent to an in-vitro paternity test. If the baby didn't have Frank's DNA, that would be the end of the story. But if the young woman was telling the truth . . .

Lila dismissed the thought. She was inclined to believe that Crystal was lying. During her eleven-year marriage, Lila had tried everything to get pregnant. Since she'd given birth to a daughter at eighteen, she knew she wasn't infertile. And Frank had two children from his first marriage. After a time, when she'd failed to conceive, she'd begun to suspect he'd had a secret vasectomy. But the coroner who'd done his autopsy hadn't bothered to check. Now it was too late. His body lay in the Culhane family cemetery on a desolate hilltop, within sight of the house.

Nerves quivering, Lila put the photographs away, stood, and walked to the window. The ranch office gave her a view of the stables, the covered arena, and the paddocks beyond, where blooded American Quarter Horses grazed in the morning sunlight. Beyond the paddocks, in the larger pasture, were Black Angus cattle, fed on the drought-yellowed grass.

For the past eleven years, as Frank's wife and business partner, she had given her time, her energy, and her heart to this ranch and its program of breeding and training performance horses. It had become her world, her life. Now, with Frank's death, everything had been thrown into chaos.

With Frank's ex and her two adult children plotting to take everything Lila had worked for, the one person she could count on had been Roper McKenna, her horse trainer and manager. But now, even his support was coming into question.

Lila was fighting battles from all sides and the last thing she needed was Frank's former mistress showing up pregnant.

Without conscious thought, she found herself leaving the house and heading down the cobblestone path to the stable, where Roper would be working the horses that were owned by, boarded, and trained at the Culhane Ranch. Weeks ago, she would have taken him into her confidence and trusted him to understand. She might even have told him about Crystal.

But all that had changed after Roper qualified for Frank's place in the reining event of the year—the Run for a Million. Lila had known he'd be getting a lot of attention. Big horse breeders would be courting him, offering him money and prestige to train in their stables and compete on their horses.

She needed Roper. He'd worked for Frank before he'd worked for her. There was no one else she trusted to manage her horse operation. That was why she'd been prepared to offer him a partnership—the one thing he wouldn't get from anyone else.

But now she was holding back on the offer. Roper, who'd been her rock, was showing signs of dissatisfaction. The loyalty she'd felt from him was gone—if it had ever been real. Lila sensed that she was going to lose him, and she didn't know what to do.

In the covered arena, Roper had just put One in a Million through his paces, the pattern of rapid circles, dashes and gallops ending in a spectacular sliding stop with a rollback. At the age of thirteen, the legendary stallion was still sharp, as sharp as he'd been a few weeks ago when he'd won Roper a place as one of sixteen riders in the Run for a Million.

The big bay roan had the heart of a champion. But at his age, did he have the speed and stamina to win again?

The decision was Roper's to make—and he needed to make it soon.

Frank Culhane had qualified for the final event at the March Cactus Classic, riding Million Dollar Baby—a daughter of One in a Million. He'd also planned to ride the promising mare in the Run for a Million. But Frank's murder, followed by Baby's tragic death, had changed everything.

One in Million had been Frank's horse, winning him more than a million dollars before being retired to stud at the age of ten. In the competition for Frank's place, it was decided that Roper would show the aging stallion, but only as a tribute to his late owner. To everyone's astonishment, One in a Million had caught fire in the arena. His scores had put Roper in first place.

Roper walked the stallion to cool him down before turning him over to the grooms. The horse snorted softly, his hooves sinking into the thick layer of sand, loam, and sawdust that cushioned the arena floor. After his retirement at the age of ten, Frank had ordered that One in a Million be exercised and kept in good condition. With luck, the big bay roan could give the ranch another decade of stud fee earnings. But was he up for the stress of competing in the Run for a Million? Would he have even a prayer of winning?

The right horse could make all the difference; but reining events were a competition between riders. A rider could compete on any horse he or she chose. If the rider was using a borrowed horse, the winnings would be divided between the rider and the horse's owner—typically a breeder, a rancher, or even a corporation.

If Roper were to compete on One in a Million, any prize money won would be split with Lila. But if Roper were to win on someone else's horse, Lila would be out of luck.

And that was Roper's dilemma.

Since his qualifying win, Roper had received numerous offers from owners who wanted him to ride their horses. Good offers. Great horses, strong and well trained, with sterling bloodlines. Some were already big money winners.

Time was running out. If his choice wasn't to be One in a Million, he needed time to try other horses and more time to work with the one he chose.

If he didn't choose the great roan stallion, he would be battling Lila all the way. He wanted to keep her happy—and to keep his job. But more than anything, he wanted to win.

He could see Lila now, standing at the entrance to the arena. Tall, blonde, and stunning in a white silk blouse and tailored slacks, she was built like the Vegas showgirl she'd been before her marriage. Roper's pulse skipped at the sight of her. He brought himself under control before he acknowledged her with a tip of his Stetson. She remained where she was, a ray of sunlight falling on her hair.

Lila was his employer, as Frank had been before her. To cross the line between them would be a mistake—especially now, while they were at odds over his choice of a horse. Still, sometimes the urge to reach out and pull her into his arms was almost too compelling to resist. She was so fiercely proud of her own strength, yet so alone and so vulnerable . . .

Roper ended the thought with a curse as he crossed the arena to the stable entrance where a groom was waiting to take the stallion. Dismounting, he turned and walked back to where Lila waited for him. In her rigid posture and the stubborn jut of her chin, he read the signs of a coming showdown.

"Boss?" It was what Roper called her—"Lila" being

too familiar and "Mrs. Culhane" too formal. Despite his misgivings, the word left his lips as a caress.

"It's time," she said. "I need to know what you're thinking."

Roper sighed and shook his head. "If you put One in a Million back in the arena, you know he'll give you everything he's got. But he's too old for this level of competition, Boss. He knows the routines, but he can't win against those younger horses."

"He did it once."

"I know he did. But his legs, his heart and lungs—they won't hold out forever. He could die out there or have to be put down. Even if he had a chance of winning, would it be worth the risk?"

Lila lowered her gaze.

"With luck and care, One in a Million could live another ten or fifteen years," Roper said. "His stud fees and his colts could earn a lot more over time than he could ever win competing."

"We have other horses," Lila said.

"We do. They've got talent and good pedigrees, but they're still in training. They don't have the experience to win the Run for a Million. We were counting on Baby for that. She had it all."

"I could buy another horse."

"You could. I thought of that. But a trained horse with champion bloodlines would bankrupt the ranch. You'd have to find an investment group and buy in. There's no time for that now. As I see it, there's only one way to win."

"You mean for *you* to win." Her gaze hardened. "I know you've had some great offers, Roper. Are you going to take one?"

His jaw tightened. "I want to win. At least I want a fair chance."

"So you'd bring the horse here, board it in my stable, train it in my arena, and then, if you win—"

"I could arrange to go somewhere else."

"You'll have to if you're not working for me anymore." Lila let the threat hang, but Roper felt the sting of her words. The lady meant business.

"Let's not fight, Boss," he said. "I know where you stand, and I want to be fair. But I've got a lot of thinking to do. Can we talk again tomorrow?"

She exhaled, clearly impatient with him. "Fine. I've got a busy day planned tomorrow. I'll come and find you when I have a few minutes. But you'd better have something to tell me. I'm tired of being strung along."

Without giving him a chance to respond, she swung away from him and stalked out of the arena.

Roper cursed his indecision as he watched her go. Lila had relied on his support since Frank's death. He despised himself for letting her down, especially when she was dealing with other problems, including the fight to keep her property. He cared deeply for her. But a chance to win the Run for a Million was the dream of a lifetime. How could he throw it away by choosing an aging stud or an unprepared youngster from the ranch?

The conflict wasn't so much about the prize money as it was about loyalty. That issue was going to make his decision even more painful. Once it was in place, he feared that things would never be the same between him and Lila.

Could he live with that?

A groom was waiting with the next horse. Forcing himself to focus, Roper strode back across the arena, mounted up, and went to work.

In her haste, Lila had taken the wrong exit from the arena. She was still fuming over Roper's attitude when she found herself in the stable wing that led back to the house.

She was facing an empty box stall, still festooned with yellow crime-scene tape. It was One in a Million's old stall, the place where Frank had been found dead from an injection of fentanyl in his neck.

The only witness to the crime had been the stallion. Removed to a different stall, One in a Million had been a bundle of nerves, trembling and snorting. Roper's skilled handling had finally calmed him. But the memory of his master's death would be imprinted on the big roan's brain for the rest of his life.

Frank's killer had yet to be found. Madeleine, Frank's ex, had confessed to hiring a hit on him—a hit that had never been carried out because Frank was already dead. Someone else, probably someone Frank had known and trusted, had injected him from behind. His daughter, Jasmine, had found his body the next morning, lying facedown in the straw.

After Madeleine's confession, the FBI agent who'd stayed at the ranch had gone back to his office in Abilene. Tomorrow he'd be returning to take up the investigation again. Maybe this time he would be able to put Frank's murder to rest—a murder that had made the national tabloids.

Everyone in the Culhane family and on the ranch was under suspicion, including Lila herself. Now it appeared that there might be a new suspect—Crystal.

If Frank had been told about her alleged pregnancy, and he'd refused to marry her, support her, or even believe her, that would have given Crystal motive to kill him.

Tomorrow Lila would be meeting Crystal at lunch. Would she be confronting a naïve young woman who'd been led astray? Or would she be facing a ruthless opportunist, capable of lying and murder?

Visit our website at
KensingtonBooks.com
to sign up for our newsletters, read
more from your favorite authors, see
books by series, view reading group
guides, and more!

Become a Part of Our
Between the Chapters Book Club
Community and Join the Conversation

Betweenthechapters.net